1

It was only the start of the second week of the summer holidays and *l*ready eleven year old Molly Peters was bored and wishing she was back at school. *S*he wandered idly along the narrow lane, swishing with a stick at the nettles and cow *p*arsley in the hedgerow and only half watching Fizz, her border collie, as the dog *p*oted around in the overgrown banks looking for rabbits and squirrels to chase. The *y*oung girl was in no real hurry to go back home. Home was a melancholy place *t*hese days.

Tears sprang sharply into Molly's eyes as she thought back over the last few *w*eeks, back to the morning when her Mother had tearfully told Molly that her father *h*ad passed away. Mother and daughter had clung together and sobbed *u*ncontrollably until Fizz had tried to climb, whining, onto Molly's knee. A surge of *e*motion and, inexplicably, anger had risen in Molly's chest and suddenly she had *j*umped from her seat, called Fizz to her and then she ran out of the door, slamming it *h*ard behind her. She'd run until she was well away from the Lego block style council *h*ouses and was out in the fields across the stream at the bottom of the hill. There, *s*he had flung herself down in the long grass and sobbed until she was exhausted, *h*ugging Fizz tightly to her as the dog licked away her tears. Nothing at home had *e*ver been the same since.

A funny little yip from Fizz jerked Molly back to the present. Fizz was in the *d*itch under the late flowering hawthorn, her excited wriggling causing the blossom to *f*all like snow onto her black and white coat. Fizz yipped again, the sound unlike any *n*oise she'd ever made before, more like the sound you'd expect from an excited *c*hihuahua. Molly was about to call Fizz away, expecting her to have found some *r*otten, maggot infested remains of a squirrel or rabbit when she heard an even *s*tranger sound, a squeaky high pitched whinny, and the cow parsley jiggled, *s*eemingly vibrating with the sound.

Molly crouched down and crept forward, shushing the excited dog. As she *t*hrust through the undergrowth she suddenly saw a pair of big brown eyes gazing at *h*er from either side of a big white heart shaped star in the middle of a black head. *M*olly froze and gasped in shock! It was a horse! Well, she admitted to herself, not *e*xactly a horse yet but a young foal with a fuzzy coat and a fluffy sparse mane, lying *o*n it's brisket and flaring it's nostrils at her.

As Molly continued to stare, Fizz yipped again. Molly glanced at the dog and *w*ent to shush her when she noticed Fizz wasn't looking at her or the foal but was *i*ntent on something further along the ditch. Molly followed Fizz for a few yards, *t*hankfully it was a hot dry summer and there was no water in the ditch. What she *f*ound made her shrink back with a cry of horror. Wedged on it's back in the ditch, it's neck bent at a grotesque angle, it's lifeless eyes staring glassily, was a black and white horse. Flies were already flocking down to feast and lay their eggs and there was a bad smell in the air, over-riding the scents of the hawthorn blossom and wild flowers. Gagging, Molly backed away, quietly calling to Fizz to follow. She moved slowly back to the foal and reached out to touch it's face. The foal snorted and jerked it's head away.

Molly's mind whirled. What to do? The lane only led up to the farm and probably only half a dozen vehicles drove along it each day. She couldn't possibly take the foal home either. They had a tiny shed in a tiny garden and it was certainly no place to keep a horse, even one as small as this! Then a thought occurred to her and she grinned to herself. The farm. Although the farmer raised mostly cattle and sheep, he did have a couple of Clydesdale horses that he kept as a hobby from a hankering for 'the good old days'. They did a few small tasks around the place and Molly often went up to the farm to take carrots for the horses. Old Sam, the farmer, sometimes let her her sit astride the great creatures as they plodded round the fields and she often helped him with grooming and other small tasks. The farm was only about a quarter of a mile from where the foal lay, but how could Molly get it there? She could only think of one way to do it. Calling to Fizz, Molly pointed to the foal and, with her hand, motioned for the dog to lie close by the foal's side.
"Fizz, stay. Stay with the baby" Molly's voice command was firm but not too loud. She didn't want to startle the foal. Fizz's tail waved slowly from side to side. "Down Fizz and stay." Fizz flopped down beside the foal and Molly gave the dog a soft pat. "Good girl, stay." Molly wriggled back out of the ditch and with a last soft command of 'stay' to Fizz, Molly ran off along the lane.

When Molly ran into the farmyard, another collie came bounding up to greet her. With a cursory pat, Molly ran on towards the barn where she could hear cattle bellowing and shouts from Sam and his men. The dog, Sam's sheepdog Meg, followed on her heels. As she entered the barn, Molly's senses were assaulted by the noise, sight and smell of about a hundred beef steers. Sam was standing to one side calling out directions to the three men who were in amongst the cattle. He noticed Molly and, with a puzzled look at her dishevelled appearance, gave a final shout to the men then hobbled over to her, his walking stick helping his progress.
"Are you okay gal?" was his opening line. Molly was gasping for breath and wasn't even aware that she looked a proper mess. She gulped some air.
"There's a horse, dead, in the ditch but the foal's alive!" she blurted out finally.
"Eh? What?" Sam struggled to hear under normal circumstances, much less amongst the clamour of the cattle.
Molly plucked at Sam's sleeve to get him to follow her out of the barn. Once clear of the worst of the din, she gasped out again "a foal, in the ditch, it's mum's dead."
"Better take a look then gal, hadn't we?" Sam hobbled off towards a battered, rusty land-rover, Molly trotting beside him. For an old fella with a dodgy hip, he could still move fairly quickly when needed!

As Sam yanked the land-rover door open with a creak, Meg leapt into the vehicle and Molly ran round to the passenger side. With a cough and a splutter, the engine roared into life. Sam crunched the ancient vehicle into gear and they bounced their way across the yard and into the lane, Meg standing between the seats, tail wagging and tongue lolling. She loved jaunts.

Just as Molly was beginning to worry that they may have passed where the foal was lying hidden, she caught a glimpse of Fizz's black and white coat under the hawthorn. The old vehicle rattled so loudly, she had to shout "There!" as she pointed to the spot. With an angry squeal from the brakes, the land-rover jerked to a halt. Molly leapt out, Meg following as Fizz came bounding out from the ditch. There was no danger of the two dogs being hostile – Meg was Fizz's mother and they had always got on well.

Molly crept into the ditch slowly, talking in low tones so as not to startle the foal. She could hear old Sam wheezing behind her and she turned and put a finger to her lips. Being a little hard of hearing meant that Sam tended to talk extra loudly, almost as though he thought everyone else was going deaf too! When he saw the foal, Sam tutted under his breath.
"You said there was a dead 'un"
Molly pointed, "There".

Sam inched into the ditch and looked at the mare, shaking his head and muttering under his breath. Then he seemed to come to a decision.
"Right gal, we need to get this little mite back to the farm. Reckon you can get it to stand up?"
"I can try" Molly felt a flood of relief that Sam was taking charge.
"There's a bit of old rope in the back of that truck, be quicker if you get it." Sam motioned towards the land-rover with his head. Molly scrambled back out of the ditch and ran over to fetch the rope.

When Molly handed over the rope, Sam started making a few deft knots and loops, one eye still on the foal. When he'd finished, Molly looked in surprise. Sam had made a perfect rope halter! He handed it back to Molly. "Gently now gal" he muttered.
Molly inched her way towards the foal. This time, when she touched it's muzzle, it gave a tiny snort but didn't pull away. Agonisingly slowly, so as not to frighten the baby, Molly inched the halter onto the foal's head. It fitted snugly but not too tightly. Sam obviously was good at judging head sizes. Once the halter was on, Molly looked back at Sam. "What now?" she asked.
"Need to be gentle but don't let go if it struggles. Just give it a gentle tweak." Sam nodded as he spoke.
Molly gently tweaked the rope. The foal shook it's head. She tweaked again. With a snort, the foal thrust out it's front legs. Molly tweaked the rope again. The foal scrambled to it's feet and leapt sideways, almost yanking the rope from Molly's hand.
"Steady gal, go with it" Sam muttered. Molly went with the rope, trying not to pull or jerk it, talking in a soft voice all the time. The foal was stopped by the far side of the ditch and stood, snorting, staring, ears flicking back and forth, it's entire body quivering with fear and tension. Molly inched forward again, slacking off the tension

on the rope foal had created, still talking softly. She touched the foal's face again and gently rubbed with her fingers. Trying to move so slowly was making her muscles ache in her legs but she ignored the discomfort as she moved closer to the foal. Soon, she was able to reach the foal's neck and she began gently scratching it with her fingertips. Closer. Ever closer. Scratching the foal's shoulder now. Then she moved her fingertips up to the withers. Time stood still as Molly scratched the foal's withers and back, inching closer all the time until she was able to press her body gently against the little horse. She was mesmerised by the soft fluffy curls. She heard a wheezy breath behind her, reminding her of Sam's presence.

"Now gal, see if it'll let you scratch the top of it's tail. Slowly now."
Molly moved her scratching fingers to the foal's dock. As she scratched there, the foal actually moved it's quarters towards her, obviously enjoying the sensation.
"Good gal. Now slowly pass me the end of the rope." Sam knelt creakily and stretched out his hand. Molly had to move back towards the front of the foal to hand the rope over. Her actions prompted another snort from the foal so, as soon as Sam had hold of the rope, Molly moved back to the foal's side and resumed her scratching of the base of it's tail.
"Okay gal. Now, I'm gonna have to pull on it's head, hopefully not too much. It won't like it but it's got to be done. You need to try and put your arms round it. I need you to put an arm round the front and one round the back. Try to keep it from struggling too much and guide it up. You ready?"

Molly's heart was racing as she put her arms around the foal's chest and quarters. As Sam took up the tension on the rope, the foal started to try to run backwards and, without even thinking about it, Molly gave it a push from behind with her arm. The foal lurched forwards, scrambled against the side of the ditch then suddenly leapt upwards onto the bank, so quickly, Molly fell forwards, her arms letting go. Recovering quickly, she leapt up the bank. The foal, eyes rolling, gave a plaintive whinny and pulled against the rope as Molly moved towards it as quickly as she dared. The foal looked at her from it's left eye. It obviously recognised her. Although still straining at the head rope, obviously trying to keep as much distance between itself and Sam as possible, the foal didn't move away from Molly as she approached. Molly resumed her scratching of the foal's withers and her quiet rambling nonsense chatter. Eventually, she felt able to take up her 'foal walking' position again. With a quick glance at Sam, she put her left arm across the foal's chest and her right arm around it's quarters. Slowly, she pushed with her right arm. The foal took a short step and Molly made sure her left arm was gently allowing the step whilst guiding the foal. She pushed again. Another step. Step by step, with Sam holding the rope loose but ready to restrain the foal if Molly should have to let go.

The two collies lay panting, watching the antics of the humans as they painstakingly inched the foal round to the back of the land-rover Finally, they were by the back door of the vehicle. Sam quietly swung the door open.
"Now gal, we're gonna have to lift this little beggar into here. It don't look too heavy though, luckily. But I don't reckon it's got the strength to walk back to the farm under it's own steam."
Molly scratched the foal's withers. "Okay." she nodded.

"Gimme a tick," Sam handed Molly the end of the rope and started to rummage in he back of the land-rover, "That's better." Molly glanced through the door. Sam had rranged some old hessian sacks on the metal floor.

"Right. Let's have a go at lifting this little 'un." Sam moved close to the foal and, opying Molly, began scratching and rubbing the foal's coat. As he scratched, he utlined the plan. "I'll lift him up as high as I can but I need you to help get them long egs in. Okay?" Molly nodded. She suddenly wondered how long they'd been in the ane. Poor Sam had more important things to be doing. As if he read her thoughts, am said "Now lass, don't worry. We'll get yer foal home, then see what we need to o next. We've got all the time in the world." He patted her shoulder then turned his ttention back to the foal. Half crouching, he put his arms around the foal's chest and uarters and then, with a grunt, stood upright, lifting the foal off the ground. Whether was shock, exhaustion or resignation, Molly would never know but the foal didn't ven attempt to struggle as Sam stepped forward and began to slide the foal into the and-rover. Molly kept an eye on the foal's legs, tucking them in as the foal lay on the acking. She was surprised that the foal didn't struggle to it's feet as Sam released is hold. It just flopped onto it's side and lay there, the only sign of life being it's eaving sides. It didn't even react when Meg and Fizz leapt in beside it. Molly felt a ımp in her throat and her eyes stung. It looked to her as though the foal was dying fter all. Her vision blurring, she stumbled round to the passenger side and lambered in, not noticing that the two dogs were laying close to the foal and eginning to wash around it's head with their tongues. Sam's face was grim as he tarted the vehicle, did a slow three point turn in the land and drove carefully back to he farmyard.

When they arrived back at the farm, Sam told Molly to stay seated for a noment whilst he went to speak to two of his farm workers. Molly watched as one isappeared into the barn, returning shortly with a collection of ropes and straps, vhilst the other hitched up a trailer to the smaller of two tractors parked nearby, the ne with a spiked attachment that Sam used for moving the large round bales of hay round the place. When Sam returned to the land-rover, he climbed in and drove it cross to one of barns, the one where Sam kept his two Clydesdale mares, each in a oomy pen with deep straw bedding. Sam climbed out of the vehicle, beckoning for lolly to follow him to give him a hand. As she walked round to join Sam, she gave a asp of delighted surprise.

Oh! Pepper's had her foal!" Before she could go over for a closer look, Sam called ut to her.

You can have a good look at him later, let's get your little tyke sorted out first." As e spoke, Sam lifted a sheep hurdle from a stack against the wall and carried it into he corner, close to but not touching, Pepper's pen. Molly had to half drag her hurdle cross for Sam to attach it to his one. They repeated this a few times until they had onstructed a roomy pen like the ones the mares occupied then they bedded the rea down with clean straw. Sam opened the back of the land-rover At first sight, lolly thought they were too late and the foal had died during the short journey up the ıne, then she saw he was still breathing. His face was damp where the two collies ad been comforting him.

Hey gal," Sam said quietly, "run over to the house and ask Jean for the orphan kit –

the calving one."

"The orphan kit?" Molly was puzzled. Sam gave a brief nod and then began to busy himself with pulling the edge of the sacks towards him so that the foal would be slid close enough for him to pick it up. "Do you need a hand Sam?"

"Nope, I can manage, you go get that kit." Sam grunted as he put his arms around the foal's body and prepared to lift it. Molly turned and ran from the barn.

Within minutes, Molly was back, carrying a large plastic box. The foal was laid on it's side in the deep straw of the pen, still breathing, just. Sam was in with Pepper, sitting on an old milking stool with a clean jug in his left hand. With his right, he was gently drawing white frothy milk into the jug from Pepper's teats. He looked up as Molly arrived, out of breath.

"Good job this old mare don't mind me doing this. If it were the other one, Shandy, she'd kick yer across the barn. 'Ere, 'old this" With that, Sam rose stiffly from his seat and handed Molly the jug of milk. "That'll do fer now, if we can get the poor soul to sup it."

"If you can't, no one can, Sam." Jean, Sam's wife, had followed Molly back to the barn. She moved across to the pen and looked down at the foal. "Poor little mite. Do we know what happened?"

Sam shook his head. "Travellers I reckon. Dead mare's a typical gypsy cob. Reckon when she died, they couldn't be bothered to raise an orphan foal so dumped the pair of 'em. Probably thought this 'un was a goner too."

"Well, we'll see about that." Jean said briskly. Taking the plastic box from Molly, Jean opened it up, revealing an assortment of plastic feeding bottles, tubes, bowls, jugs and teats, all wrapped in cling film. She glanced up at Molly's puzzled face and explained "We always seem to have one or two orphaned calves or lambs so we made up kits so we're always prepared."

"What's that?" Molly pointed to a clear polythene bag full of a creamy coloured powder.

"A colostrum substitute and milk replacement. It has lots of added stuff to make up for a baby missing out on it's mum's first milk."

"Colostrum?" Molly asked with a puzzled frown. Jean smiled and explained that the milk produced in the first couple of days was called 'colostrum' and contained lots of antibodies to help guard the baby's system against illnesses until the baby had built up it's own antibodies. Molly nodded, thinking she understood what Jean meant but vowing to look it up later when she got home.

"That won't be much good for this little one though, it's for cattle, not horses." Jean went on ruefully.

"Wouldn't there be some in Pepper's milk?" said Molly nodding down at the jug she still held.

"Naw," Sam piped up, "Pepper's foal is over two weeks old now, past the time for colostrum." As Sam spoke, Jean took the jug of milk from Molly and busied herself filling a bottle and fitting it with a teat from the orphan kit.

"Okay, let's see if we can get a drink into this little one." She went into the pen. Again, Molly felt panic rise in her throat as the foal lay motionless, not responding to Jean's presence at all. Then, yet again, she breathed a sigh of relief as she saw the foal's ribs were moving.

Jean propped the bottle in the straw and moved towards the foal's back end.
"First things first." She muttered, almost to herself. Gently, she lifted the uppermost of
the foal's hind legs and peered beneath it. "Okay, little man, let's get you sorted." She
put the leg gently down and moved back to the foal's head.

"It's a boy?" Molly asked, to make sure she had heard Jean right.

"Yep, a boy. A little colt. Why don't you pick a name for him?"

Molly shrugged. "I'll see what I can think of." she said. Jean nodded, seeming to
understand that Molly was reluctant to name the colt whilst it's survival hung in the
balance.

Jean quietly settled herself down in the straw whilst gently lifting the foal's
head into her lap. The foal didn't even twitch an ear. Molly swallowed hard, blinking
back tears. She watched as Jean gently touched the corner of the foal's mouth with
the teat. Gently wiggling the bottle, she managed to get the tip of the teat just
between the foal's lips and gave the bottle the tiniest squeeze so a few drops of milk
dribbled onto the foal's tongue. Molly held her breath. Nothing happened for a few
seconds. To Molly it seemed like hours. Then she saw the foal's mouth move slightly
and a tiny pink tip of his tongue flicked out between his lips. Jean gently squeezed in
a few drops more. Again the foal's mouth moved. Molly let her breath out with a rush.
When Jean dribbled a third lot of milk into his mouth, the foal carried on moving it's
tongue and lips as if seeking more. Quietly, Jean handed the bottle to Sam and then
slowly altered her sitting position so that the foal's shoulders were now in her lap and
she could hold the colt's head at a better angle for him to be able to drink properly.
As the sound of the tractor returning was heard outside, Sam handed back the bottle
to Jean. Picking up another clean jug, he grunted "back in a minute" and hobbled out
of the barn.

Molly watched, fascinated, as Jean, finally satisfied with the position of both
herself and the colt, eased the teat into the front of the foal's mouth. The foal, eyes
still closed, opened it's mouth slightly. Jean gently wriggled the teat further in and,
with a gentle squeeze, again dribbled the milk onto the foal's tongue. The foal gave a
tentative suck, then another. Then he got into a rhythm. It wasn't the normal frantic
sucking small animals usually did, just a small suck every few seconds, but at least
he was drinking and Molly watched happily as the level of milk in the bottle slowly
went down.

"Oh!" Molly could barely speak as her emotions welled up inside her chest. "He's
drinking! Does that mean he's going to be okay?"

"There's a long road to tread yet." Sam's voice made Molly jump. "But the little fella
looks a bit better and maybe this'll help." Molly turned and saw that Sam was holding
a small jug. The milk in it looked watery compared with what the foal was currently
drinking. "I reckoned this little fella ain't more than half a day or at most a day old an'
that mare weren't long dead so I decided to see if I could draw summat off 'er." He
shook his head and sighed sadly. "I 'ate milkin' dead 'uns."

"Is that colostrum then?" Molly asked.

"Aye, near as dammit I reckon." He plucked another bottle from the orphan kit and
hobbled away again. Molly looked back at Jean and the colt. The foal had stopped

sucking and let go of the teat having drunk about half the bottle's contents. Better yet, he'd opened his eyes and seemed to be holding his head up without Jean's help.

"That'll do for now." Jean said softly. She held the bottle out for Molly to take and gently eased the foal up so he was lying on his brisket. The foal looked a lot happier as Jean eased the stiffness out of her body and stood up. She left the pen and took the bottle back from Molly. "Back in a tick" she said as she toddled off in Sam's wake.

A sudden whine caused Molly to look down. Fizz and Meg hadn't made a sound until now, in fact Molly had forgotten that the dogs were there. It was Meg who had whined and she was pushing her nose at the join between two of the hurdles.

"Let her in." Sam and Jean had returned and Sam nodded down at his dog. Molly eased the hurdles apart so that Meg could squeeze through the gap and into the pen. She crept up to the foal and sniffed at it's face before starting to lick the traces of milk off. After a few minutes, the dog settled in the straw, lying curled up against the foal's chest. Sam grinned broadly. "Come on then folks," he said, "Meg will keep an eye on him, I need a cuppa after all the excitement!"

Molly could barely tear herself away.

"Let them settle." whispered Jean, placing her hand on Molly's shoulder. Together the three of them walked out into the sunshine, Fizz trotting at Molly's side.

*   *   *   *   *

2

Molly woke up to the sound of snuffling in her ear. As she opened her eyes, Fizz licked her face briefly the jumped off the bed. Running to the bedroom door, tail wagging wildly, the dog looked back at Molly and gave a small whine. Molly glanced at her bedside clock. It was only half past seven in the morning. Mum wouldn't be up for at least another half an hour. Fizz whined again, her whole body now wagging. Molly frowned slightly. It was unlike Fizz to get so excited first thing in the morning. Then, in a rush, Molly remembered her adventures the day before. Scrambling out of bed, she quickly gathered up the clothes she had discarded the night before when she had finally come to bed, so exhausted that she hadn't even read her book before going to sleep.

She could only find one sock. She began to search for the other one then, as Fizz whined again, Molly waved the one sock she had found and spoke in a whisper, not wishing to disturb her sleeping parent in the next room.
"Fizz, find my sock. Find it!"
Wriggling madly, Fizz began rushing round the room, nose twitching, eventually locating the missing sock on the windowsill, behind the curtain. How it had got there, Molly would probably never know. Molly dressed quickly then carefully opened the bedroom door as quietly as she could. To her surprise, she could hear noises from the kitchen downstairs. Her mother was obviously already up! Oh well, Molly thought, at least she didn't have to sneak around trying to be quiet now.

As Molly entered the kitchen, her mother was reading a newspaper and drinking a mug of tea, her morning routine for as long as Molly could remember. As she heard Molly coming through the kitchen door, Mrs Peters looked up and smiled warmly at her daughter.
"Don't forget Gary's coming home on leave today." She said.
Molly paused as she reached for the cornflake packet. Oh crumbs, she *had* forgotten! How on earth could she had done that? Although he was ten years older than Molly, her brother Gary had always looked out for his little sister and she missed him terribly since he had joined the army when he was eighteen. Even more so since Dad had died. That was the last time she had seen her big brother, when he came home on 'compassionate leave' for a few days.
"Um." Molly felt herself blush slightly at her memory lapse. "What time is he going to be here?"
Mrs Peters shrugged. "You know your brother. He'll get here when he arrives as usual. Did you have any plans for today then?"
Molly felt her blush deepen. She wasn't sure why she hadn't told her mother about the colt. Maybe because, for once, it was *her* secret. She wasn't even sure she'd tell Gary about it when he finally arrived. She busied herself with putting milk and sugar

on her cereal so she had an excuse not to look at her mother.

"Um, not much really. Just that I saw old Sam yesterday and Pepper's had her foal so I was going to go up today to see it." Molly thought over her words. Not a word of a lie. Just not the whole truth. In fact, nowhere near the whole truth!

"How lovely!" Molly's Mother enthused. "I'm sure Gary would love to see the foal as well so, if you think Sam won't mind, I'll get Gary to come and pick you up from the farm if he arrives early enough, shall I?"

Molly nodded, swallowing the last of her breakfast. "Yeah, sure. See you later, Mum." She gave her mother a quick kiss on the cheek then, calling Fizz, she ran from the house before her mother could think up some chores for Molly to occupy herself with instead.

Molly ran all the way to the farm in an emotional turmoil. What if the foal had died during the night? As she went through the farm gate, she saw Sam and his men in one of the fields with a small digger gouging a huge hole out of the ground. Meg spotted Molly and Fizz first and raced across to greet them, causing Sam to look up. He waved, turned and said something to his men then began to hobble in Molly's direction, smiling broadly. Molly felt a rush of relief. Surely Sam wouldn't be smiling if there was bad news about the colt?

"Alright gal?" Sam called as he approached. "Come to take a turn at feeding the little guy have yer?"

"Is he okay then?" Molly asked.

"Aye, he's okay. Proper fighter that one. Even been on his feet a few times." He glanced at the digger. "They're burying his Mam."

"Oh." Molly looked sadly at the men as they worked. "I'm sorry."

"What yer apologising for? Weren't your fault she died, nor your fault she were dumped like that. Come on, let's go and see this colt."

Pepper and Shandy were out in the field at the front of the barn, Pepper's foal stretched out asleep beside his mother, almost obscured by the daisies. Seeing her owner and Molly going past, Pepper whickered. She liked Molly, although probably only because the girl always had mints or treats in her pocket. When Molly gave no sign of going up to the fence with any goodies, Pepper went back to her grazing whilst her foal slept on.

As they entered the barn, Molly was overjoyed when the colt, standing looking at the door, greeted them with a high pitched whinney. Molly was about to rush up to the pen when Sam stopped her with a gentle but firm hand on her shoulder.

"Now then, gal, you know better than to run towards 'em like that."

Molly blushed. Of course she did! She'd just got a bit carried away. "Sorry Sam." She mumbled.

"Slow and steady then gal," Sam gave her shoulder a small squeeze, "off yer go."

Molly walked sedately towards the pen whilst the colt watched her intently. She realised she hadn't really had a chance to look at him properly the day before. She'd been too concerned with watching Jean trying to save his life. Molly realised hat he wasn't completely black as she had thought. As well as the white star on his orehead, she saw he also had a long white 'stocking' on his off hind leg and a splodge of white under his tummy, as if someone had thrown a handful of white paint up underneath him.

"He's lovely!" Molly exclaimed. "Is he drinking okay?" She turned to Sam.

"Aye, he's got the hang of that right enough. Had the stuff I got off his Mam last night. Got plenty of Pepper's milk into him since then. He can have some more now if you'd like to try feeding him yerself?"

"Can I really?" Molly asked eagerly. "Oh! Yes please!"

"Right enough. Come with me then."

Sam took Molly across the barn to a small room built onto the side. In the room there was an electric kettle on a long worktop, a huge shiny sink, a fridge and several cupboards. Sam filled the kettle with water and switched it on. Then he opened the fridge and took out a bottle of what was, presumably, more milk from the generous Pepper. He removed the top of the bottle and replaced it with a rubber teat. When the kettle had boiled, Sam poured the water into a bowl and dropped the bottle in so it stood upright in the hot water. Every so often, he took the bottle out of the water, gave it a good shake, then dripped a few drops onto the inside of his wrist. Soon, Sam gave a grunt of satisfaction and handed the bottle to Molly.

"That's about just right. Come on gal."

As he went back out into the barn, Molly followed behind, clutching the bottle of warm milk tightly. Her heart was thumping with excitement. Sam smiled down at her as they reached the pen and the colt gave his tiny little whicker at the sight of the bottle.

"He's happy to drink standing now. Do yer want the old stool to sit on or will yer stand yerself?" he asked.

"I think I'll be fine standing." Molly whispered. For some reason, she was feeling a little overawed.

Sam opened up a gap in the hurdles so that Molly could enter the pen. The colt looked at her a little warily at first so she gently reached out her hand and scratched his neck. That seemed to reassure him and he stepped forward, nudging at the bottle in Molly's hand.

"Careful now gal," Sam muttered, "you need to keep the bottle at a bit of an angle so that he don't just suck air."

Molly nodded, murmuring to the foal the way she had the day before during his rescue. She touched his lips with the teat of the bottled and was surprised at how quickly he grabbed hold of it and began to drink. So different from the day before when he hardly seemed to have the strength to suck at all! It seemed almost no time at all before the bottle was empty and the foal was nudging her, dribbling the last few drops of milks onto her hand. Molly handed the bottle back to Sam and stood with the foal, scratching him around all the places his mother would have caressed him.

"Try this." Sam said from behind her. Turning, she saw he was holding a small body brush. She took it and began brushing the foal's coat. "You okay staying with him fer now?" Sam asked, "only I should really go and help the lads with that poor mare."

"Yes, I'll be fine. Thank you Sam." She smiled at the old man as he grunted and walked out of the barn towards his gruesome task.

Using the body brush, Molly groomed the colt all over his body with firm but gentle strokes. She grinned to herself as the little horse arched his neck and, as she brushed what she now thought of as his 'itchy spots' he leaned into her as if asking her to brush him harder.

"Have you thought of a name for him yet?" Jean's voice made Molly jump, causing the foal to jump sideways. "Whoops!" Jean said apologetically, "Sorry, I didn't mean to startle you both. I should have known better!"

Molly reached out towards the foal and, talking softly to him, rubbed the edge of the brush against his shoulder. He began to relax again and stepped forwards to wards Molly.

"Tyke." Molly whispered.

"Pardon? Did you say Tyke?" Jean asked.

"Yep." Molly nodded firmly. "Sam keeps calling him a 'little tyke' so I guess he already named him.

"Tyke" Jean repeated and gave a chuckle. "It's a good name, suits him. Did Sam tell you we've named Pepper's foal 'Buster'?"

"No, he didn't. But it's a good name. I like that." Molly grinned at Jean. I've decided on a posh name too, for when we go to shows."

"Oh?" Jean raised her eyebrows. "What's that then? 'Little Tyke'?"

"Nope." Molly shook her head vigorously. "His show name's going to be 'Secret Gypsy'."

Jean nodded in her turn. "Yes, I like that. It'll look good on his passport."

"Passport?" Molly frowned. "What do you mean about a passport?"

"It's the law in England," Jean explained "that every foal is passported and microchipped before it's six months old."

"Oh." Molly looked at the foal. "Doesn't that cost a lot of money?" Molly hated to admit it but money was scarce at home since Dad had died. She knew horses were expensive. A horrifying thought suddenly occurred to her. "Oh my gosh!" She exclaimed, "I can't keep him! There's no way I can pay to keep a horse!"

"Calm down, Molly." Jean said gently. "I'm sure we can work something out. At the moment, at least, you don't need to worry. His main cost is in time. Pepper has plenty of milk to spare so you've no need to think about money, not yet anyway."

But Molly couldn't help herself. Tears filled her eyes as she look at Tyke. She already adored him so much, she hated the thought of not being able to keep him. The foal gazed at her for a few moments then turned and, on long, still wobbly, legs, he wandered over to the corner of the pen and flopped down, obviously deciding it was time for a nap. Molly was vaguely aware of Jean walking away. Swallowing the lump in her throat, Molly went slowly up to Tyke and sat down beside him, gently stroking him with the brush and still desperately fighting back her tears.

"Wakey, wakey, sleeping beauty." Her brother's voice woke Molly from her doze. Blinking in the daylight, she found herself looking up into Gary's grinning face with it's deep blue eyes. She smiled up at him and went to get up, then she realised there was something heavy resting on her stomach. She glanced down, expecting to see Fizz lying across her but instead she saw that Tyke had decided to use her as a llow. Fizz was curled up in the straw beside him. Molly stayed where she was, not anting to disturb the sleeping animals, although in truth Fizz was already awake nd trembling with excitement at Gary's presence. Somehow, the dog knew that ving in to the urge to greet Gary in her usual boisterous fashion was not appropriate hilst she was lying close to Tyke.

Molly gently stroked Tyke's head, rousing him from his snoozing. He woke up uickly, the deep-seated instincts of the prey animal already fully developed and inging him to full alertness in a heartbeat, causing him to leap to his feet and snort alarm before ramming himself against the back of the pen. Taking advantage of e opportunity, Fizz leapt the hurdle, causing Tyke to give out another snort of arm. Wriggling and whining with excitement, Fizz jumped up at Gary, almost using him to overbalance in her excitement.

ley, there, steady girl!" Gary held out his arms to the dog and she leapt up into em, whining as she licked his face.

Tyke's ears were flicking back and forth and his eyes and nostrils were wide lth alarm as he watched the display. Molly turned to him, speaking nonsense in soft nes as she slowly approached, stretching her fingertips out towards him. When she uched him, Tyke's skin quivered but he didn't move away so Molly started with her cratching again. She was vaguely aware of Gary putting Fizz down and telling the 0g to settle. Fizz went into a typical collie crouch, eyes flicking between Gary and olly. Obedient enough to stay still but also alert so as to be able to obey any ommand immediately it was given.

ary looked at his little sister.

5o, Sis, what have you got there? Sam said you found him in a ditch?"

Fizz found him really." Molly said, still scratching Tyke's withers where he seemed like it the most. "He was in the ditch down the lane. His mum's dead."

Yeah, Sam said. They're just filling in the hole where they've buried the poor thing. am reckons the mare was still a baby herself, only about two or three years old. oody evil, some people."

3ary! You shouldn't swear!" Molly realised she sounded a bit like her mother.

Nell, do you blame me sis?"

olly had to admit that she couldn't blame him at all really. She'd actually sworn erself when she had found the mare mare and foal, albeit only inside her head. She irugged.

5o sis, you appear to have got yourself a horse. Have you told Mum yet?"

No!" Molly ran towards Gary, making Tyke jump. "I haven't told her anything! ease, don't tell her!" Molly half sobbed on the words.

Nhy not?" Gary frowned down at Molly. "What's the big deal?"

3ecause I don't want to worry her! I won't be able to keep him anyway! We've no oney for a horse!" Despite herself, Molly burst into noisy sobs.

*　　*　　*　　*　　*

3

It was Gary's last full day of being on leave. Molly wished he could stay longer but she knew that the army were very strict about their soldiers getting back to camp on time. The two weeks he had been at home had flown by. Gary had finally agreed to keep Tyke a secret, at least for the moment and, if Mrs Peters was curious about Molly and Gary spending so much time up at the farm, she kept her thoughts to herself.

Gary's time in the King's Troop of the Royal Horse Artillery had proved to be a useful asset to Molly during his leave. Gary had bought a nice new foal slip and lead rope and Molly thought her horse looked really smart in it. With Gary's help, in just two weeks, Molly had taught Tyke to lead. Molly had also, again with Gary's help, taught Tyke to pick up his feet so that she could clean them out the way her brother had shown her. Molly had used some of her precious Christmas money to buy Tyke a grooming kit too. The foal was even starting to nibble proper horse food, and pieces of carrot and apple, as well as nibbling at the grass whenever he was outside. For the most part though, Tyke still relied on Pepper's generous donations of milk. Feeding him was easier now, since Sam had adopted the routine he used with his calves and taught Tyke to drink from a bucket.

As Molly and her brother arrived at the farm, Sam was waiting for them by the gate, almost as though he'd been watching out for their arrival. Molly felt a surge of panic.
"Sam, what's wrong?" She asked as she rushed up to the old farmer.
"Hush gal, nothing's wrong." Sam put his finger's to his lips. "Come and look at this." he whispered. Then he walked off in the direction of the horse paddock.

For the past week, Tyke had been going out in the paddock during the day, in his own little section. Sam had placed a couple of strands of electric fencing tape across the corner of the paddock so that Tyke could see the other horses but not get bullied by them. The fence wasn't connected to the electric but Shandy, Pepper and Buster respected the fence and Tyke had followed their example. As the three humans approached the paddock, Molly couldn't see any sign of Tyke but she noticed Pepper was standing right up against the tape fence, the hind leg nearest the tape stretched out behind her and raised slightly off the ground. Molly looked at Sam in alarm.
"What's wrong with Pepper's leg? Has she hurt herself?"
"Shhhh!" Sam put his finger to his lips again. He beckoned Molly and Gary to follow him into the shade of the huge barn wall. Pepper seemed to be half dozing and, on the ground nearby, Buster was laid flat out on his side, fast asleep. Shandy was in the middle of the paddock, quietly grazing. As they drew level with Pepper's quarters, Molly's eyes widened in surprise as she spotted Tyke. His head was lowered and

tipped slightly sideways as he thrust his muzzle between the two strands of tape.

"Oh!" She gasped, "She's feeding him!"

"Aye" Sam said, "she's feeding him on the quiet. I noticed she was often by the fence when Buster was asleep and Tyke'd be close on the other side but they'd both walk off whenever they saw me coming so, today, I hid down near the barn door where they couldn't see me.

Gary chuckled. "Well that explains why he's never very eager for his bottle when he comes in!"

"Actually," Sam said, "while yer both here, I'd like to try an experiment, just to see what happens."

"What were you thinking of?" Gary asked.

"What say we try putting Tyke in with Pepper and Buster, as I say, just to see what happens." Sam suggested.

"What about Shandy?" Molly piped up, glancing over at the other horse still grazing nearby.

"Well I did wonder about that." Sam looked at the young mare speculatively. But then I saw her grooming Tyke over the fence earlier so I reckon she'll be fine. They all have head-collars on anyways so, if needs be, we can grab 'em."

"Sounds okay." Gary nodded. What do you think Molly? He's your foal after all."

"If you think he won't get hurt, I think it's a good idea. I'm sure he gets lonely on his own."

"Right." Said Gary. He turned to Sam. "So, what's the plan of action then?"

"Molly, you go and get Jean to come across, just in case there's trouble. I'll go and get some food and some lead ropes. Can't take too many precautions when you're doing summat new with horses."

By the time Jean and Molly arrived back at the paddock, Sam was all prepared.

" Right folks, here goes. I reckon we may as well just open the gate tape and let Tyke through then just wait to see what happens. If there's a problem, we'll just have to try and grab 'em again."

"Sounds like a plan." said Gary. "So what are we waiting for?"

First things first, Sam sent Fizz and Meg away. They didn't need to add a pair of excitable collies into the mix. Then he walked into the paddock and Pepper moved away from the tape fence and into the field whilst Tyke scuttled away from his side, both of them looking, for want of a better phrase, as though they were trying to act innocent. Molly giggled nervously as she followed Gary and Jean in Sam's wake.

Spotting Molly, Tyke trotted over, his whickering greeting causing Buster to lift his head to see what was going on. Seeing people in the field and obviously curious, he scrambled untidily to his feet and trotted over to his mother. Shandy looked up from her grazing, her curiosity also aroused. Molly approached Tyke and scratched him for a moment then, taking a gentle hold on his foal slip, she led him towards Sam as Sam unhooked the tape to let them through. Molly led Tyke through into the main part of the paddock, gave him a small pat then released her hold on the foal-slip and stepped away from him.

Buster was the first to respond. He walked over to Tyke, champing his lips in the classic greeting of very young horses, his ears flicking back and forth. Tyke mimicked Buster's moves. The two foals touched noses then Tyke gave a high pitched squeal and stamped his tiny hoof. Suddenly there was a bellowing neigh and the ground began to shake. Shandy, ears pinned flat back, teeth bared, was bearing down on the foals. Molly screamed. Gary rushed forwards to try and head the mare off but the huge Clydesdale showed that, despite weighing almost a ton, like most horses she was very agile if she needed to be. She dodged round Gary, although her shoulder banged against his and he fell to the ground. Molly screamed again as Shandy reached the foals. Sam was shouting and waving a lead rope and Jean was running towards Tyke.

Shandy opened her jaws wide and grabbed Buster! She sank her teeth into his neck and flung him away from Tyke before turning to the the younger foal in his turn. Before the humans could react to this unexpected turn – they never dreamed Shandy would have attacked Buster – Pepper cannoned into Shandy, causing the mare to stumble and almost go down. As Shandy recovered herself, Pepper spun and lashed out with both hind legs, catching Shandy a heavy blow on the ribs with her hooves. Tyke spotted Molly and started to gallop towards her but, before he could reach her, Shandy had caught up with him. Before Molly could scream again, Shandy had circled around Tyke and, instead of attacking him, herded him across the paddock, away from the humans and the other horses. Pepper had gone over to Buster, now back on his feet, and was nuzzling him all over. Sam watched Shandy and Tyke as the mare cantered around the perimeter of the paddock with the little black foal beside her. Gary scrambled to his feet as Jean went over to Molly and put her arms around her.

Muttering under his breath, Sam went across to Pepper and Buster and checked the foal over. Just as he was reaching up to take Pepper's head-collar to lead her into the smaller section, Shandy and Tyke galloped past, the little colt looking tiny next to the huge bulk of the draught horse. Pepper flung her head up, snorted and flung herself forward into a flat out gallop, Buster by her side.

Molly was shaking as she watched the four horses thundering around the paddock, changing direction after every few circuits. Dark patches of sweat were starting to appear on all their coats. Gary came to stand with Molly and Jean and they watched whilst old Sam went to stand closer to the imaginary 'track' the horses seemed to be following. Each time they thundered past him, he gave a long, drawn out 'whoa' in a low but carrying voice, following it up with "steady there girls, whoa boys". Whether or not it was the sound of Sam's voice, or simply that they were getting tired, Molly didn't know but after a few more circuits, as if responding to a hidden signal, all four horses dropped back into trot. They all trotted for a couple more circuits and then Pepper, with Buster still close at her side, veered off the invisible track and trotted over to Sam, where she halted and stood, sides heaving, sweat darkening her neck and flanks. Buster was even worse, looking as though someone had thrown a couple of buckets of water over him. Meanwhile, Shandy and Tyke had started cantering again. Sam watched them for a moment then took hold of

Pepper's head-collar and led her over to the taped off section. With Buster still close, Pepper allowed herself to be led into the enclosure. Sam released the mare and put the loose strands of tape back across the gap before walking back to join the others. "Let's see if they settle now," Sam said. The four people stood watching quietly as Shandy and Tyke slowed slightly then continued to trot around the paddock. Again Sam began calling in low, carrying tones.
"Whoa there Shandy, steady old gal."

It seemed an age to Molly before the mare and foal finally slowed to a walk and then, within a few strides, they halted and Shandy stood looking around her, breathing heavily. Poor Tyke looked exhausted. Suddenly, Shandy gave a low whicker and strode towards the tape fence. Pepper approached from the other side with an answering whicker. When they had both reached the fence, the mares stood as close to each other as they could and began to groom each other's necks, withers and shoulders with their teeth. Ignored now by the mares, Buster and Tyke had both flopped down on the ground, each as exhausted as the other by their adventure.
"So what now?" Molly asked.
"I reckon we need a cuppa after all that excitement." Sam said, Jean nodded her assent.
"Sounds good." agreed Gary, flexing his arm.
Jean glanced at him "Did the mare hurt you?"
"Not really." Gary grimaced as he rubbed his shoulder. "It's more the way I hit the ground than any damage the mare did. She didn't mean it anyway."
"Naw, yer right, she didn't" Sam agreed. "That's the thing about horses, they'll try to avoid running you down if they can – unless they're in a proper blind panic. Though sometimes you can get a proper nasty tempered one, luckily not often."
"Yeah, we've got one like that at Woolwich." said Gary, "Kick a fly's eye out he could. I wouldn't stand in front of him if he was galloping towards me, not for any money! Especially when he's hauling the gun carriage!" They all laughed at the thought then, together, they made their way out of the paddock and across to the house, leaving the two mares grooming each other over the tape fence and the foals both deep in an exhausted sleep.

In the kitchen, they seated themselves around the big wooden table, welcome mugs of hot tea in hand and freshly baked scones piled high on a plate before them. Finishing off his second scone, Gary leaned back in his chair.
"I wish you could come and cook at the barracks Jean." He grinned at the farmer's wife.
"Don't be daft." Jean said, giving Gary a playful tap on his shoulder with her hand. "Oops, sorry!" she apologised as Gary winced. Gary waved away her apology. He looked at Molly.
"So sis," he said, "you now have a horse of your own. When are you going to learn to ride?"
"Last time I mentioned riding to mum she said it was just too expensive so it looks like I'm not." Molly looked down at her cup of tea sadly.
"Actually, we may be able to help you there." said Jean as she began buttering another plate of scones. "A friend has asked if she can keep her daughter's old pony

© Chrissie Turner 2017

here. The girl's outgrown him but they don't want to sell him. He's in his twenties but I gather he still has plenty of life in him! I'm sure, if I explain, his owner would be happy for you to ride him."

"Really? Molly looked at Jean excitedly. "Do you think I could?"

"Well, I can but ask, I'm sure it won't be a problem."

"Well, that solves my little quandary then," Gary piped up, "I was wondering about buying my little sister a present before I go back but couldn't think of what to get. I guess we'd better visit the tack shop first thing tomorrow, get a riding hat at least."

Molly threw her arms around her brother, "Oh Gary, thank you!"

"Ah well," Sam mumbled, "better go and check on them horses I suppose. See if they've settled down yet after all that excitement this morning.

When they got to the paddock, the first thing they saw was yards of fencing tape, most of the posts still attached, strewn across the field. Molly felt a moment of panic then she noticed the horses. The two mares were grazing side by side and both foals were lying flat out on their sides nearby, soundly sleeping.

"Well," Gary chuckled, "I guess that solves that question then. But what about when you bring them in? Are you going to put Tyke in with Shandy?"

Sam looked up at the cloudless sky. " No, I don't think so. In fact, the weather's so good at the moment, we'll probably leave then out full time for a while."

Gary nodded, "That's a good idea."

Molly heaved a huge sigh of relief as she watched the four horses. She hadn't quite realised how worried she'd been. She leant on the top rail of the post and rail fencing, watching the peaceful scene. She didn't even notice Gary taking Sam to one side and handing him a wad of money. Then Gary's voice broke into her reverie.

"Come on then sis, we may as well go to the tack shop now instead of tomorrow. I reckon, after his adventures this morning, Tyke will be too tired to have any leading lessons today."

*　　　*　　　*　　　*　　　*

4

A week later, Molly was running towards the farm with Fizz by her side in the arly morning sunshine. Today was a busy day. A special day. This morning, the vet as coming to do the foals microchips and to fill out the identification forms for the assports. Then, later on, the new pony was arriving!

Molly had been worrying about the vet, about how she could possibly pay for verything. She'd researched it online and discovered that, in total, it could easily ost over a hundred pounds! When she had emailed Gary in a panic, he replied that ne had no need to worry, that he, Gary, had sorted everything out with Sam. Molly new she was lucky to have a brother like Gary, even though he did keep harassing er about telling their mother about Tyke.

About half way along the lane, Molly noticed a strange man poking around nder the bushes with a big stick. Fizz growled low in her throat, hackles rising, as olly ran past the man, determinedly not looking at him. Hey! You there!" the man shouted. Molly ran faster. Young girls didn't stop to talk to range men in lonely lanes, even if they did have a protective dog like Fizz to protect em. The man shouted again. Molly ignored him, called Fizz to come close to her nd ran as fast as her legs could carry her towards the farm.

When Molly arrived at the farm, she saw that Jean and Sam had already ought the horses in to the barn. For some reason, Molly was relieved that Tyke asn't out in the field. Although the horse paddock wasn't in full view of the lane, olly felt better knowing that the foal was out of sight. She felt uncomfortable about e man who'd been poking in the hedges but she wasn't quite sure why. Jean alked over to Molly, holding a sheaf of papers. These are the forms for the passport and microchip." She showed the forms to olly. On one, there were some line drawings of a horse showing each side, front d back of a horse's body. Jean pointed out, "This is where the vet draws all the orse's marking and hair whorls where the coat changes direction." Molly nodded. It as one of the things she'd discovered when she had googled 'horse passports' last ght. "Okay," Jean went on, "Now, I hope you don't mind but we got Gary to sign ese forms before he went back to camp so Tyke will be registered in his name. Is at alright?" olly nodded again. She was quite pleased about the idea really but, even if she had inded, she couldn't really protest about it. After all, Gary was paying for everything! olly suddenly remembered the man in the lane and decided to tell Jean about it. Whereabouts in the lane?" Jean asked, frowning, as Molly explained what had appened. Near where I found Tyke and his Mum I think." Molly replied. As she spoke, she ddenly thought she knew what the man had been looking for, although, after three weeks, would there really be anything left to find?

"Hmm." Jean looked at Molly, then she smiled. "Don't worry too much about it. I'll speak to Sam and get the men to keep their eyes peeled. Maybe we'll keep the horses in tonight, just in case, eh? In the meantime, whilst we're waiting for the vet, how about a nice cool drink?"

Feeling much better now she had told someone, Molly followed Jean back to the house. Neither of them noticed the shadowy figure of a man standing under the trees by the farm gate, watching them intently.

"So Molly, are you excited about Fred coming?" Jean asked as she cut thick slices from a still warm fruit cake.

"Fred?" Molly looked up, puzzled.

"OH! Sorry, I forget to tell you his name. Fred is my friend's pony. She says they should arrive around two O' clock."

"Um, yeah, I guess so." Molly mumbled before biting into her cake.

"Well, I must say, you don't seem to be very excited. Or are you still worried about the man in the lane?"

Molly looked at Jean with a frown. "What if he's looking for Tyke?"

"After all this time?" Jean shook her head. "I doubt it."

Molly wasn't convinced.

The sudden noise of barking dogs caused Molly to jump up from her chair, causing her to spill her drink down the front of her jeans.

"Hey! Steady on!" Jean grabbed a cloth to wipe up the mess and rub Molly's jeans down. "It'll just be the vet. You know what Meg and Fizz are like, especially Meg, she hates the vet!"

"Fizz too," Molly admitted with a smile, grateful that it had been a cool drink rather than hot tea that she had spilt. Jean finished her mopping up and threw the cloth into the washing basket by the utility room door.

"Come on then." Jean jerked her head towards the door. Together, she and Molly headed for the barn.

Tyke wasn't at all keen on this strange woman searching over his body as she looked for hair whorls. Nor was he keen on standing still as she drew the shape of his white markings on the passport form, despite Molly scratching his itchy spots. He was even less impressed by the needles, first vaccinations and then the thicker needle to insert the microchip. Finally though, the vet had finished. She handed Molly Tyke's paperwork. "There you go," she said with a smile. "Now, who do I send the account to?"

Jean, who had been holding Buster, spoke, "Put it on the farm account please."

"That's fine then." The vet looked down at Tyke. "He looks a lovely little chap, what's his breeding? He's obviously not a Clydesdale!" She laughed loudly, sounding not unlike a braying donkey. Tyke jumped at the sound.

"Er, he's a Cob cross." said Jean. "His mother died giving birth, sadly."

"Ah, sorry to hear that." replied the vet. "So he has a foster mum in that big bay mare?" She nodded towards Shandy. Luckily, she didn't seemed to notice Shandy wasn't 'in milk'. The vet shut her back of needles and medications. "Well, I'll see you soon." With a nod at Sam and Molly, the vet walked out of the barn towards her car. Suddenly she stopped and turned back.

"By the way," she said, "as I drove through the gate, I noticed a dodgy looking chap standing under the trees in the lane. Looked like he was watching the place so be on your guard, eh?" Without waiting for a reply, she turned away and left the barn.

"He's after Tyke! I know he is!" Molly cried, tears springing into her eyes.

"Now, now gal, don't fret yourself. I'll sort this." Sam looked at Jean and nodded. Taking hold of Molly's hand, she headed back to the house, calling Meg and Fizz as she went.

As Jean started to make some sandwiches for lunch, Molly was startled to hear deep throated barking from outside. Even though the sound was obviously made by something much bigger than a collie, Molly glanced across to where Fizz and Meg were lying quietly by the door, looking alert but staying quiet. Molly looked up at Jean.

"What's that noise?" She asked.

"Ah. I guess you've never met Bruno and Tyson, have you?" Jean carried on buttering slices of bread.

"Er, no." Molly shook her head. "Who are they?"

"They are a pair of Tibetan Mastiffs." Jean put down her knife and went to the fridge to get fillings for the sandwiches, talking as she went. "Put it this way, you wouldn't want to meet them, especially after dark!"

"So how come I've never seen them? Or heard them before?" Molly had seen pictures of Tibetan Mastiffs online when she did a school project about dog breeds earlier in the year. They looked distinctly unsociable.

"They live in one of the old stables round the back during the day." Jean explained. "When we've locked up for the night, Sam let's them out so they're loose in the yard until he gets up in the morning and puts them away again. Only Sam handles them. The men can't start work until the dogs have been shut in!"

"They're guard dogs then?"

"Oh yes. Much better than the German Shepherds we used to use. Even our chickens are safer. No fox would even get close to the the chicken coop! Talking of chickens," Jean crossed to the old fashioned pantry and rummaged around for a few minutes. "The chickens have been laying so many eggs lately.... Here, take these home with you." She handed Molly a carrier bag with at least two dozen eggs inside.

Lunch was over and Molly was in the barn grooming Tyke. Every day she went over the lessons she had taught him – with Gary's help – then tried to think of new things to do. Today she had an old bath towel which she had hung over the hurdles for the moment. She finished her grooming session by picking out Tykes feet. He was still a bit funny with the back ones, jerking his leg back and forth rapidly to try and snatch his foot out of Molly's grasp but Molly held the foot firmly, the way Gary had shown her and, eventually, Tyke would give in. Every day, the battle was a little bit shorter as Tyke realised he wasn't going to win.

It was cool in the barn. Being the middle of August, the heat outside was almost unbearable. Hence Jean and Sam had now adopted a new routine for the horses whereby they turned them out at night, after the heat and the flies had gone, then brought them into the barn first thing in the morning. Molly fretted about that now. With a strange man hanging around, would Tyke be safe out in the paddock all night? Then she remembered Jean saying that they would keep the horses in tonight and she began to relax. Especially since it meant that anyone trying to get into the farmyard would have to get past Tyson and Bruno first!

Her grooming finished, Molly picked the towel off the hurdle, glancing over at the new pen that had been constructed a few feet away for the new pony to go in when he arrived. Molly felt a flutter of excitement. Suddenly, Tyke nudged her hand to remind her that he was still there. She stroked his neck and then showed him the towel. Tyke sniffed at it then took it in his mouth and started chewing it. Molly laughed as Tyke shook his head up and down and the towel flapped up against his face, startling him. He dropped the towel and leapt back in surprise. When Molly laughed again, Tyke inched towards the towel on the floor, snorting. He sniffed at it then mouthed at it, before picking it up again. Molly grabbed the other end and there was a brief tug of war before Tyke let go. Molly spent the next half an hour playing with Tyke and the towel. She flapped it around him, put it on his back, dropped it over his head, wrapped it around his body – in fact anything she could think of until Tyke wasn't bothered by the towel at all. Just as she was beginning to run out of ideas, she heard the sound of a vehicle pulling up outside and Jean calling her name. Giving Tyke a last hug, Molly climbed out of the pen and ran outside. Fizz, who'd been dozing by the pen, trotted behind her.

A land-rover, even older looking than Sam's – and certainly muddier – pulling a battered looking old green trailer, had pulled into the farmyard. As Molly approached, she could hear whinnying coming from inside. The horses in the barn called back. The woman who climbed out of the driving seat of the vehicle also looked older than either Jean or Sam but her movements were much more sprightly than Sam's. She strode up to Molly.
"Hello!" Her voice was quite loud but it was clear she wasn't actually shouting. "You must be Molly! Jean's told me a lot about you!" She shook Molly's hand vigorously. "I'm Marion!" Dull thumping sounds were beginning to issue from the trailer. "Let's get this little beggar off then, before he wrecks the joint!" With that, Marion marched brusquely up to the back of the trailer and deftly undid the clips on the ramp before lowering the ramp to the ground.

Molly peered at a round, dark brown rump with a bushy tail that reached almost to the ground as Marion went through the empty left hand stall of the trailer to get to the pony's head. As Marion untied the pony's lead-rope, Jean stepped forward and unclipped the chain that ran across the pony's quarters.
"All set?" Marion called out. At Jean's affirmative, Marion replied, "Jolly good! Okay boy, back you go!" This last was obviously a command to the pony as the brown rump began to carefully emerge from the trailer, followed by the rest of the pony's body as the pony backed down the ramp. Finally, the front end of the pony emerged, followed closely by Marion. She patted the pony on the neck and turned to face Molly.

"Meet Fred. Believe it or not, he's a pure bred registered Fell pony, despite the fact that he's a bay." Marion saw the puzzled look on Molly's face. "The more traditional colour is black, my dear. There are some judges who would actually mark him down in the show ring, simply because of his colour. Of course, they shouldn't. Bay is a perfectly acceptable colour for a Fell pony but, hey ho, there you go! Luckily we aren't really into showing and this chap loves hacking and jumping!" Marion smiled. "Now, I rather you're going to be riding this little chap for me while he's here?" Molly simply nodded, feeling more than a little bit over-awed. "Jolly good!" Marion patted Molly's shoulder heartily then handed Molly the end of the lead-rope "I brought his tack, though it could do with a bit of a clean. It hasn't been used for a while!" Marion disappeared into the back of the land-rover and began rummaging around. Molly took the opportunity to have a good look at Fred.

The pony was dark bay, about thirteen-two hands high, stockily built and very hairy. His tail almost brushed the floor and his black mane was over half the depth of his neck. Molly had to push his forelock to one side so she could see his eyes. They were kind eyes, she thought, but maybe there was a glint of mischief too? Molly's musings were interrupted by Marion reappearing with a saddle and bridle. When Marion handed the tack over, Molly thought Marion's comment that it 'hadn't been used for a while' was definitely an understatement! Both the saddle and the bridle were almost completely white with mould and so stiff, they seemed made out of wood! Jean took the items from Molly. "We'll soon have this sorted." She smiled at Molly, "Why don't you take Fred into the barn so he can see his new home and meet his new friends? You can come to the house afterwards and Marion can tell you all about your new pal."

After Marion had left, leaving strict instructions about Fred – namely that he was to be left completely 'natural', no trimming or mane pulling or even shoes – Jean retrieved the saddle and bridle from the back porch and dumped it on the kitchen table. Molly grimaced. It was filthy, mouldy and stiff. It didn't even smell like leather! Fill the washing up bowl with warm water and I'll be right back." Jean instructed Molly. Jean returned just as Molly was carefully placing the bowl of water on the table beside the leather-work "Right," Jean said, seating herself beside Molly. "First things first. We need to undo every buckle and take everything apart." With that, Jean picked up the bridle and began to wrestle the stiff leather out of the buckles, tugging at the straps. Molly pulled the stirrup leathers off the saddle and slid the irons off the leathers. Jean dropped the snaffle bit into the bowl of water. "Drop those stirrup irons in here too," she told Molly. "Thank goodness all the metalwork is stainless steel, otherwise it would be rusted to bits! That girth is webbing so it can go in the washing machine with the numnah."

Once all the buckles had been undone and all the parts of the bridle were separated, Jean showed Molly how to use a damp – not wet – sponge to clean all the mould and dirt off the leather. As Molly looked at the jumbled pile of straps, she wondered how earth they were going to get it all back together again! However, it would seem that was a job for another day. Once all the leather was clean, though still stiff, Jean pulled the lid of a small bucket. Molly saw it was half full of a clear, golden fluid.

"Neatsfoot oil" Jean explained. She gathered up all the straps, including the stirrup leathers and dumped the whole lot into the bucket of oil, making sure everything was under the surface of the liquid. Then she handed Molly a small paintbrush, about an inch wide. "Obviously, we can't get the saddle into the bucket Molly, so you need to paint the oil onto the saddle. I think it will soak in quite quickly so you'll need to do several coats. Keep going until it stops soaking in. Molly picked up the brush and got to work whilst Jean busied herself cleaning the bit and stirrup irons, then she took the numnah and girth into the utility room where Molly could hear Jean putting the things into the washing machine and turning it on.

After about half an hour, Jean announced that it looked like the saddle had taken as much oil as it could, at least for the present. Asking Molly to bring the saddle, Jean picked up the bucket of oil, still containing the dismantled bridle and stirrup leathers, then she grabbed the now gleaming stirrup irons and bit and headed for the back door with Molly close behind. Jean led Molly round to the back of the barn where there was a small stable yard of six boxes, together with a tack-room and feed store. Jean briskly unlocked the two combination padlocks on the tack-room door and swung it open, stepping aside to let Molly enter the room first. As Jean flicked on the electric light, Molly's eyes widened at what she saw. Down either side of the room, several highly polished harnesses hung along the walls. At the far end, there were half a dozen saddle racks and bridle brackets. Only three racks held saddles and four bridles hung on the brackets.

"We do ride Pepper and Shandy occasionally," Jean explained, having seem Molly staring at the saddles, "and we always ride them a few times in December so we can take them to the Boxing Day Meet. Mind you, I had to go on my own last year because poor Sam's old bones weren't up to it really."

"Oh!" Exclaimed Molly, "Where's the meet?"

"Up at the Half Moon Pub in the village. Great social occasion!" She grinned at Molly. "You never know, you and Fred might be able to come along to the next one, after all, you've got four months to get ready for it!"

Molly looked uncertain. "I'm not sure my Mum would let me go hunting. She doesn't agree with it you see."

"Oh, don't worry about that. We don't actually follow the hunt, just go to the meet and move off with them. They always cut through the farm so that they can go round the cross country course on the farm over the back of us, so we peel off when they get here. There's no way I have the time to get two Clydesdale horses hunting fit!" She grinned again. "Maybe, if he's home for Christmas, your Gary would like to come along on Shandy?"

"I can ask him." Molly said. "If he goes too, Mum might be okay with it, I guess."

"Good. Now, pop your saddle on one of those racks at the end there dear while I sort out this bridle."

As Molly placed the saddle on one of the racks, Jean started started carefully lifting the leather-work out of the bucket of oil and hanging it on a four pronged hook that hung from the tack-room ceiling. Making sure the bucket was directly underneath the hook, to catch the drips of oil dropping off the leather, she wiped her hands on an d towel before glancing at her watch.

3ood grief!" Jean exclaimed, "It's half past four already! Doesn't time fly!"

Half four?" Molly was shocked at how late it was. "I need to go. Mum wants me >me before five!"

That's okay dear, you run along home now. No doubt we'll see you tomorrow?"

Don't you need me to do anything with Tyke and Fred before I go?" Molly didn't ant it to seem that she was shirking her horsey chores.

No, that's fine. It's been a busy day, hasn't it Molly? You get off home. It wouldn't do r you to get yourself grounded now, would it?"

f you're sure?" Molly was still reluctant to take advantage.

Dh, get on with you child!" Jean gave Molly a playful push towards the door. "Go on rl!"

Dkay Jean, I'll see you tomorrow. Thanks for everything!" Calling for Fizz, Molly ran >m the tack room. A low growl from the end stable reminded her about the guard >gs. Grateful that she didn't have to pass their stable as she left the yard, even ough they were securely locked up, Molly ran past the barn, just as Fizz came >unding around the corner. Although she had plenty of time, Molly still ran all the ay down the lane, still worried about the strange man she had seen that morning, it there was no sign of him now.

"Look at the state of you!" Mrs Peters looked exasperatedly at her daughter as olly ran into the house. "Dinner's almost ready so, if I were you, I'd at least wash my ands and drag a brush through my hair!"

Yes Mum." Molly mumbled as she turned to go upstairs to the bathroom. As she oked at herself in the mirror, Molly wasn't really surprised at her mother's reaction. here was a big smudge of oily dirt on her cheek and her shoulder length hair had :caped from her hair band. Taking a flannel from the side of the bath, Molly began fill the sink with warm water and tried to make herself look a little more esentable. Five minutes later, she was back in the kitchen helping her mother set e table, ready for their evening meal.

"We need to go and get your school uniform tomorrow." Mrs Peters inounced as she scraped the leftovers from dinner into Fizz's bowl, adding a tin of >g food and a handful of dog biscuits before putting the bowl down on the floor in >nt of the patiently waiting dog.

3ut I'm going to the farm tomorrow!" Molly protested.

Not tomorrow you're not! You're starting senior school in just over two weeks and e've got to get all the uniform, there's a huge list, goodness knows how we'll be able afford it all!"

3ut Mum, I promised Jean I'd go to the farm tomorrow! She's got a new pony for me ride!" Although Molly still hadn't told her mother about Tyke, she felt safe telling her ›out Fred.

Don't be silly girl, you can't ride!"

know that!" Molly glared at her mother. That's why Jean's going to teach me. arting tomorrow!"

've barely seen you all summer. I'm sure Jean won't mind if I have my daughter to yself for just one day. Getting the uniform isn't something I can do without you –

you need to try everything on you know! Now, get on the phone and tell Jean you won't be up tomorrow, or I'll ban you from the farm for the rest of the holiday!"

Finally admitting defeat, with tears stinging her eyes, Molly went into the lounge to call Jean. Despite herself, she couldn't hold back the sobs as she explained to Jean that her mother had forbidden her going to the farm the next day.

"Don't worry Molly, one day won't hurt and it will give Fred more time to settle in. Which school are you starting at?"

"Badger Road." Said Molly, between sniffs, wiping her nose on her sleeve.

"Oh, that's a good school I hear. That's where Marion's daughter went I think. You'll like it there.

"I hate school." Molly sniffed again. "I want to be with the horses!"

"Now, now, calm down." Jean said, "I'll see you the day after tomorrow. You take care." With that, Jean hung up. As she went through the hallway to head upstairs to her room, Molly glared at her mother, but it was a waste of time since Mrs Peters was busy at the sink, doing the washing up. Molly stomped off up the stairs. After a long shower, Molly was lying on her bed, already wearing her pyjamas, reading 'Black Beauty' for the umpteenth time. She heard the phone ringing downstairs, cut short as her mother answered the call. She could hear her mother's muffled voice but not the actual words as Mrs Peters spoke to the caller. Molly allowed herself to become lost in the narrative of Black Beauty meeting up with his old friend Ginger in the streets of London and she mentally braced herself for the next bit when Beauty sees Ginger on the knackerman's cart. It always made her cry, that bit, but she never skipped over it.

Molly had just finished the chapter and wiped her eyes when she heard her mother calling her from downstairs. With a sigh, she put the book down on her bed and padded out onto the landing.

"Yes Mum?" She called down.

"Could you come down here for a moment please?" Mrs Peters called back.

Molly went back to her room for her dressing gown and slippers then went down into the kitchen. At least her mother hadn't sounded as if she was annoyed about anything so, hopefully, it was something good.

"There you are." Mrs Peters smiled as she filled the kettle. "I've just had Jean Smithers on the phone."

Molly's heart sank. What had Jean said? "Oh." Was all Molly could think of to say, at least until she knew exactly what was afoot.

"Hmm." Mrs Peters started lifting mugs down from the cupboard. "Does she prefer tea or coffee, do you know?"

"Err, te... tea." Molly stammered.

"Okay. Could you grab the biscuit tin for me please?" Mrs Peters bent down to reach into the cupboard under the sink and retrieved a cake stand. As she wiped it over with a damp cloth, Molly put the tin of biscuits on the table. Mrs Peters glanced at the tin then back at the cake stand, shook her head in exasperation and replaced the cake stand in the cupboard it had come from. She then lifted the lid off the biscuit tin and peered inside. "Hmm. It's a good thing Gary's not home or this would be empty!" Replacing the lid, Mrs Peters busied herself with making three mugs of tea.

When the doorbell rang, it made Molly jump. Fizz, however, went into a frenzy of barking, racing towards the door, trying to sound like a vicious guard dog but her tail wagging frantically kind of spoiled the effect. Before Molly could react, Mrs Peters hurried to answer the door. It was obviously someone Fizz knew because she stopped barking as soon as the door was opened, rather than having to be commanded to 'shut!' and to 'go to bed!'. Molly's curiosity overcame her and she wandered out into the hall, stopping in surprise as she saw Jean stepping over the threshold, carrying a huge box.

"You must be Molly's Mum." Jean said cheerfully smiling at Mrs Peters.

"Yes, I am. So nice to finally meet you Jean, I'm Barbara Peters." Mrs Peters went to offer her hand for Jean to shake, then realised Jean had her hands full with the box. "Come through to the lounge, would you like a cup of tea?"

"Oh, yes please." Jean nodded. "Hello Molly, I've got something for you."

As Molly went to follow her mother and Jean into the lounge, Mrs Peters turned to her daughter. "Could you finish making the tea please Molly? And bring the biscuit tin." With that, she escorted Jean into the lounge.

Molly's heart was pounding as she made the tea and placed the three mugs and the biscuit tin on a tray to carry them through to the other room. She did so hope that Jean wouldn't let slip anything about Tyke. Cautiously, she entered the lounge where Jean and Barbara were now seated, the box on the floor between them. She placed the tray on the coffee table and handed Jean and Barbara their drinks before taking her own and perching on the edge of a chair, wondering what was going on. Barbara Peters opened the biscuit tin and offered it to Jean.

"Not at the moment, thank you, I've only just finished my dinner." Jean said with a smile. She turned to Molly. "Now, young lady, as I told you on the phone, Marion's daughter used to go to Badger road, she left last term and starts at a sixth form college in town in a couple of weeks I think. Anyway, after speaking to you, I called Marion. Not only is Marion a bit of a hoarder – hates to throw anything out – but also her daughter isn't much taller than you are, even with the five year age difference. So, I decided to see if Marion still had any of Andrea's old school stuff and, Voilà!" Jean patted the box in front of her.

Molly was astounded. "That's awesome, isn't it Mum?" Mrs Peters smiled, looking somewhat bemused. "Thank you so much Jean." Molly went on.

"Now, now. Don't get over excited. It may not fit you or be too careworn. I suggest we have a look and see what we have. Oh and Marion said she'd put a few bits of riding kit in there too!" Jean began to open the box.

Half an hour later, to Molly and her mother's amazement, they had sorted out enough stuff to tick off everything on the school clothing list except footwear. Sadly, Andrea obviously had very petite feet as all the trainers and shoes were at least half a size too small, as were the two pairs of riding boots. But the jodhpurs fitted nicely.

"Well, that was good, wasn't it?" Said Jean. "And as for the riding boots, I do actually have a pair at home that may fit you, so no worries there. If the worst comes to the worst, you could always wear wellies to start with!"

"I thought wellies weren't safe to ride in?" Frowned Molly.

"Well, looking at Fred, I'd say he needs to slim down a bit before that saddle of his will fit him so you can start by riding him bareback. Doesn't matter what you have on your feet then. Besides, it will be better for your balance!"

"Oh!" Exclaimed Mrs Peters. "So you are definitely going to be teaching Molly to ride then?" She looked at Molly and Jean in surprise.

"Of course!" Jean nodded. "Marion's sent this pony to us because she has no room for him at home with Andrea moving on to something bigger now. They don't want to sell him either so we need to be able to exercise him and Molly's the only one small enough!"

"Oh." Mrs Peters said again. "Only we can't afford....."

Jean held up her hand. "I know, I know. There's no need to worry. Marion is paying for the pony to live at the farm so there will be no costs involved there and I won't be charging for teaching Molly either. She's such a help around the farm, she deserves a treat – and besides, I'll enjoy it!" Unseen by Mrs Peters, Jean winked at Molly.

"In that case... If you're sure.... then thank you." Mrs Peters smiled "Thank you so much, for everything."

"No problem. Happy to help!" Jean looked at her watch then stood up to leave. "I'd better get back before Sam thinks I've left home!" she chuckled.

Mrs Peters stood up to show Jean out. "Thank you again, Jean."

Molly was still sitting in the lounge, gazing at the piles of clothing when Mrs Peters came back from saying goodbye to Jean.

"Well, what a lovely lady Mrs Smithers is!" Mrs Peters plonked herself down on the sofa. "Do you realise she's just saved us a couple of hundred pounds by bringing all this stuff!" She smiled warmly at her daughter. Now, gather it all together and go and put it all neatly in your wardrobe."

Molly began folding everything neatly and placing it all back in the box so she could carry it easier. Blazers, skirts, shirts, ties – at least two of everything, three or four of some things. In fact, it looked as though Molly would be kitted out for next year too! As Molly stretched her arms wide and picked up the box, her mother spoke again.

"I suppose it would be a bit rude of me to deprive Jean of her 'little helper' after she's been so good as to sort out your school stuff." Molly paused by the door as her mother went on, "so I guess you can go to the farm as usual tomorrow."

Molly dropped the box, span round and ran to her mother, throwing her arms around her in a massive hug. "Oh thank you Mum!"

"Steady there girl!" Mrs Peters cried, even as she hugged her daughter back. "You've just dropped that box! Good thing nothing in it is breakable!"

Molly gave her mother another quick squeeze then stepped back and retrieved the box. Then a thought occurred to her.

"But what about shoes and trainers?" Molly asked.

"Well, I know your size so I suppose I could go on my own to get them. If they don't fit, we can always take them back."

Molly picked up the box. "Thank you Mum. I guess I'd better go to bed now, I'd like to get to the farm early so I can ride Fred before it gets too hot." she smiled again at her mother. "Night, night."

Mrs Peters rose from the sofa and crossed to her daughter then gave her a quick kiss on the cheek. "Night, night, sweetheart."

*   *   *   *   *

5

It was just coming up to seven the next morning when Molly jogged through the farm gate and stopped suddenly in surprise at the sight of a police panda car parked in the middle of the yard. Sam was talking to two policemen whilst Jean stood nearby, listening quietly to the conversation. Molly accelerated and made a beeline for Jean.

"What's happened? Are the horses okay?" Molly shouted.

"Hush girl. Everything's fine." Jean said.

One of the policemen turned towards Molly as she skidded to a halt, gasping for breath.

"And who might you be young lady?" He asked.

Jean stepped forward. "This is Molly Peters. Her brother owns the black and white foal and, since he's in the King's Troop, Molly looks after the foal for him. She also has the Fell pony on loan from a friend of mine."

The policeman nodded as he made some notes in a small black notebook. "Ok." He looked at Molly, pen poised over the notebook. "Now, young lady, could you tell me if you've seen any strangers hanging around lately?"

Molly glanced at Jean who nodded slightly. "Erm. There was a man in the lane when I came up yesterday." she said.

"Can you describe him?"

Molly wracked her brains and told the policeman what little she could remember of the man in the lane.

"Was he doing anything? This Man? When you saw him?" The policeman had been scribbling the whole time Molly was talking.

"Um. He was poking around under the hedge with a stick. He shouted to me to stop but I ran away. I wanted to get to the farm." Molly said firmly.

"Ok. That will do for now." He turned towards Jean. "Your husband says the vet saw him as well. Do you have a name and contact details for us?"

"I'll get them." Jean headed off towards the farm office.

Sam and the other police officer came over.

"Well gal, never a dull moment, eh?" Sam said.

"Why, what happened? Is Tyke okay?" Molly looked at Sam with scared eyes.

"Tyke's fine, all of them are. Bruno's a bit sore though but he'll be fine." Sam shrugged

"So what happened?" Molly asked again.

"We think that dodgy fella tried to do a bit of breaking and entering last night. Obviously, my showing him Tyson and Bruno hadn't put him off." Sam paused, then went on. "I heard an almighty commotion out in the yard about three in the morning. Both dogs going ballistic, which of course, set Meg off. So I grabbed my shotgun and haired it out here!" Sam grinned but the police looked disapproving.

"And?" Molly was feeling impatient. The policemen both frowned at her.

"Well," Sam went on, "Just as I came round the corner, I saw that dodgy bloke just

ear the gate. Both dogs were having a proper go, though they hadn't touched him
et, just plenty of growling and snarling so he knew they meant business. I shouted
: him and the dogs both went quiet – sound of my voice I guess. Next thing, he
med a kick at Bruno, catching him in the ribs so I fired the gun." Sam laughed.

You shot the man?" Molly was horrified.

No, no," Sam shook his head, I'm not that daft! I fired over his head. Frightened him
 death I reckon cos he leapt the gate in one move and legged it! Not before Tyson
ot a souvenir though!"

Eh? What souvenir?" Molly asked.

am nodded towards one of the policemen. "I gave it to 'im."

ooking across, Molly saw that the policeman was holding a clear plastic bag with a
crap of grubby looking blue cloth in it. Seeing the futility of not telling Molly anything,
e policeman held it up briefly.

t looks like a piece of denim from a pair of jeans." he said.

So what then?" Molly turned back to Sam.

Well, as I say, he legged it so I went over and checked Bruno. He was fine, just a bit
inded. Then I called these fellas. They only just got 'ere though!" Sam frowned at
e two policemen.

Well sir, as we explained, the intruder had already left so there wasn't much point in
ur attending at that time. We did, however, send a local patrol car out. He had a
ive round and reported all was quiet so we left it until a more sociable hour before
oming to collect your statement." The officer flipped his notebook shut. "Now sir, if
at's all for now?"

suppose so." Sam said. I'll call you if anything else happens shall I?"

Yes please sir. Oh, and a word of warning, even though you have a licence for it,
scharging a shotgun in the direction of a person could have nasty consequences
o, if you must use the gun, leave it unloaded, eh?"

Gun's not a lot of use if it's not loaded." Sam said.

he policeman shrugged. "Well sir, you've been warned. Good day to you." With that,
oth officers went over to their car and climbed in. Molly and Sam stood silently
atching as they drove away.

"Right!" Jean walked briskly round to the barn. "I think it will be best if we give
ou a lesson now, before it gets too hot. Then, in view of the fact we had a prowler
st night, we'll pop everything out in the field for a couple of hours, then they can
me in for the night, just to be safe. Okay?"

Will Fred be okay out with the others?" Molly asked as she trotted along behind
ean, her new riding hat dangling from her hand.

Oh, Sam's putting the tape fence back up. A couple of proper posts should make it
ore pony proof, I hope!"

Oh. Okay." Molly entered the barn behind Jean and was greeted by Tyke's whinney.
he went up to the foal and rubbed his face, promising to groom him later.

Let's have another look at this saddle." Jean said, lifting the saddle onto the hurdle
efore letting herself into the pen. She lifted the saddle from the hurdle then gently
aced it on Fred's back. Even Molly could see that it was much too high over the
ony's withers. "Hmm." She said. "Well, Marion insists that this is his saddle so we
ed to get him a lot slimmer before we can use it! So, bareback it is then! How are

the boots?"

Molly glanced down at her feet which were now clad in the battered pair of brown jodhpur boots Jean had given her. "Fine." she muttered.

"Okay then. Let's get started. Have you got that bridle?" Jean held out her hand and took the now clean bridle from Molly. Although all the straps were through the buckles, Jean hadn't put them through the keepers yet. Molly pointed this out. "Oh, I did that for a reason." Jean said. "Because I don't know which holes the cheek pieces and noseband need to be on, I've left them like that so it will be easier for me to alter it if I need to. Okay?"

Molly nodded then watched carefully as Jean fitted the bridle to the pony's head. When she was satisfied with the fit, she finished fastening all the straps, slotting them into the keepers. Then she picked up what looked like another head-collar but Molly saw it had three big rings across the front of the noseband.

"This is what is called a 'lunging cavesson'." Jean explained. "You'll see how it works in a minute."

They led Fred out to the small paddock in front of the house where there were often a couple of dozen sheep grazing. The paddock was empty but the sheep had obviously been there recently since the grass was shorter than a well kept lawn! Distant bleating told Molly that the sheep had been moved into one of the cattle fields.

"Right." Jean said. "The easiest way for you to get on without a mounting block is with a 'leg up'. Even if you have a saddle, it's better for both the saddle and the horse's back if you don't mount from the ground all the time." Jean patted Fred. "Mind you, you can also learn to vault on!" To demonstrate, Jean grabbed a handful of Fred's mane in her left hand, bounced on the balls of her feet a couple of times then jumped upwards, throwing her body across Fred's back then swinging her right leg over his rump and sitting upright, all in one smooth movement.

"Wow." Molly said.

"Wow indeed!" laughed Jean. "I can't remember the last time I did that! Helps he's only 13.2hh though. Wouldn't even dream of trying it with the Clydesdales!" Leaning forwards, Jean swung her right leg back over Fred's rump and dropped back to the ground. She looked at Molly. "We'll try that another day. Today, I'll leg you up."

"Okay." Molly said doubtfully.

"Right. Put your left hand on his neck, near the withers and grab a chunk of mane. Then put your right hand just about where the back of the saddle would be."

Molly positioned herself expectantly.

"Okay," Jean said, "now bend your left leg back at the knee so your shin is parallel to the ground. I'm going to put one hand on your knee and the other just above your foot. I'll count to three. As I count three, spring off your right foot and I'll lift at the same time. Just lay on your tummy across his back for a moment then swing your right leg over and sit upright. Okay? Think you can do it?"

"Um, I can try" Molly said, feeling uncertain.

"Okay, here goes. One, two, three!"

Molly was surprised at how easy it was to get on with a 'leg up'. After a few seconds of laying across Fred's broad back, she cautiously threw her leg over and sat up gingerly. She'd done it! She was sitting on Fred! Jean handed Molly the reins and showed her how to hold them. Firmly but gently, with her hands relaxed and her little finger outside. Jean then showed Molly how to shorten the reins and explained about maintaining a 'contact' with Fred's mouth, through the reins.

"Now Molly," Jean said, "the key word with horses, whatever you're doing with them, is to relax. Sit up straight, close to Fred's withers and let your legs hang down. Riding is mostly about balance you see. If you are relaxed and balanced, you will move with the horse. If you tense up, you won't. Also, to the horse, tension means fear so the horse will get worried but not know what it's worried about, which can be a disaster. Most importantly, keep your hands and wrists relaxed, otherwise it's like trying to drive a car with the handbrake on. Understand?"

Molly nodded. "I think so."

"Okay. Now, give Fred a gentle squeeze with your legs and off we go."

That first morning, Jean led Fred around the little sheep paddock mostly in walk, although they did do a few strides of a very bouncy trot, which made Molly giggle. Then Jean got Molly to do a few exercises, swinging her legs up above Fred's neck or quarters and clapping her feet together, touching her toes – both together then touching her right toe with her left hand and visa versa. Next, Jean sent Fred to the end of the twenty-five foot lunge line and, with a gentle wave of her long lunge whip, sent Fred around her in a large circle, telling Molly to correct her posture etc. as Fred walked round.

"Would you like to try a trot again Molly?" Jean asked. "Remembering that I'm not close enough to catch you if you fall off!"

"Um. Yeah, okay. I think." Molly grabbed hold of Fred's thick mane.

Jean laughed. "Here we go then, remember to sit up nice and tall, weight down into your heels and try not to grip up! That will definitely make you fall off! Trot on, Fred." Jean clicked her tongue and Fred moved forward into a steady trot. Molly tensed and began to bounce as Jean called to her to relax and take the bounce through her seat bones. When Molly realised that Fred's trot wasn't so bouncy after all, she began to relax and enjoy herself. After half a dozen circuits though, Jean said a long drawn out 'walk' in a sing song voice and Fred came back to walk, plodding round with a martyred expression on his face. Jean said 'whoa' and then 'stand' in the same drawn out sing song voice and Fred stopped.

"Oh!" Said Molly. "Is that it?"

"Not quite." Jean smiled, stepping forward and patting the pony. "I'm sure Gary told you that you should always try to do the same thing on both reins to avoid the horse becoming 'one sided'. Molly nodded solemnly. "Right then," Jean went on, "so we need to change the rein now and have a trot round the other way." With that, Jean turned Fred around to face in the opposite direction and stepped back to the middle of the circle. "Walk on then Fred" she called. Fred started to plod round. This time, before trotting, Jean got Molly to practise stopping and starting. "Right, sit tall, drop your shoulders back slightly, drop your weight into your heels and stop following his movement with your body. Then close your hands gently on the reins and say 'whoa'." Fred halted. "Okay Molly, now sit tall again, gently close your legs on his sides, relax your fingers a little and say 'walk on'." Molly did so and Fred plodded forwards. They practised halt and walk a few more times then Jean told Fred to trot on, getting Molly to give a squeeze with her legs to encourage him.

Molly's legs trembled slightly as she slid off Fred's back at the end of the lesson, grinning widely.
"Did you enjoy that?" Jean asked as Molly hugged Fred.
"It was great!" Molly hugged the pony again. "Much easier than I thought!"
Jean laughed. "You have what we call a 'natural seat'. Some people have it, some don't. You do."
"A natural seat?" Molly looked at Jean, not sure if the older woman was winding her up or not.
"I reckon. We'll soon know for sure. Now, instead of cordoning off part of the big paddock, I think Fred would be better off in here. Not as much grass either after the sheep grazing it so we'll just pop his bridle off, give him a couple of polos and let him go." Jean helped Molly undo the noseband and throatlash of the bridle and, after a pat and a treat, Fred wandered off to explore his new home. He didn't seem at all fazed about being on his own in the paddock.

In the tack room, Molly went to hang the bridle straight up on it's bracket.
"Oh no you don't, young lady! That's how tack ends up in the state that bridle was in when we got it!" Jean took the bridle from Molly and hung it on the tack cleaning hook. "Look, I'll show you. It doesn't need a thorough clean every time, just a wipe over with leather conditioner. Oh and get a clean wet cloth to wipe over the bit please." Jean briskly wiped over the leatherwork whilst Molly wiped Fred's saliva off the bit. "Good." Jean said when Molly had finished. "Now, what we do next is 'put up' the bridle. So we pass the throatlash across the front of the bridle, round the back and loop the reins on it, then back across the front and fasten it." Jean finished wrapping the throatlash around the bridle then hung it on it's bracket. "There. Doesn't that look neater?"
Molly had to admit that all the bridles looked very neat indeed.
"Now Molly," Jean said seriously, "you must make sure you do that every time you use your tack, especially if it gets wet for any reason. And once a week, I like to give all my tack a proper clean. Okay?"
Molly nodded and glanced at the gleaming harnesses.
"Oh, I don't touch those," Jean said with a laugh, "they're Sam's province. He won't let anyone else near them!" With that, they left the tack room, Jean locking the door securely behind them.

As Jean and Molly wandered round to the farm yard, Molly was surprised to see the police car there again. There was no sign of any policemen. Molly looked worriedly at Jean.
"Sam must have taken them into the house." Jean said.
Panic gripped Molly. Why on earth had they come back? She realised there was only one way to find out. Wanting nothing more than to run back to the main horse paddock, grab Tyke and somehow just disappear, Molly reluctantly followed Jean into the kitchen.

It was the same police officers who had been to the yard earlier that morning.

Both were seated at the kitchen table opposite Sam. One was scribbling in his notebook whilst the other talked to Sam.

"Okay sir," said the officer, "You say you haven't seen a black and white cob mare wandering around anywhere in this vicinity."

"Naw, not at all." Sam stated, looking the officer straight in the eye.

Molly and Jean glanced at each other. Well, strictly speaking, Sam wasn't lying. The mare had been dead in the ditch so definitely not wandering anywhere.

"Only, as I say, we found your intruder. Easy enough to identify with half the leg on his jeans missing. He reckons he came here to collect his mare. He says you contacted him when you found it in the lane."

Sam shook his head. "Nope. Definitely not. If I'd found it, I'd have contacted you lot wouldn't I? Don't want no travellers round here."

"So, what horses do you have here at the moment?" The officer asked.

Jean chipped in. "Two Clydesdale mares, two foals and this girl's pony, as we said this morning. That's all."

The police officer leaned forward. "Could this chap have thought one of your mares was his?"

Jean gave a short laugh. "Not a chance! Here, I'll show you." With that, Jean opened a cupboard and pulled out a laptop computer, opened it and switched it on. "It's a bit old and takes a few minutes to boot up. Would you chaps like a drink while you wait?"

Both officers declined.

"Right. You can see the pictures of our Clydesdales on the walls of this room."

The officers looked round and nodded.

"Okay." Jean said. "Now, if we google 'Clydesdale Horses', look what we get." Jean tapped a few keys on the laptop then turned the screen so both officers could see it. "Both our mares look like that." She turned the screen back and tapped a few more keys. "And these are 'gypsy cobs', such as you say that chap is looking for." She turned the screen to face the officers again. "Not only are they a lot smaller but I'm sure even you can both see the differences between them."

"So what about this girl's pony?" The officer asked.

"It's a gelding." Jean stated, flatly. "He's a neutered male. He's also only thirteen two and a plain dark bay." She went on as both officers looked confused. "So no, even a traveller wouldn't mistake him for a gypsy cob mare!"

Then came the bit Molly was dreading.

"May we see these horses?" One of the officers asked.

"Of course!" Jean said briskly. They're all out in the fields at the moment. Follow me."

Molly opened her mouth to protest but shut it again as Jean threw her a warning look.

One of the officers asked Sam to show him inside all the buildings and they wandered off towards the cow barn. The other officer followed Jean and the increasingly worried Molly. They went to look at Fred first. He was rapidly chomping at the grass as though he was starving but looked up and called to Molly as they approached the fence.

"See?" Jean waved her hand towards Fred. "One plain bay Fell pony gelding. Not a gypsy cob mare."

"Okay, I concede that." Said the officer. "So where are the others?

"This way." Said Jean as she headed off towards the main paddock.

Afterwards, Molly thought it was as if the horses knew something was amiss. When they got to the paddock, both mares were standing nose to tail under the trees, flicking away flies with their tails. Both foals, on the other hand were laid flat out on their sides, also in the shade of the trees, only the occasional flick of a fluffy tail showing any sign of life. Jean stopped at the gate.

"There you go. Two mares, two foals, just as I told you. All fully passported and microchipped." Jean said.

"Sorry? Did you say 'passported'?" The police officer looked confused.

"Yes. You know about that though, surely?" Jean smiled sweetly and raised her eyebrows at the flustered looking policeman.

"Horses have passports?" The officer frowned in puzzlement.

"It's the law?" Jean said. "Did you not know that?"

"Er." The officer seemed at a loss for words.

"Look," Jean said, "follow me." With that, she headed back to the house.

"There you go. Horse passports." Jean tossed three passports onto the table. "It is a legal requirement that a horse is passported and microchipped by the time it is six months old. The same as dogs have to be chipped and ID'd by eight weeks. Weaning age you see?"

"There's only three passports here." Said the officer, flicking though the documents.

"Because the foals' have only recently been applied for." Jean pointed out. "Even though we have six months from the date of foaling, I like to get it sorted sooner, rather than later. Here's the paperwork."

The officer barely looked at the documents Jean put in front of him. Molly suddenly realised that it was probably because he didn't have a clue what he was looking at! Suddenly, Sam and the second officer came through the back door.

"Lots of black and whites." The second policeman declared. "Shame they're all cows!" He actually gave a small chuckle, especially when he saw the expression on his colleague's face.

"Okay. I think we're finished here for now." said the officer who'd been so bemused by the information that horses needed passports.

"May I make a suggestion officer?" Jean smiled sweetly. "Well, two actually." Both policemen looked at Jean as she went on. "First of all, this is a very horsey area so I suggest you do your homework with regards horses and passports etc. Secondly, I also suggest that you ask the gentleman who is accusing us of stealing his mare to show you the passport for her. That way, you'll have a very accurate description of what you're looking for, complete with drawings of the mare's markings."

"Thank you for the information madam, and the suggestions." The 'scribbler', as Molly thought of him, closed his notebook, sliding it into a top pocket. "Erm, we'll be off now. Good day." With that, they both headed for the door as though they couldn't get away fast enough!

Jean and Sam both sank onto chairs and looked at each other.

"Erm, Shall I make tea?" suggested Molly.

"That would be lovely." Jean smiled at her.

olly filled the kettle and switched it on. "Do you think we'll get into trouble?" she
sked Jean, worriedly.

Over what?"

Stealing Tyke." Molly swallowed hard as tears sprang to her eyes.

Stealing Tyke?" Sam bellowed. "Who's stolen Tyke?"

We did, when we took him from the lane." Molly sniffed and wiped her nose with the
ack of her hand.

We rescued him. He would have died if we had left him." Sam pointed out.

But he obviously belongs to that traveller. And he wants him back!" Molly was
anicking now. "The police will come again and they will take him away!"

Calm down Molly." Jean got up and began making the tea herself, since it was
ovious that Molly was too upset now.

Sit down gal." Sam pointed to a chair. Molly sat. "Now, them coppers didn't even
now about passports and now, thanks to the missis here, they do. And who's name
on Tyke's passport?" He answered before Molly could. "Yer brother's that's who."

But the man will say we stole him. That we stole his mare." Molly sniffed again and
ean handed her a piece of kitchen roll.

He has to prove there WAS a mare first." Sam stated and leaned back in his chair
oking smugly at Jean.

Sorry? I don't understand?" now Molly felt really confused.

Look," Sam leaned forward again, "it's simple. A lot of travellers are just that,
avellers. They move around all the time so are of 'no fixed abode' as they say. So, a
t of 'em don't see the need for things like driving licences, car tax, vehicle
gistration, dog microchips or," Sam glanced at Jean, "horse passports."

Therefore," Jean piped up, "when the police contact him again, they will ask for a
assport for the mare. If he does produce one, chances are it won't be for Tyke's
um anyway. If he doesn't, he'll be breaking the law and be fined about five
ousand pounds. Not that he'll pay it of course." Jean carried three mugs of tea over
the table and sat down herself. "If, by some chance, he does have a passport for
at poor mare, no one will be able to find her now anyway." She took a deep drink
om her mug.

But what if he produces a foal passport? Even a fake one! He can take Tyke!" Molly
as still panicking.

Calm down." Jean patted Molly's hand. "Think about it. There's been no mention of
foal and, even if there was, Tyke is now chipped. How could that man produce a
assport with the correct chip number, and accurate drawings of Tyke's markings
d accurate positioning of all his hair whorls. There's no way it could happen!"

He might just decide to steal him then!" Molly couldn't help feeling this was exactly
at was going to happen.

Then he will be arrested. As I say, police didn't mention a foal. That man has no
eans of proving Tyke's out of his mare. We can prove he belongs to your brother.
ase closed."

Are you sure?" Molly sniffed again.

Positive. Now, how about some lunch?"

Okay." Molly sniffed then blew her nose. Whatever Sam and Jean said, she still
asn't convinced.

*   *   *   *   *

6

The last two weeks of the summer holidays flew past. Molly spent every day at the farm, riding Fred and playing with Tyke, still trying to quell the feeling of unease that she felt every time she thought about the police and the traveller, despite nothing having been seen or heard from any of them.

It was just four days before the new school term when Jean finally announced that Fred had slimmed down enough for his saddle to fit him. Molly paid close attention to what Jean was saying about how to put the saddle on – slightly too far forward then slide it back to the right place so the hair underneath lay smooth and to make sure there were no creases in the numnah. She then showed Molly how to do the girth and to stretch out Fred's legs to smooth the skin out. Then Jean showed Molly how to check the length of the stirrups before getting on by placing her knuckles on the stirrup bar and seeing if the iron fitted into her armpit. Next Jean showed her how mount using the stirrup, both from the ground and using the mounting block. Jean then gave Molly another short lunging lesson, making sure Molly was happy and relaxed. For the first time, Molly was able to have a go at 'rising trot'. It took two or three goes but, eventually, Molly got the hang of the rhythm. After about ten minutes, Jean halted Fred and smiled up at Molly.
"Okay, you ready to go it alone?" Jean asked the grinning girl.
"Really? Do you think I can?" Molly felt a surge of excitement.
"Sure. After all, he can't go far in this small paddock, can he? Remember what I said and just relax. If you feel you're losing your balance, grab his mane. If you think you can't stop, turn him towards the fence-line. Okay? Off you go then."

Tentatively, Molly squeezed her legs against Fred's sides and he set off across the paddock at a sedate walk. As they approached the fenceline, Jean called to Molly to turn left. Molly remembered the practise they had done when Jean was holding the leadrope. Gently, Molly squeezed the left rein, looked emphatically left and pressed harder with her right leg. Fred turned left and carried on. Following Jean's instructions, Molly did lots of turns and even a few wonky circles. Towards the end of the lesson, Molly even managed a short trot on her own! When the time came to finish for the day, Jean got Molly to do even more exercises, including 'round-the-world', 'half scissors' and 'thread-the-needle'. It felt a bit like doing acrobatics but Jean pointed out the benefits to Molly's balance and confidence by being able to do all the different movements on horseback.

After lunch, Molly took Tyke for a walk around the farm as part of his education, making sure he got a good look at the cows, sheep and even the monster tractor! She felt a little more relaxed about Tyke these days, mainly because his passport had arrived at home the other day. Mrs Peters had been curious to know what was in the envelope, especially as it had 'Horse Passport Agency' as the return address but, since it was addressed to Gary, she assumed it was something to do with the King's Troop horses and she popped it in the kitchen draw with the rest of his post. Normally, she would pop everything into a bigger envelope every few days and send it on to him but he was due home on leave for the weekend so she didn't need to this time. Molly was itching to see the passport but couldn't open the letter. She knew Gary wouldn't mind but her mother would be appalled at Molly opening her brother's post. At least Tyke was now legally registered in Gary's name!

When Molly arrived home, her mother was flitting around, hoovering, dusting, changing the bedding on Gary's bed and, generally, getting agitated. Molly sighed. Ever since Gary had joined up, every time he came home, Mrs Peters acted as though royalty were poised to visit! It was amusing and irritating at the same time.

When Mrs Peters saw Molly come through the front door, she turned off the vacuum cleaner and smiled. "I got your shoes and trainers for school today, finally." Such had been the demand for the specific style of shoes the school had stipulated, the shop had sold out and had to order them in. "If you go and try them on now, Gary can take you to change them tomorrow afternoon if needs be." Before Molly could reply, Mrs Peters began hoovering again.

Molly wandered into the kitchen and spotted a carrier bag from the shoe shop on the floor by the fridge. Not expecting much, she opened the bag and discovered that both the shoes and the trainers were the better quality ones, not the cheaper version she had expected, in view of the shortage of money these days. Trying them on and walking around the kitchen, she was pleased that they not only fitted well but were comfortable too! Nice to have decent stuff for once! Then it occurred to her that it was because of the fact that her Mum hadn't needed to buy any other things on the school uniform list, thanks to her having all the stuff from Marion's daughter. So that was something else she needed to be grateful to Jean for. Molly sighed. She'd speak to Gary getting about some sort of 'thank you' gift for Jean. With another heavy sigh, Molly re-packed the shoes and trainers back in their boxes ready to take them upstairs to her bedroom.

Gary was due early the next morning so Molly had arranged with Jean to go up to the farm later than normal so that Gary could go with her. More exciting though was that, when Gary opened his mail, they would at last have proof that Tyke was Gary's horse – and, by default, was HER horse. She hugged herself. Now she could really get to work on training Tyke, without worrying about the police trying to take him away. Then she felt a cold shiver. There was still the possibility that the travellers might try to steal him!

Molly was fretting so much about Tyke that it wasn't until the early hours that she finally fell asleep so she didn't even hear her alarm go off at it's usual time of six thirty. She only woke up when Fizz jumped off her bed and began scrabbling and whining at the bedroom door. Still half asleep, Molly got up and opened the door. The dog raced down the stairs, barking with excitement. Molly heard her mother trying to calm the excited dog, then heard Gary's voice. Suddenly she was wide awake! Looking at the clock, she saw it was after nine! She quickly pulled on her clothes and dragged a brush through her hair before running down to the kitchen, where Gary was already tucking in to a full English breakfast. Molly stopped in the doorway and grinned at her big brother.

"Hi Sis." Gary grinned back. "How's the riding going?"

"Okay I think." Molly took the seat next to her brother and grabbed the cornflake packet. "You can come and watch me today if you like."

Gary nodded, his mouth full of bacon and egg. He swallowed. "Yep, sure. When I've finished this." He popped another fork full into his mouth.

Molly busied herself with her breakfast, then almost choked on her cornflakes as her mother opened the kitchen draw and took out the variety of envelopes that had arrived for Gary over the past few days. Still forking up his breakfast, Gary used his free hand to sift through the pile, nodding to himself. He singled out the passport envelope then handed the others back to Mrs Peters. "Pop those back in the draw and I'll sort them out later." He said.

"So what's that one?" Mrs Peters asked, her eyes on the envelope which was still laying on the table.

"Nothing much." Gary glanced at Molly.

"Why have you got a letter from a horse passport company?" Mrs Peters looked at her son.

"It's for a horse I'm looking after." Gary shrugged. "As I say, nothing much."

Mrs Peters didn't look convinced by Gary's explanation but she realised he wasn't going to go into any details so she busied herself with making more tea. Gary winked at Molly. Molly began to relax.

Gary finally pushed his empty plate away and took a last swig of his tea.

"You ready to go Sis?" He looked at Molly as she was swallowing the last mouthful of cornflakes. She nodded eagerly. Picking up the brown envelope, Gary stepped across and gave Mrs Peters a quick kiss on the cheek. "We'll see you later, Mum". Fizz and Molly rushed after Gary as he headed down the hallway.

As Molly and Gary walked along the lane towards the farm, Molly told Gary all about the strange man and the police.

"Well," Gary said, waving the brown envelope, "at least we can prove Tyke's all ours now."

"But he isn't really, is he? He really does belong to that traveller bloke!" Molly still worried about it all.

Gary stopped and turned to face his little sister. "Molly, if someone threw some stuff in a skip that they didn't want any more, but you did want it and took it, who's is it?"

"Um. Mine I guess."

"Right." Gary went on. "Marion doesn't need her daughter's school uniform any more. She could have thrown it in the bin or given it to a charity shop, instead she passed it on to you. Is it yours or Andrea's?"

"Erm, mine."

"Right again. Now, let's say that someone had dumped a load of wood in the lane. Say Sam came along and decided it would be good to use for firewood, for whatever eason. Whose wood is it now?"

"Sam's I guess."

"Okay. Look at me Sis," Gary took hold of Molly's shoulders and turned her to face im. "Someone dumped that dead mare in the ditch, like a load of rubbish. They left 'yke with her, not caring that he was going to die by inches. You found him so, as far s I can see, he is yours. It was weeks before anyone came looking for that mare nd foal. Sam said that, from the way the mare was laid in the ditch, she was dead /hen they dumped her. So they didn't give a damn. No one can prove that the foal ved, or that the foal is Tyke. End of. Okay?"

Molly nodded slowly. Maybe Gary was right.

"Right Sis, now, lets get going. You promised me a demonstration of your new riding kills, remember?"

The first thing Gary did when he and Molly got to the farm was to hand Jean he letter containing the passport. Jean opened the envelope and took the passport ut, flicking through the pages. Nodding, she went to hand the documents back to ary but he waved it away.

Am I right in thinking that the law states the passport must stay with the horse at all mes?" He said.

Well,yes, theoretically." Jean replied. "But livery yards tend to mostly leave the assports in the owner's possession and just take a photocopy. If DEFRA do a assport check, you have, I think, four or five hours to produce the original."

I think," Gary said, "that in view of the recent 'funny business' with that traveller and he police, it may be an idea for that passport to stay here, don't you think?"

ean glanced at the passport, then nodded. "I think you're probably right. Okay, I'll ut it with the others in the office." She laughed. "I'm getting quite a collection! I have red's here too, since he is 'on loan', so to speak and Buster's arrived this morning."

That's fine then." Gary smiled at Jean then turned to his sister. "Now Molly, where's his pony you've been terrorising the countryside on?"

While Molly gave Fred a thorough grooming session before riding him, Jean ooked speculatively at Gary.

Being in the King's Troop, I gather you can ride?"

For my sins, yeah." Gary laughed.

So, do you reckon you could handle that mare?" Jean nodded in the direction of handy.

Well, it's a bit bigger than what I normally ride but, yeah, I reckon so."

Okay. I know you can do 'ride and lead' cos that's how you control the gun carriage orses so, how would you like to give your little sister a treat and take her out for a ack, just gently, walk and a bit of trot?"

Sounds fun." Gary grinned. "But I haven't got any kit with me."

Come with me." Jean toddled off towards the house. "We'll be back in a minute lolly." she called out as she and Gary left the barn.

Molly couldn't help giggling when Gary and Jean reappeared. Gary was ressed in Sam's breeches which were too big round the waist and were gathered in y an old leather belt. On his feet were a battered pair of 'dealer boots' with thick Dr

Martin soles borrowed, it transpired, from one of the farmworkers. They also look like they were a couple of sizes too big and flapped slightly as he walked, reminding Molly of the clowns you saw at the circus. A quick glance at Jean, who stood behind Gary with Shandy's tack and a spare riding hat in her arms, told Molly that Jean was also trying not to laugh. Gary was carrying Fred's tack and also had brought Molly's riding hat out for her.

"Stop giggling or I'll refuse to ride" said Gary sternly, although the twinkle in his eyes showed that he too was on the verge of laughing out loud. Molly choked back another laugh.

"Ride?" She looked at her brother in surprise, "Who are you going to ride?" Molly glanced across to Jean and spotted the tack in Jean's arms. "Oh! That's Shandy's tack!" she exclaimed.

Jean grinned. "I thought you'd like to go for a bit of a pootle out with your brother, rather than plodding round in the paddock again. Nothing too strenuous and Gary will have you on a lead rein but, well, it'll make a nice change, won't it? That is, if you want to?" Jean turned and went across to Shandy's pen. Gary put Fred's tack and Molly's hat on the hurdle of Fred's pen then smiled at his little sister.

"So Sis, would you like to hack with me?"

"Yes please!" Molly couldn't think of anything she would like more.

"Right. You finish getting Fred ready and I'll go and sort out my own trusty steed." With a chuckle, Gary headed over to lend Jean a hand with Shandy.

"I've never ridden anything this tall before." Gary said as he looked down at Molly from the back of the eighteen hands high Shandy. As he guided the mare out of the farmyard, Fred calmly plodding by her side on the end of the lead rein, Gary glanced at the ground. "It's a long way down!"

Molly laughed. This was so exciting! Okay, so Fred was wearing his headcollar over his bridle and the leadrope attached to it was being held in Gary's left hand but, as they ambled out into the lane, Molly really felt as if she was in control of Fred and that Gary was only there in case of emergencies. It even seemed that Fred felt different under her, as though he too was enjoying the change in routine. Shandy ambled along, ears lolling, not in a hurry to go anywhere but not reluctant either. Fizz trotted along behind them, making little detours to sniff along the hedgerow but never letting them get too far ahead before running to catch up.

As they rode along the lane, Molly was struck by how straight and tall Gary sat, yet totally relaxed in the saddle. She tried her best to copy him. When they turned off the lane and onto a grassy track, Gary suggested they try a trot. Molly readily agreed but soon realised that, to keep up with the longer strides of the Clydesdale mare, Fred had to trot much faster than normal and it took a while for Molly to get into the quicker rhythm. Embarrassingly, she even had to hold onto Fred's mane to keep her balance at first. Suddenly, Fred's rhythm changed. It became less bouncy, not unlike sitting on a rocking horse. It took a few strides for Molly to realise that Fred had broken into a canter beside the still trotting Shandy. He'd obviously decided it was less effort and the best way to match his stride to Shandy's long, loping trot.

As Gary brought Shandy and Fred back to a walk at the end of the track, the other and sister were both laughing and their mounts were snorting and tossing eir heads in satisfaction.

That was fun!" Molly laughed. The next second, Shandy stopped abruptly and Fred apt sideways with a snort of alarm. Molly screamed and grabbed Fred's mane, only st preventing herself from falling off!

What the …..!" Gary cried out.

man had suddenly stepped out of the hedge and stood in front of them, blocking e exit from the track. Gary glanced down at Molly to make sure she was okay then ared at the man. Molly, meanwhile, felt her heart start racing. It was the man who d been hanging around the farm! She managed to whisper to Gary that she had cognised the man. Meanwhile Fizz had stopped beside the horses and her throat as rumbling with a low, menacing sounding growl. The dog was staring at the man, ff legged, her hackles rising along her back.

5hh." Gary said, whether to Molly or Fizz, it wasn't clear. He then called politely to e man. "Hey there, could you let us past please?"

stead of stepping off the track, the man stepped forwards and took hold of nandy's bridle, glaring up at Gary.

Where's my horse?" The man demanded.

What horse?" Gary feigned innocence. "We haven't seen any horses except the nes we're riding." Gary looked directly at the man as he spoke. After all, for the oment at least least, he wasn't lying.

My best cob. Black and white mare. She was in foal to a good blood horse. She's ne missing. I reckon you and that lass" he jerked his head at Molly "know summat out."

5o, she's wandered off somewhere then?" Gary asked.

Naw, she was on a chain so she couldn't have wandered. She's been pinched and I ckon you two had summat to do with it."

You should call the police then." Gary suggested. The man looked down at the ound, avoiding Gary's gaze.

did speak to them about her being missing. Sort of."

5ort of? What do you mean by that?" Gary knew what the man meant, but wasn't ing to let him know that.

Nell, I sort of mentioned it when they came to talk to me about summat else. But ey ain't interested in helping folk like me." He lifted his head and glared at Gary ain. "Was worth a lot of money that mare."

_ook," Gary said, "we haven't got your mare, we haven't even seen your mare but, if e do, we'll let you know. Now, please will you let go of my horse's bridle?"

uttering what sounded to Molly like some very rude swear words, the man let go of nandy and stepped off the track. Gary didn't go to ride away immediately but looked wn at the man and said, "As I say, we don't know anything about your mare. owever, I do know that you've been hanging around the place where these horses e kept. So, I will say this. If you harass me, my sister or anyone around the farm ain, I will report it to the police. Do you understand me?"

ne man just glared at Gary and then spat on the ground. He swore again, louder s time, then turned and walked off across the fields.

Phew." Gary said, as he nudged Shandy into a walk. "He's a dodgy character if ever there was one. What have you got me into?"

"I'm sorry! I couldn't just …."

"Shh!" Gary hissed. "Don't speak for now. Lets get back to the farm"

"I'm calling the police!" Jean said indignantly when Gary and Molly related their encounter with the traveller.

"No!" Molly cried, on the verge of tears. "They'll search and find Tyke!"

"Calm down Molly." Gary said quietly. "Think about it. Sam called the police when the guy was trying to snoop around the farm so, it will look odd – to both the man and the police if we don't report what happened."

"I won't be doing anything much Molly." Jean said. "Just informing them that he has been hanging around again and that he stopped you two when you were riding. Gary can speak to them. Okay?"

Reluctantly, Molly nodded, though she had a horrible churning feeling in her stomach. Suddenly, she turned and ran from the kitchen. When she got to the barn, she forced herself to walk calmly over to Tyke's pen then she climbed in. Putting her arms around the foal's neck, she buried her face in his fuzzy mane and burst into tears. Young as he was, Tyke seemed to understand that he was being used as a source of comfort and pressed himself against the sobbing girl.

Molly had cried herself out by the time Gary came to find her. He almost had to prise her arms from around Tyke and as soon as he had gently drawn her away from the foal, Molly flung her arms around Gary's waist and buried her head against his chest, almost choking as she tried to hold back her hiccuping sobs. Gary hugged his little sister close.

"It's okay Molly. All the police have done is make a note of what happened this morning and they said they will go and have a quiet word with the guy and warn him to stop this stupid harassment. It will be alright, you'll see."

"But what if it isn't?" Molly stammered out between sobs. "What if he comes to try and take Tyke?"

"Do you know something sis, I'm not even sure he will. There's been no mention of a foal, except for that man saying that the mare was *in* foal. So I don't think he knows about the foal being born. If he did, surely he would be asking about both? Not just the mare?"

"So why was he poking around the hedgerow near where I found Tyke?" sniffled Molly. Gary pulled a handkerchief from his pocket and handed it to Molly for her to blow her nose and wipe her eyes.

"I don't know, Molly. But, as I say, don't worry. As far as the police are concerned, there's no sign that we have had the mare here, no one has mentioned the foal and all the horses here are legally passported. Now, this is the last leave I have before Christmas so let's make the most of it, eh?"

Blowing her nose loudly on Gary's handkerchief, Molly gave Tyke another hug then followed her brother back to the house where Jean was preparing lunch.

During the afternoon, Gary and Molly worked with Tyke. Molly was pleased when Gary complemented her on how much progress she had made with all Tyke's lessons. The little foal would stand still to be groomed and lift his feet for them to be picked out. He moved over at the slightest touch. He would walk, trot and even canter on the lead rein, responding to the voice commands instantly. He happily walked past the noisy vehicles and things like flapping plastic around the farm, ignored the cows, sheep and chickens. Then Molly showed Gary how, even if she took the lead rope off, Tyke would follow her in all three paces as she ran around the paddock, over ground poles and even walking over an old tarpaulin. As they finished the session, Gary patted the baby horse.

"He's coming on great, Molly. You've obviously been working really hard with him." Gary stepped back a couple of paces and studied the foal for a few moments. "He's really grown too! I think he's going to be a good size when he's fully grown! That will be the Thoroughbred in him I reckon."

"Thoroughbred? He's a gypsy cob, isn't he?" Molly looked confusedly at Gary.

"His mum was. That traveller chap said she was in foal to a 'blood horse'. A 'blood horse' is what the travellers call Thoroughbred horses."

"Oh." Molly looked at Tyke. "Is that why he's not getting very hairy? I noticed Buster's getting hairy but Tyke isn't."

"He may develop a bit of 'feather' round his legs I suppose but not as much as his Mum I don't think, or even as much as your Fred."

Molly looked at Tyke's legs. They were very long and showed no signs at all of developing any feather. Then she realised something else. Gary had commented on how much Tyke had grown and Molly suddenly realised it was true. When Tyke had first arrived, his withers were just a little above Molly's waist but now, when she laid her arm across him, she could feel his withers were almost up to her armpit. Yet it seemed to be his legs rather than his body that was growing the most. He was fast too. When he was out in the field, he always managed to outrun the Clydesdales.

Tyke was also shedding his baby fluff and, underneath, his darker patches were not quite completely black but a very dark brown so that it looked black in certain light. Gary watched Molly running her hands through Tyke's coat.

"What colour did the vet put on the passport?" he asked.

"I dunno." Molly shrugged. "Piebald I think because of the amount of white he has."

"Hmm." Gary reached towards Tyke and ruffled the coat himself. "Let's go and check it, shall we?"

Gary flicked through the pages of the passport.

"Ah. Here we are." He studied the page for a few seconds. "Oh, that's good!"

"What is?" Said Molly.

"Well your vet obviously realised that Tyke was likely to change colour, at least a bit. She's put him down her as 'skewbald'.

"Skewbald?" Molly frowned slightly. "So he's not just black and white?"

Gary shook his head. "Skewbald is white with any colour except black. I'd say that this will make it even harder for our traveller friend to claim Tyke is out of his missing mare."

"Really?" Molly was thrilled. "That's brilliant!"

"Well yes, we can hope so." Jean said as Gary closed the passport and handed it to her. "Now, would you like some tea before you head off home?"

Gary glanced at his watch. "Better not. I promised Mum we'd be back early and go

out for a meal tonight. We'll see you in the morning though."
With that, Molly and Gary said their goodbyes to Jean and Sam before calling Fizz
and heading off home.

There was no sign of the traveller for the rest of the weekend. Jean had heard
that some of then had left the local gypsy camp to go to some huge horse fair which
was popular with so many of them. Gary and Molly rode out together on both the
Saturday and the Sunday, even doing a few 'official' canters which Molly revelled in.
On the Sunday, Gary even unclipped the lead rein from Fred as he and Molly rode
along a narrow bridleway through the woods. On a long straight stretch, they
cantered again, Fred following the Clydesdale's rump but, as if he knew he couldn't
overtake, he was content to canter a couple of lengths behind. Molly was overjoyed!
She was really riding! On her own! Molly expected Gary to clip the rope back on
when the got back into the lane and headed back to the farm but he didn't even
suggest it, just watched Molly closely and quietly made suggestions like 'shorten the
reins slightly', 'sit up taller', 'keep your heels down', etc.

The afternoons were spent playing with Tyke. On the Sunday afternoon, Molly
mentioned to Gary that she had been reading about something called 'Natural
Horsemanship' and she had been thinking of trying some of the techniques with
Tyke. Gary frowned as he looked at his sister's earnest face.
"The thing is, Sis, you don't want to believe everything you read, nor think everything
you read will work on every horse. There's a very old saying: 'It's all well and good
reading the book, but remember, the *horse* hasn't read it!'
Molly laughed at that but then noticed the serious look on Gary's face.
"So, what do you mean?" she asked.
Gary sat on a nearby straw bale.
"The thing is, Sis, a lot of these so called 'modern' techniques are more about sorting
out horses with 'issues'. No two horses are the same, just as no two humans are the
same. As far as training is concerned, the best trainers know, instinctively, what will
work best for each individual horse. They are all so very different! And no one will
ever know everything there is to know. If you get involved with horses, you will
always be learning. The thing is though, some people have a knack of locking in to
their instincts, even if they don't really know very much yet. Take you for example.
You're already using your instincts to work with Tyke and it's proving to be the right
way to go. In a way, you've already developed your own style of 'Natural
Horsemanship'.
"So you don't think I should try 'Join-Up' with him then? Or some of the games I've
seen people teaching horses on 'You Tube'?" Molly felt a bit confused now. It looked
so easy and the way the horses interacted with their owners looked *so* cool! She
wanted Tyke to be like that too!
"Right." Said Gary with a sigh. "Now, let's think about this. If you studied the subject
properly, you would learn that 'Join-Up' is based on the way the Matriarch mare in a
wild herd disciplines the other members of the herd. Therefore, it's a method best
used for sorting out issues between horses and humans, rather than an everyday
basic training method. Join up is especially useful if you have a horse with has some
sort of mental barrier which prevents it from responding positively to a trainer. It

establishes the trainer's status as a leader and creates a bond. But Tyke already has a strong bond with you, already acknowledges you as his leader. So why put him in a round pen to 'punish' him? You and he are already 'joined up' so 'round penning' is pointless. Do you see?"

Molly nodded, although she still wasn't quite sure she understood.

"Some of the games could be useful though." Gary went on. "I gather you've already played a few with him using a towel?"

Molly grinned. "He keeps trying to eat it!" she said, laughing.

"Okay." Gary chuckled. "When we get home tonight, I'll find some stuff on line for you to do to help him develop mentally as well as physically but remember not to do so much at a time, he is just a baby after all."

Molly agreed to do just short, ten minute lessons with the foal. Then she and Gary finished up in the barn, feeding the horses and settling them for the night before going over to the house, saying goodbye to Jean and Sam, then heading for home.

*   *   *   *   *

7

Molly's first day at her new school wasn't too bad, considering. There were a few people she knew from junior school so it wasn't quite as daunting as it could have been. The school was a lot bigger than junior school though so, like most of the others just starting, Molly spent most of her day getting lost, despite having been given a detailed map of the building.

There were, however, two things about the new school that *did* upset Molly. The first one was that, whereas her old school had just been a ten minute walk from home, this new one necessitated Molly getting the school bus. Unfortunately, where the Peters family lived was near the beginning of the school bus route which meant that Molly had to leave home at eight in the morning. It also meant that she was amongst the last to be dropped off in the afternoon so she wouldn't get home until after four! Even worse than that though was the dreaded homework. Even on the first day, Molly's bag felt weighed down with a mountain of books and the prospect of over two hours worth of stuff to do at home – some of which had to be handed back at school the next day! It wasn't fair. It meant that the first thing she had to do when she got home was to phone Jean and explain that she wouldn't be able to go to the farm on school nights.

"Don't worry about it Molly." Jean was sympathetic, "We'll look after Tyke and Fred for you. To be honest, I fully expected this to be the case."

"Yes but...." Molly was near to tears.

"Look at it this way, love. If you don't do your homework you'll get into trouble at school. Then your Mum will probably ground you!" Jean said, echoing what Gary had said to Molly earlier when she had emailed him, trying to persuade him to contact Mum to plead her case for going to the farm every day. Molly sighed as Jean went on. "Look on the bright side. It will be half term in six weeks! And there's still the weekends."

"I suppose so." Molly said, sulkily. It felt like a conspiracy. All the adults in her life conspiring together to stop her doing the only thing she wanted to do – to ride and to play with Tyke. Then Molly brightened up a little. "Mum did say I can come up on Friday evening – if that's okay with you?"

"That would be great Molly. It's still light in the evenings so you can still do plenty so, I'll see you on Friday. Work hard and don't be too miserable. Okay?"

After dinner, Molly took Fizz for a quick walk and then ploughed through her homework, not wanting to give her mother any excuse to ground her. She even did the stuff that didn't need to be handed in for a few days. Friday seemed so far away, Molly wondered, yet again, whether or not to explain to Mrs Peters about Tyke. Maybe then her mother would understand that the pull of the farm was more than just going riding on Fred. As she watched her mother sign her 'homework diary', Molly ghed. Tyke's story was all too complicated really and Mrs Peters may worry if she ought that her daughter had fallen foul of the local traveller group. Instead, she ssed her mother goodnight and went to bed. She still hadn't finished reading 'Black eauty' and she was getting near to the bit near the end when Joe found him again. nat was another part of the book which always made her cry.

Mrs Peters was impressed by her daughter during that first week of term. olly diligently did ever piece of homework she was given, on the same day it was ven, so that she had no backlog to take up her time at the weekend. On Friday, owever, Molly changed her routine completely. Whereas, on the previous four ternoons, she had rushed home and, after walking Fizz, started on her homework raight away - only breaking for dinner - on Friday Molly raced upstairs to get ıanged into her jodhpurs and was out of the door and on her way to the farm within teen minutes of stepping off the school bus. Watching her daughter running across e field, Fizz at her heels, Mrs Peters decided that dinner that evening would be best it were a simple microwave type meal that could be heated up when Molly rentually came home. Meanwhile, Molly had only one aim – to waste as little time ₅ possible getting to the farm.

Gasping for breath, Molly unlatched the farm gate as Jean came out of the ₅use. Seeing Molly, the older woman waved and smiled broadly. ₅o, Molly, how was your first week?" ￼eah. Okay." Molly managed to pant. ₅ome on then. I think there's a couple of chaps in the paddock that have missed ₅u as much as you've missed them I reckon." ₅rely able to contain herself, Molly walked round to the paddock at the back of the ₅rn. To her surprise, the tape fence that had cordoned off an area for Fred had ₅en taken down again and all five horses were now grazing together. Tyke had ₅viously taken to Fred as he was grazing nose to nose with the pony. Buster had ₅cided he would stay with the mares. ￼ou know, I do wonder if Tyke and Fred have become such good friends because ey both share a bond with you." Jean said. ₅o you really think so?" Molly felt a buzz of pride at the thought that she could ₅uence the horses in such a way." ₅mm. Anyway, let's get them all in and then, since Gary let you off the leadrein on ınday, I think we could go for a hack around the farm. What do you think?" ₅h, yes please." Molly said.

Molly would never have admitted it but she felt a bit nervous about going ₅ough the big open fields without anyone holding on to Fred. Jean, riding Shandy, ₅d a rolled up leadrope clipped to a 'D' ring on her saddle, just in case. But it emed she had no intention of needing it, unless she really, really had to. ₅ow Molly, just relax. If you are tense, Fred will be tense." Jean said calmly as they ₅ved into the first field, a huge – it seemed to Molly – open space, although it was ₅ly about twenty acres in size. ₅spite her best efforts, Molly felt herself tense even more. "But what if Fred takes ₅?" She asked Jean, nervously.

"Okay," Jean said, still very calm about it all, "let's be honest here. If that little chap decides he wants a gallop, you will probably not be able to stop him. I can advise you about what to do but, chances are, that will all fly out of your mind and your only concern will be staying on!"

"I'm not sure I want to ride in this field." Molly said in a small voice.

"Don't worry about it, Molly." Jean manoeuvred Shandy so that she could close the field gate behind them. "Now, *if* a horse takes off, the key is, as with any riding, to try to stay relaxed and to give before you take. Turning in ever decreasing circles is a good tactic, as is aiming for the hedgerow. The main thing is not to pull. You pull, he will pull back. He's stronger than you so he will win that argument."

Molly swallowed hard. She felt more than a bit sick. Jean looked at Molly's green looking face and her expression softened.

"Molly, Fred is an experienced pony who is unlikely to go any faster than you want him to. However, if he does get over excited, then try to remember what I said. Failing that, if I do think you're out of control, the best thing I can do is stop Shandy and stay put – this mare will not be able to catch that pony. In that event, try to stay on and steer around the outside of the field. At then end of the day, Fred will eventually run out of steam and then you will be able to stop him. Okay?"

Molly just nodded, not trusting herself to speak. She still felt sick.

"I think we'll do a circuit of this field in walk to begin with and, Molly, if you stay between Shandy and the hedge, it should make it less likely that Fred will decide he wants to take off across the field, okay?" Jean smiled at Molly.

"Okay." said Molly, in a small voice. In her head, she was repeating the word 'relax' whilst she tried to slow her breathing but it didn't seem to be working. Fred, meanwhile, was flicking his ears back and forth as his tried to gauge his rider's mood and work out why she was so tense. Fred was an old hand at carrying novice riders though so, although the field looked inviting, he kept himself in check.

By the time they had completed a whole circuit of the field, with Fred striding along calmly beside Shandy, Molly had begun to relax. Grinning up at Jean, she quickly agreed to trying a short trot as they started a second circuit.

"What we'll do," Jean said, "is just trot as far as the corner, then walk to the next corner, then trot again, then walk the last stretch to the gate. How does that sound?"

Molly grinned, feeling much happier now. As they started to trot, Jean had her work cut out slowing down Shandy's trot enough so that Fred could keep up without having to trot too fast. Just before they got to the corner, Jean instructed Molly to sit tall, and gently ask Fred to walk. To Molly's delight, Fred responded to her immediately. As planned, they trotted again on the third side and then, without a word, Jean carried on trotting into the fourth side, then, again without saying a word, she quietly pushed Shandy into a canter, causing Fred to follow suit. Molly gave a small squeak of surprise but then, when she realised that Fred was happy to stay level with Shandy, she began to relax and enjoy it.

Back at the gate, Jean suggested to Molly that she try taking Fred round again but on his own this time while Jean waited for them. Molly's nerves fluttered again.

"Just take it steady, Molly. Up to you what pace you go at and remember what I said, even if he does take off, he can't get out of this field and he's bound to run out of steam eventually."

"Uh. Okay." Molly said. She took a deep breath then squeezed Fred forward along the hedge-line

Molly had never felt so nervous about anything. Even starting the new school earlier in the week hadn't been *this* scary. Fred walked calmly and then, as they rounded the next corner, Molly went to squeeze him into trot but, because of her nerves, she accidentally kicked him! Fred, obedient as always, went from walk to canter! Molly began to panic but then, in her mind, she heard what Jean had said and, instead of trying to stop the pony, leaned forward slightly, holding a piece of mane to keep her balance. Suddenly, Molly realised they were approaching the next corner! She sat up and pulled hard on the reins.... and nothing happened! If anything, Fred began to speed up! Molly grabbed his mane again as they rounded the corner in a fast canter. In doing so, she had stopped pulling and Fred took it as a cue to steady up. Molly decided to do what Jean said and simply sit quiet, hoping that Fred would stop when he got back to Shandy. As they round the last corner, Molly prayed that Fred would stop at the gate and felt a surge of relief when she realised that, as they approached the big Clydesdale, Fred was actually slowing himself down. Fred brought himself back to trot a few strides from Shandy then stopped abruptly as he reached the mare, causing Molly to slide up his neck. Luckily, she managed to stop herself falling off and laughed up at Jean who was smiling broadly.

"Well done Molly! Did you enjoy that?"

"It was great!" Molly felt really good now. She felt that, at last, she was really starting to ride! She looked up at Jean eagerly, "Can I do it again?" she asked.

"Maybe tomorrow." Jean laughed. "Probably best to use a different field though so Fred doesn't start anticipating things. Although I did think that, tomorrow, you might like to try a bit of pole-work?"

"You mean jumping?" Molly said excitedly.

"Hmm, not quite jumping, not yet. Just some basic stuff in preparation I think."

"That would be really cool, if that's okay, I'd love to!" Molly felt really good now.

After their ride, Jean helped Molly do some work with Tyke. His main problem was with his feet. Sometimes he would pick them up first time, other times he would be silly about it and keep jerking his foot away, so the more they could practise with him, the better. After all, it wouldn't be too long before he needed to have his hooves trimmed by the farrier so he needed to be good about his feet by then!

Molly's first jumping lesson on Fred wasn't quite as exciting as she first thought it would be. When Molly arrived at the yard on the Saturday morning, she was surprised to see half a dozen poles laid out in a line across the middle of the small paddock. There were pairs of jump wings either end of alternate poles but all the poles rested on the ground. Molly went over to the barn and found Jean already there, giving Buster a good grooming. Knowing that it would be best if she were already riding Fred before Jean turned the mares and foals out, Molly quickly fetched Fred's grooming kit and started getting him ready to ride. Tyke watched over the side of his pen, almost begging for Molly's attention. Molly leaned across and gave Tyke's face a quick rub then carried on with Fred. Once she had got Fred ready, she led him out to the paddock whilst Sam and Jean took the other four horses round to their field and turned them out.

By the time Jean got back, Molly was already on Fred's back, riding him round the paddock in a steady walk. Jean told Molly to do a few circles and turns then, still in walk, go in a nice straight line down the line of poles.
"Now, remember, it's Fred's job to work out where the poles are, your job is to keep him straight and moving forwards. Do not look at the poles as you go over. Look for the first pole, to make sure you're nice and straight then look up and look straight ahead. I want you to do at least half a dozen strides after the last pole, in a nice straight line, before you turn. Okay?"
Molly nodded. This was going to be so easy, it would be boring she thought. She soon discovered she was very wrong. It was hard not to look down, hard to keep Fred straight and even harder to stop the pony turning as soon as they stepped over the last pole. Jean seemed to be constantly shouting, "look up", "Stay straight", "More energy in that walk", "Don't turn too soon!". It was so much harder than it looked!

After half a dozen goes in walk, from both directions, Jean came over and showed Molly how to 'fold' over a fence. "Even though these are ground poles at the moment, it's good to practise your position over a fence from the start." Jean explained. "So, we'll trot the line now and I want you to fold over each pole, looking up and ahead, back straight, then sit up as soon as you are over the pole. So it will be fold, sit up, fold, sit up etc. If you feel wobbly, grab his mane. Don't ever use the reins for balance. Off you go."

Trying to remember everything at the faster pace of trot was agony! It seemed every time Molly rode down the line, she forgot one thing or another. After another half a dozen goes down the poles, Molly was fighting back tears of frustration. Jean seemed to notice this and told Molly to walk around the paddock a few times to settle down again. When Jean called her back over, Molly noticed that the last pole in the line had been raised at one end and the second last pole had been moved to join it, raised at the other end, so the two poles formed a cross in the middle, between the jump wings. The centre of the cross was about eight inches high. As Molly rode up to Jean, she realised that this was to be her first 'jump'.
"Right Molly, I want you to trot down the line as before. Now, that cross pole is still low enough for Fred to step over but he may jump it so, after he goes over the pole before it, grab his mane, just in case. Okay?"
Molly nodded, her mouth feeling dry. She rode Fred away from Jean, then asked him to trot. As she turned down the line again, Molly felt herself start to tense up.
"Try to relax and just go with it" called Jean "remember, Fred knows his job and he'll look after you."
It took three or four tries but, eventually, Molly was trotting calmly down the poles and popping over the cross pole neatly.
"We'll call it a day there I think before Fred gets too bored." said Jean. "Did you enjoy that?"
Molly nodded "can we do it again tomorrow?" she asked.

"Not tomorrow, no." Jean shook her head. "If you jump every time, you can make the pony go stale. So it would be best if you do something different tomorrow and we'll do the pole-work next weekend."

"Oh, okay." Molly felt a bit deflated at that but she supposed Jean was right. "May I ride in the big field again tomorrow then please?"

Jean thought for a moment. "I may not be able to come with you tomorrow though."

"Could I try riding in there on my own then please? I'll be sensible, I promise."

"Maybe." Jean patted Fred. "We'll see what tomorrow brings. Let's get this lad turned out and sort out the barn, shall we?"

*   *   *   *   *

8

Half term arrived before Molly really knew where the time had gone. What with her new school, homework, weekends spent at the farm etc. the days seemed to have galloped by. Molly couldn't wait to have a whole week to play with Fred and Tyke. Tyke was getting bigger by the day it seemed and was, at times, over boisterous. Sam had spent the Saturday morning at the start of half term examining both Tyke and Buster closely before declaring that he felt it was time to get the vet out. Jean, beyond a comment about them both being very young, seemed to agree.

"Why do we need the vet?" Molly asked, a surge of panic in her stomach. "Tyke's not ill is he?" She looked worriedly at the colt.

"No, he's not ill Molly." Jean said reassuringly, "It's just that he's getting really big now and stronger. He's also very developed for his age – so is Buster actually – so we think it's time to have both colts gelded. The sooner the better really, before the weather gets too cold."

"Gelded? An operation?" Molly was even more worried now.

"Don't worry Molly, it's a very common operation. The majority of male riding horses have it done. Gary has said for me to let him know when we felt it was time so I'll email him tonight. Now, how about a hack out?"

Although Molly enjoyed hacking out, this time with Jean on Pepper, in the back of her mind she was still fretting about Tyke. Jean seemed to notice how quiet Molly was, rather than being her usual chatty self.

"I was thinking, Molly, there's a little pony club open show on Wednesday and I thought you might like to take Fred along."

"Eh?" Molly came out of her reverie. "A show? What would I need to do?"

"Well, it's up to you, of course. But there's 'clear round' jumping, some low level jumping competitions and some showing as well. I have the schedule back at home so we can look at it over lunch. Would you like that?"

"Oh, okay." Molly shrugged. Not bothered about shows, still worrying about Tyke. "Erm, won't I need proper show kit though?"

"I already thought of that one." Jean laughed. "I phoned Marion and, as I thought, she still has Andrea's old jacket. She'll drop it over later with some other bits."

"Oh. Okay. Cool." Molly still didn't feel very enthusiastic. Jean looked at her with a frown.

"Please stop worrying about Tyke being gelded Molly. We have a very good vet and he will be fine, trust me."

In the afternoon, Molly began to realise that, perhaps, Jean and Sam were right about Tyke. As she went through his lessons, the colt seemed distracted and was fidgety. He also tried to bite Molly several times, despite being told off. Even hen she resorted to a slap on his neck [emulating an older horse biting him back] nd a sharp "NO!", he still didn't stop. Several times he pushed sideways into Molly, most knocking her over at one point. Then, without warning, he reared up, yanking e lead-rope out of Molly's hands, and galloped gleefully away. As he galloped und the paddock, lead-rope swinging dangerously around his legs, Molly tried to ll to him calmly, despite the fact that her eyes were filling with tears of pain from the pe burns on her hands. Molly was about to call for Jean to come and help when ie saw that the older woman was having problems of her own at the other side of e paddock. Jean had been doing some leading practise with Buster but now was ruggling to hold onto the young Clydesdale as Tyke charged around. Molly turned er attention back to Tyke. He had slowed to a trot now, tail in the air, snorting citedly. Molly winced every time the rope went near his legs and tears started to ream down her face with the combination of panic over Tyke and pain from her ands.

Suddenly, Molly saw Sam coming into the paddock. He went up to Jean and ok Buster from her, deftly wrapping the leadrope around the colt's nose. As he ained control over Buster, Jean began to walk swiftly across to Molly. 5o what happened?" Jean asked. don't know." sniffed Molly. "He's been in a strange mood all day really. I just uldn't hold him any more." Molly sniffed again and wiped her hand across her eyes.)on't worry." Jean put her arm around Molly. "Look, he's calming down now." Molly anced across at Tyke. He was walking now, grabbing the occasional mouthful of ass. "You stay here, Molly, I'll go and get him." Jean gave Molly another quick hug en began to walk slowly towards Tyke, talking to him in a soft voice.

Ten minutes later, Jean walked Tyke into his pen in the barn and removed the pe from across his nose before taking the headcollar off. She looked at Molly with a rious expression on her face. "Now do you see why he needs to be gelded?)oner rather than later?" Her expression softened. "It's for his own good and the fety of the people around him. If we don't do it soon, he will only get worse." 3ut he might die!" Molly's eyes were still full of tears. .ook Molly, I won't deny that, as with any operation on any living creature, there is me risk, but vets geld thousands of horses every year and only a handful would ffer any ill effects. He'll be a better horse for it, trust me. And he won't be alone cause we'll be having Buster done at the same time." Jh, okay." Molly sniffed again. She looked at Tyke who was now calmly munching s hay as though it was some other horse that had been so boisterous such a short ie ago. With a resigned, heavy sigh, she turned and walked slowly out of the barn.

The next few days were exciting ones for Molly, taking her mind off the fact at Tyke's life may be put at risk by his impending operation. Carefully avoiding the bject of gelding, Jean had Molly practising for various events at the coming show Wednesday. Not only did Molly practise over some low jumps but also gymkhana mes and even showing classes. Fred was also groomed thoroughly every day and s tack cleaned and polished until it was gleaming. On the Tuesday afternoon, it was warm day for October. Jean took the opportunity to help Molly bath Fred and then

© Chrissie Turner 2017

Molly cleaned his tack yet again. Marion had brought over a navy jacket for Molly to wear, along with a white saddle cloth and a leather girth. Because Molly wasn't in Pony Club, she couldn't wear a pony club tie so Jean was lending her a plain navy one of Sam's. Molly already had jodhpurs and boots from the stuff Marion had sent over with the school uniform so, with a clean school shirt, she was all set.

It was an early start on the morning of the show, since the 'clear round' started at nine in the morning and was going to be raised every half hour through to lunchtime. Molly was just going to do the lowest height, as it was her first time. Luckily, as a 'Native' pony, Fred didn't need to be plaited for the showing classes.

The show was to be held on a neighbouring farm and was only a couple of miles away along the lanes. Jean said she would 'bunny hop' as Molly and Fred rode along. This meant that Jean would drive the landrover to a point just out of sight of Molly and Fred then, when they reached her, Jean would drive on a few hundred yards to the next bend. And so on. This meant that, although she was riding on her own, Molly would never be far from help if she needed it. Jean was also bringing a picnic and a selection of extra equipment.

Before they left the yard, Jean insisted on taking some photos of Molly and Fred in all their 'posh' show kit so she could send a couple to Gary. Then, once she had made sure that Molly knew the way she needed to go, Jean got into the landrover and drove out of the farmyard. Trying to quell the butterflies in her stomach. Molly gave Fred a squeeze with her legs and set off down the lane.

Despite the fact that she knew Jean would always be waiting just around the next bend, Molly felt a tingling thrill that, only three months since she started riding, she was, technically, riding out on her own. She rode quietly in walk, as Jean had suggested, so she could save Fred's energy for the actual show. It was a sunny morning with just a hint of Autumn in the air. Fred seemed to know what was going on. He walked along the lane energetically, ears pricked, blowing contentedly through his nostrils now and again. When they rounded the first bend, there was Jean standing by the landrover a about fifty yards ahead. As Molly and Fred approached, Jean came forward with a bottle of water.
"How's it going? Is Fred behaving?" Jean asked, handing the bottle to Molly so she could have a few sips.
"He's being really good. I think he knows we're going somewhere." Molly grinned.
"He probably does. He's an old hand at this lark, after all." Jean patted the Fell pony.
"Right, I'll see you round the next bend."
Molly waited until Jean started to drive away then asked Fred to walk on again.

When Molly and Fred arrived at the show ground, Jean was waiting by the entrance, a copy of the schedule in her hand. It was just coming up to half past eight so they were in plenty of time. Molly dismounted and ran her stirrups up before loosening Fred's girth and then walked with Jean across to where the landrover was now parked, quite close to the rings where the various competitions were going to be taking place.

"Okay Molly. I reckon that we try and get the clear round out of the way first – I got you two tickets so you can go round twice. Then there's the showing classes. I've put you down for Veteran and 'Mountain and Moorland'. I think you would be better doing the in hand stuff for today. Does that sound okay?" Molly nodded numbly. The butterflies had started again. "So," Jean went on, "that takes care of the morning. We'll see how you are feeling after lunch before we decide on the fun classes and the gymkhana." With that, Jean set off across the show ground to 'ring three' where there was a small course of about eight show jumps. At the moment, they were all set out as 'cross poles' and were only about a foot in height in the centre of the cross. Molly suddenly felt queasy. She was certain she would never remember the course! Jean seemed to sense her worries and patted her arm as a young girl approached carrying a box of rosettes and a clipboard. Jean walked across to the girl and spoke to her quietly, glancing at Molly and Fred as she talked. When the girl nodded, Jean beckoned Molly and Fred over.

"Melanie here has kindly agreed to hold on to Fred for us while we walk the course." Jean glanced at her watch. "It won't take long, then I'll help you warm Fred up." Handing Fred's reins to Melanie, Jean smiled at the girl. "We'd like to be first in if possible, we've got lots of other stuff to do!"

Melanie gave Fred a pat. "I'm sure you will be fine." She smiled at Molly in a friendly way. "The start is over there." she added, pointing towards a small board, with the word 'START' on it, a few feet in front of a red and white jump that bore the number one. Too nervous to open her mouth, Molly nodded at Melanie and gave a nervous smile before following Jean into the ring.

Even though there were only eight tiny jumps, set in a simple figure of eight course, Molly could feel her stomach churning and her mouth going dry as they walked around the ring. She could barely take in what Jean was saying, instead her attention was taken by the arrival of other ponies and riders, including a tiny child who looked to be only about three years old and who was mounted on a tiny black Shetland, the smallest equine Molly had ever seen! Molly suddenly became aware that Jean was talking to her.

"So Molly, what's the course?"

"Erm." Molly looked around at the jumps. Several more people were walking around the ring now. Molly looked at Jean. "Erm. I know the first jump is that red and white over there."

Jean gave an exasperated sigh and began to run through the simple course, pointing to each jump in turn. "Do you think you know it now?"

Not wishing to annoy Jean, Molly nodded, uncertain still.

"Okay. Lets go and warm up then." Jean marched briskly out of the ring.

Fred seemed unimpressed by the fact that no one was allowing him to snatch a quick snack of grass during the waiting around but he soon perked up when, after tightening his girth, Molly remounted and rode him across to the warm up area adjacent to the clear round ring. Jean instructed Molly to ride round quietly whilst she put up a small cross pole. She then told Molly to trot quietly round a couple of times and then, still in a steady trot, come in a nice straight line and pop over the little jump. The first time, Molly got so flustered that she forgot to ride Fred forward. This, coupled with her tense hands, meant that Fred ground to a halt in front of the jump. Jean went across, patted Fred and told Molly to try to be a bit more positive. The second time, Fred hopped over the jump but then stopped on the landing side and tried to put his head down, almost causing Molly to fall off. Molly felt the inevitable tears of frustration welling up. Jean walked around with Molly and Fred for a few moments.

"Don't worry so much, Molly. Just ride forward, not only towards the jump but away from it too. Trust the pony. Remember, your job is to ride him to the fence, his job is to get you both over it. He knows that so *trust* him."

Molly nodded then had another go at the practise jump. This time, she managed to jump it properly. Grinning, Jean declared that they should go over to the ring and do their rounds.

Molly's heart was racing as she rode Fred into the ring. Where on earth was the first fence? Jean had said for Molly to take it quiet and steady, just trotting quietly round so she could get the hang of it. Molly was so nervous that, when she finally spotted the first fence, she kicked Fred so hard, he shot forward into a surprised, very fast canter, thundering towards the tiny cross pole, then leaping it as though it was three foot high! Molly was flung upwards but managed to cling on to Fred's mane as Fred trotted merrily towards Jean in the entrance to the ring. Jean calmly reached out and grabbed Fred's bridle.

"Steady there Fred. Now Molly, calm down and concentrate." Jean turned Fred round to face the course again. Molly was shaking but managed to stop herself bursting into tears. Jean patted Fred and smiled up at Molly. "Okay girl, keep going. Fence two is the green and white one just over there." With that, Jean let go of the pony and stepped back to stand beside Melanie once more. Molly took a deep breath, sat up straight and squeezed Fred into a much calmer stride as she trotted him towards jump number two.

Molly and Fred managed to pop over the next three jumps without incident, although not very tidily as Molly kept fiddling with the length of her reins and zig zagging between the jumps as she struggled to remember the course. Jean called out to tell Molly which one was the fifth jump just as Molly was about to ride past it – despite there being a large number five resting against the wing. Molly yanked Fred's head round and kicked him forward as they turned. Fred ground to a halt then stepped slowly over the jump, dragging his last hind leg across the pole and knocking it to the ground. Molly thought of a swear word she had heard Gary use once, when he though no one was listening. She halted Fred, sat up straighter then looked round for number six. Spotting it, Molly pushed Fred into a trot again. Concentrating hard, she trotted over the last three jumps then gratefully trotted over to Jean at the entrance.

"You know, that wasn't too bad Molly," Jean said, patting Fred and giving him a polo mint. "Considering you've not been riding long and this is your first show, it was a very good effort!"

"I was useless." said Molly, crimson with embarrassment when she saw how many people were standing around, on foot or mounted, in the collecting ring.

"Well," Jean went on, "I got you two tickets so I think you should go round again straight away. Get it over with. And this time, *concentrate!*" She gave Fred another pat. "Off you go."

Taking a deep breath, Molly gathered up her reins again and rode back out into the ring. A couple of young kids had put the poles back on jump number five and the course was ready for her to jump. Trying hard to remember all Jean's lessons and advice, Molly squeezed Fred into a trot and headed for jump number one.

"Well done Molly!" Jean came up and patted Fred. Molly had a huge grin on her face. She'd done it! There had been a couple of 'iffy' moments when she had turned a corner a bit tighter than she should have and Fred had scrambled untidily over the jump but she had done all eight, in the right order and without knocking anything down. To prove it, she now had a pretty pink rosette with the words 'Clear Round' embossed in gold in the centre.

"Jolly well done!" Came a voice from the other side of the collecting ring. Molly looked across and there was Marion, striding towards them. "I agree with what Jean told me, you're a natural girl! My Fred couldn't be in better hands!"

Molly smiled weakly, feeling very self-conscious at the praise. She managed to mutter 'thank you' before Marion gave Fred a pat and announced that, since Andrea was about to compete in ring one, she had better go and help her out. Jean waved Marion off then looked up at Molly.

"Okay, Molly, showing classes now, in hand. We have about half an hour before the veteran class starts and then the Mountain and Moorland is next but one afterwards. So we need to get that saddle off and smarten this little chap up a bit."

In hand showing was a bit boring, Molly decided as, along with about ten other competitors, she led Fred around ring two, in a huge circle with the judge and the steward standing in the middle, looking at each horse or pony critically. Before going into the ring, Jean had Molly practising getting Fred to stand 'square' and also trotting up and down calmly beside Molly's shoulder. Now Molly scanned the other entrants as they all plodded around the ring. They were all shapes and sizes, all looking very smart. Some even had tiny bobbled plaits in their manes and what looked like a 'French Plait' running down the tops of their tails. Molly had noticed this earlier and had asked Jean why they hadn't done the same to Fred.

"Natives are never plaited" Jean had said. "Nor are they trimmed or pulled in any way either. They are always shown as natural as possible"

Thinking on Jean's words, Molly deduced that was why the Shetland in the ring was also not plaited, nor another one which was bigger than Fred and not quite as hairy round it's legs. Molly made a mental note to ask Jean what breed it was.

The steward calling across jolted Molly out of her reverie. Following the steward's instructions, the line of horses and ponies were all turned towards the middle of the ring and stood in a long line side by side, facing the judge. Molly thought the woman looked very much like the queen mother, with her long tweed skirt, brogue shoes and a flowery, wide brimmed hat. Since Molly was about half way along the line, she was able to watch closely what was happening with the other competitors.

The judge stayed in the middle of the ring and the steward beckoned to the first competitor. A young woman led her horse out and halted it squarely in front of the judge. As the judge looked over the horse, feeling it's coat, running a hand down it's legs, picking up it's hooves, she was obviously asking the handler questions and the steward was making notes on her clipboard. Then the judge straightened up and stepped back. The steward spoke to the handler and, clicking to her horse, the young woman walked off across the ring in a straight line then turned just before the fenceline, clicked again and ran back with her horse trotting easily beside her. She ran right past the judge then, after a few more strides, brought the horse back to a walk and walked back. All the time the judge was obviously scrutinising the horse. When they reached the judge, the woman halted the horse. The judge stepped forwards, patted the horse and then, with a nod, turned her attention to the next in line whilst the first one returned to her spot.

It was soon Molly and Fred's turn. Trying to quell the butterflies, Molly did what she had seen the others do and led Fred out to stand neatly in front of the judge. Fred was obviously an old hand at this game as he stood stock still, ears pricked and allowed the judge to prod and poke at her whim. As she looked over Fred, the judge asked Molly about his age, how long she had had him etc. Then the steward instructed Molly to copy the others by walking away, turning and trotting back. As she set off, Molly reminded herself to turn Fred to the right so he turned around himself, rather than turn him left around her. Jean had pointed out that, not only was this correct but it was the safest way to turn a horse. The run back wasn't as easy as Molly thought! Fred was feeling energetic and was trying to trot faster than Molly could run but, with an effort, Molly managed to keep him under control as they trotted past the judge. They came back to a walk, turned and walked back. The judge had one last look at Fred, thanked Molly then turned her attention to the next one whilst the steward directed Molly to walk Fred around the back of the line and back into his place.

When all the competitors had been scrutinised by the judge, the judge asked them all to walk around the ring again, as they had at the beginning of the class. Molly grinned as she saw Jean standing at the ringside, smiling and giving her a 'thumbs up'. As the steward pointed at a big grey, Molly watched as it was led into the middle of the ring and halted. The Shetland was called in next, then a plain looking bay. Molly sighed then jumped as the steward waved at her, beckoning her out of line. Molly took her place and watched as two more were called forward to stand in line and then the steward quietly asked the others to leave the ring. Molly was surprised when the judge stepped forwards and presented the handler of the first horse with a blue rosette. She thought the winner got red. But no, the next one got red. Then the next one got green and Molly was presented with a yellow rosette and a 'well done' from the judge. Molly thanked the judge and looked at the rosette which clearly stated that she had got fourth place. When everyone had their rosettes, the steward waved her arm and the line moved off and began to trot around the outside of the ring in a 'lap of honour'.

"Well done Molly!" Jean hugged her as Molly led Fred out of the ring. "Fourth

brilliant!" Jean patted Fred. "Now, we just have time for a quick burger I think.
here's another class before your next one. Come on" and Jean set off towards the
ndrover.

atching her up, Molly looked at her rosette again.

don't understand the colours" she said. "I thought that first was red, then blue, then
ellow, then green"

Oh, normally it is." Explained Jean, "but the Pony Club is an international
ganisation so they use the international colours which are blue, red, green then
ellow. After fourth, I think people just choose what they want though. I've seen some
eird combinations for minor placings. Now, you wait here and I'll get some food.
hat would you like?"

Erm, cheeseburger with onions please, if that's okay?"

ean nodded, "Yep sure. And a coke too no doubt." With a smile, Jean headed off
wards the snack van. Molly fed Fred a couple of polos then opened the back of the
ndrover and took out a bucket that Jean had obviously half filled with water since
eir arrival at the showground. Not sure if he could drink with a bridle on, Molly
fered the bucket to Fred. He lowered his head, took half a dozen sips, then stepped
vay and started to crop at the grass.

Molly felt more confident as she went in for the Mountain and Moorland and it
eemed to help that she had eaten something now too. Her nerves this morning had
eant she had skipped breakfast but she hadn't told Jean that. Fred was still quite
erky and Molly was thrilled when they were called into second place! Afterwards,
ean took Fred's bridle off and replaced it with his headcollar. She then tied him to
e bumper of the landrover with a long rope so that he could graze whilst she and
olly ate a picnic lunch. Molly got the water bucket and placed it where Fred could
ach it easily then sat on the blanket Jean had laid out on the grass, grinning to
erself as she studied her red and yellow rosettes.

After lunch, they headed for ring three again. The jumps had all been
smantled and the poles and wings were now neatly stacked to one side of the ring.
ean had put Fred's bridle back on but was carrying his saddle whilst Molly led the
ony.

Fun classes now Molly." Jean said. "I put you in for 'Handsomest gelding' and
ongest Tail'. Okay?"

olly nodded, grinning. She felt as though she was an old hand at this showing
ame now. Jean and Molly watched as the 'prettiest mare' class was judged, then it
as Molly and Fred's turn. Jean gave the pony a quick flick over with a body brush
fore Molly led him into the ring.

'Fun' class it may have been but it seemed to take even longer than the
oper' showing classes in ring two! The judge didn't call them into line, nor have
em do an individual trot up but they seemed to be walking around the outside of the
g for hours whilst the judge deliberated. As Molly and Fred passed where Jean
as standing for what felt like the hundredth time, the steward called out "Number
y-four please." Molly didn't even register the words until Jean called to her and
inted out that fifty-four was Molly's number! Fred had won 'Handsomest Gelding'!

Molly turned him in to stand where the steward indicated and hugged him hard. Once the other five had lined up, the judge and steward began handing out the rosettes. As the judge handed Molly the blue rosette, she patted Fred and said "Sorry I took so long to decide but, actually, this little chap was already the winner as soon as he walked into the ring. It was sorting out the others that took the time." With a smile at Molly, she patted Fred again and then moved on to the next in line. Molly grinned broadly as she led the lap of honour around the ring. 'Longest Tail' was next so Molly stayed in the ring as some of the others left, to be replaced by different competitors.

'Longest Tail' didn't take so long. A couple of circuits of the ring and then they were asked to line up. Fred's face was a picture as the judge approached with a tape measure! She measured, not only the actual length of Fred's tail but also how far above the ground it ended. As the judge moved along the line, Molly noticed that some of the entries were definitely suspicious of the tape measure. Molly suppressed a giggle as a Shetland pony flatly refused to allow the judge anywhere near it's rear end with a 'snake'. Eventually though, the judge finished her measuring and the steward asked them all to start walking around again. Obviously, Fred *didn't* have the longest tail as he was called in fifth. Molly though, thought that the purple and pink rosette she was given was by far the prettiest she had won so far.

"Gymkhana's next!" Said Jean cheerfully as she began saddling Fred up. "Now, because of your age, you can't do the novice type games so I've just picked out the easiest ones for you. I don't think you're ready for the 'Bending' race yet but you should be okay with most of the others."
"What are they then?" Molly asked as she watched the people in the ring setting out lines of tall, thin, flexible poles.
"Er," Jean pulled the schedule from her pocket, "ride and lead, sack race, egg and spoon and apple bobbing."
"Okay." said Molly, wondering what, exactly, she was going to have to do but not really wanting to ask.

It was fun, Molly had to admit. Even though she was last in the sack race and the egg and spoon – she had never even thought of how hard it was going to be to ride a pony and balance an egg at the same time – she had managed to win the ride and lead by a whisker and now was just waiting for the apple bobbing to start. Jean grinned down at Molly.
"The key is to take a deep breath and to push the apple to the bottom of the bucket to grab it. Don't forget, the rules say you must put your hat back on and fasten it before you ride back. Okay? Good luck!" Jean legged Molly up onto Fred.

Molly clung hard to Fred's mane as he galloped towards the bucket of water with the apples floating in it. It helped to have a pony that was an old hand at this sort of thing. As he skidded to a halt, Molly yanked her hat off and threw herself down on her knees beside the bucket then, following Jean's advice, took a deep breath, selected an apple and plunged her head into the water. As she bit into the fruit, she lifted her head out of the water, spluttering around the apple still clenched in her teeth. She plonked her hat onto her soaking hair, fastened the chin strap then, still with the apple in her teeth, scrambled onto Fred's back, grabbing his mane again. She didn't even have a chance to sort out her reins or put her feet in her stirrups as Fred spun round and thundered back across the field, in hot pursuit of a boy on what looked like a miniature racehorse! As Fred crossed the finish line in second place, Jean stepped forward and caught hold of his bridle, bringing him to a halt.

"Well done Molly! You're second!" she said.

Laughing, Molly dismounted and took the apple from her mouth before offering it to Fred. Even with his bit in, Fred managed to bite chunks of fruit and chew them thoroughly, causing sticky, frothy apple juice to form around his mouth. When he had finished his treat, he wiped his muzzle down Molly's sleeve. "Oh, yuk. Thanks Fred." Molly wiped the mess away, then heard the ring steward's voice.

"Unfortunately, the winner of the apple bobbing will have to be disqualified because he neglected to fasten the chinstrap of his riding hat so the winner is now Molly Peters on Fred!"

Astounded, Molly hugged Fred hard, and Jean was hugging both Molly and the pony as the steward came and handed Molly another blue rosette. As they left the ring and headed back to the landrover, Marion appeared.

"Jolly well done!" She cried, hugging Molly then giving Fred and enthusiastic pat. "It's so good to see this old boy looking so well and happy and enjoying himself."

"He's brilliant" Molly said grinning. "Thank you so much for letting me ride him."

"No problem at all." Marion smiled. "So pleased for you both!" Giving Fred a last pat, Marion strode away towards ring one.

Jean suggested that she and Molly gave Fred a bit of a breather before heading home and they tied him up to graze again whilst they finished off the picnic.

"Well, you've got a good haul of rosettes for your first show." Jean said.

Molly arranged the bright ribbons on the picnic rug. "I wish Gary could have been here to see though." she said quietly.

"Tell you what," Jean said, "Let me take a picture on my phone and I can send it to him."

"That would be cool." Molly, smiling broadly.

Molly felt as though she was going to fall asleep on Fred's back on the ride home. She was exhausted from the early start and all the excitement of the show. But she was happy. She couldn't remember the last time she felt *this* happy. She sat quietly on Fred's back as he plodded along the lane, knowing exactly where he was going, as Molly relived her day. She felt a moment of sadness as she thought of how proud her father would have been. Then she thought to herself that, perhaps, if there was an afterlife, he would have been watching her and he would be proud. It was a thought she often nurtured. The thought that, even after death, her dad was still there, somewhere, keeping an eye on her. As Fred carried her back to the farm, at his own steady pace, Molly daydreamed about what life would have been like had fate not decreed that her father had passed away.

* * * * *

9

Molly had a bit of a shock waiting for her when she got back to the farm. Jean had driven straight back from the show, trusting that Fred would carry Molly safely home. As Molly dismounted in the farmyard, she noticed that the vet's car was by the barn and that Jean was hurrying across from the huge building, smiling at Molly.

"You got back safely then," she smiled, "I knew I could trust Fred." Jean patted the pony.

"Why's the vet here?" Asked Molly, a worried frown on her face.

Jean drew a deep breath. "Well, you remember we spoke about gelding the colts?" Molly's frown deepened as Jean went on. "We decided that it would be best if they were done during the holiday so that you would be able to make sure Tyke was okay before you went back to school. So we had them done this afternoon. In fact, the vet's just getting ready to go."

"What! Is Tyke okay?" Molly dropped Fred's reins and went to run into the barn. Jean put her hand on Molly's are to stopped her.

"Both colts are fine, although still sedated. Now, I think you should get hold of Fred and get him untacked and settled, don't you?"

"What?" Molly looked round to see that Fred had taken advantage of Molly's lapse in concentration to grab a snack from the long grass by the driveway. She hastily reached out and took hold of his reins.

Once Fred had been untacked, brushed off and was happily munching his haynet, Jean allowed Molly to go into Tyke's pen where the young horse was standing, head down by his knees, blood running down the inside of his back legs.

"What's wrong with him?" Molly cried, on the verge of bursting into tears.

"Don't worry Molly," Jean said, give Molly's hand a squeeze. "He's still sedated at the moment. He'll feel a bit sorry for himself for a day or two but he'll be fine, honest. Look, Buster's the same." Jean nodded across to the next pen where Buster, separated from Pepper, was also standing with his head low and blood covered legs.

"Did the vet knock them out?" asked Molly as she sadly stroked Tyke's neck.

"No, not at all. Just sedated them heavily so she could do what they call a 'standing castration'." Jean looked at Molly, "Much less risky than using a full anaesthetic. Now, you wait here a moment." She smiled at Molly then bustled off.

Jean arrived back within a few minutes with a bucket of warm water, two large bowls and a large pack of cotton wool. A faint smell of antiseptic filled the air as Jean poured water into the two bowls. She pull a large wad of cotton wool out of the packet then handed the bowl and cotton wool to Molly.

"Use this to clean up his legs and to gently bathe the wound." Jean told Molly. "There are no stitches so we need to make sure we keep it clean."

"How come there are no stitches?" Molly was puzzled.

"They leave the wounds open so that the blood can drain." Jean explained. "Now, off ou go and clean him before he wakes up fully."

Tyke didn't move at all as Molly gently bathed his legs and the wound up behind his sheath. The water turned red as she rinsed the cotton wool out frequently. Eventually, Tyke's legs were clean and his wound too, although it was still seeping a little blood. Jean came into the pen and examined Tyke, then handed Molly a clean towel to dab him dry. As Molly finished, Jean checked him again. "Yep, that's fine." Jean said, smiling. "Now, let's leave these two boys to wake up and go and have some tea. Okay?" Giving Tyke another gentle pat, Molly followed Jean out of the barn.

By the time Molly was getting ready to go home, both Buster and Tyke had woken up enough to be able to have a small amount of feed and hay. Feeling a lot better about the situation, Molly gave Tyke a hug and then went in to hug Fred too, since it was he who had been so good all day and earned the small pile of brightly coloured rosettes that Molly was proudly taking home.

Even Mrs Peters seemed impressed when Molly showed her the rosettes she and Fred had won at the show. She hugged Molly and, wiping tears from her eyes, made a quiet comment about wishing that Molly's father had been alive to see what Molly had achieved. Dinner was eaten in an atmosphere which was a mixture of pride and sorrow. Later, Molly logged on to the computer and found an email from Gary who had obviously received Jean's picture of Molly's rosettes. He too commented on how proud he was of Molly. He also asked about Tyke and how his operation had gone. Molly wondered how he knew but then realised that, since Gary had been paying for Tyke's keep etc., it was logical that he would have been told about the gelding operation, if only so that he knew to expect another vet bill! Molly quickly wrote a long reply to Gary, detailing her day and then describing how Tyke had been before she'd come home that evening. Finally, feeling exhausted now, Molly got ready for bed. Although she'd finished reading *Black Beauty* a few days ago, she hadn't dug out a new book to read so she decided to read the last bit of her old favourite again. Reading about how Joe found Beauty again and how the old horse at last found a peaceful home always made Molly feel happy as she snuggled down under her duvet to relive her eventful day.

Molly slept so deeply, she didn't wake up until after nine O clock! Opening her eyes, she sat up with a start. She was late! She must have slept through her alarm! As she went to leap out of bed, she suddenly remembered what Jean had said to her the evening before. Jean had pointed out that, since Fred deserved a 'rest day' after his efforts at the show, there was only the foals to be walked out so there was no need for Molly's usual early arrival at the farm. With a sigh of relief, Molly relaxed. She remembered that she hadn't even set her alarm last night, having decided to let herself wake up naturally for once. She looked again at the clock on her bedside table. She ought to get up now though, she'd told Jean she'd be at the farm for around half past ten. As she started pulling on her clothes, she looked at the line of colourful rosettes strung across her headboard. Her mother had given Molly a long piece of string specifically for the purpose. Smiling and feeling a warm glow inside her, Molly finished dressing and headed downstairs.

When she got to the farm, Molly was thrilled to see that Tyke and Buster were both a lot perkier, although both had dried blood down the inside of their back legs again. Jean explained that the vet wanted the two young horses to just walk out 'in hand' for about fifteen minutes a time, three times a day.

"We need to wash them down again first though." Jean said, handing Molly the bowl of water and roll of cotton wool. "Same as we did last night."

Molly took the bowl and, talking quietly to Tyke, began gently cleaning away the dried blood. When she'd finished, She and Jean put headcollars on the two young horses. Molly suddenly noticed something.

"Where are the others?" she asked.

"Out in the field." Jean said. "We've been gradually getting these boys used to being separated for short periods, ready for this. Pepper will go back in with Buster tonight though." With that, Jean opened Buster's pen and led the young horse out. Buster walked stiff legged beside Jean as Molly and Tyke followed behind. Molly tried to see if Tyke was walking stiffly too but, every time she tried to turn to look at his back legs, the foal turned with her. In the end, she gave up. She supposed it was logical that both foals would be feeling stiff today.

To keep the youngsters as calm as possible, Jean avoided walking near the paddock where the other horses were, instead just walking round and round in the small paddock where Molly had her riding lessons. Molly wasn't sure who was most bored with this game, herself or Tyke. After a few minutes, Tyke tried grabbing Molly's sleeve with his teeth which earned him a sharp slap on the neck and a shout of 'NO'! Jean glanced back over her shoulder at Molly and Tyke.

"You okay?" Jean asked.

"Yeah fine." Molly replied, giving Tyke's rope a sharp tug as he tried his luck at grabbing her again. "He's still trying to bite though."

"Well," Jean chuckled, "the operation won't have an instantaneous effect you know! It will take a few weeks for all the hormones to settle down. Tell you what, try giving him the knotted end of the rope to chew on."

Molly jiggled the end of the rope in front of Tyke's nose and he grabbed it, chewing on it as they walked round the paddock again. It seemed to work. Every time he let go of the knot, Molly jiggled it again until he caught hold. He seemed to enjoy this new game. At the end of the fifteen minute session, Jean and Molly took the foals back to the barn. Molly offered to groom the both of them whilst Jean went off to do some housework and also to prepare lunch.

"Good idea," Jean smiled. "but don't forget another job you need to do today, will you?"

"Oh! What's that?" Molly asked.

"Your tack. It didn't get cleaned after the show yesterday." Jean pretended to look severely at Molly. Molly laughed.

"Oh, yeah. No problem. I can do it when I've finished grooming these two."

"Don't worry, Molly. Jean chuckled. "It can wait until after lunch, I'm sure." With that, Jean headed out of the barn and Molly went and fetched her grooming kit so she could give the two foals a good brush over.

After lunch, Jean and Molly, with Fizz trotting beside them, took Tyke and
ister along the lane. Molly tried hard to quell her nervousness. She felt her heart
immering in her chest for two reasons. One was not knowing how the foals would
have walking out down the unfamiliar route and the other was in case the strange
iveller man was still hanging around. Her fears were unfounded though. Apart from
iving a good look around, both foals behaved well and they didn't see a single soul
they walked to the end of the lane where the bridleway started, then turned
ound and walked back to the farm. Molly decided not to voice her fears to Jean.
ie couldn't fully relax though until they turned back through the gate to the
myard. As they put the foals away and gave them a small amount of hay, Jean
minded Molly about her tack cleaning duties. With a grin, Molly jogged off to the
ck room. Tack cleaning was one of the many horsey chores she enjoyed. In fact,
olly mused, there weren't really any chores with the horses she didn't enjoy. Even
icking out wasn't too bad. Although, Molly admitted to herself, the current exercise
gime with the foals was pretty boring but at least it wouldn't be for long.

Friday saw the foals exercise sessions increased to half an hour, twice a day,
th Jean closely checking the wounds after each session. In the afternoon, the vet
pped in and announced that, since everything seemed to be okay, the foals should
able to be turned out on the Saturday, although she stressed that, if they galloped
ound too much, they would need to be brought back in, just as a precaution against
e wounds reopening and infection getting in. Feeling much better about the whole
ng, Molly looked forward to the time when the other horses came in. Jean had
omised that they would take Shandy and Fred for a quiet hack before settling the
rses down for the night.

As Jean and Molly rode along the bridleway, Fred suddenly pricked up his
rs and gave out a loud whinney. Surprised, Both Jean and Molly scanned the
rizon to see what had caught Fred's attention. Molly spotted something moving
ong the hedge-line of a big stubble field to their left.
Vhat's that?" She asked Jean, pointing.
ooks like a horse and rider" Jean frowned, squinting. "They're riding along the
adland, though they shouldn't be in that field. Come on." Jean turned Shandy off
e track and into the stubble field, riding onto the headland and heading towards the
itant horse and rider. The strangers were riding anti-clockwise around the field so
an turned left to go clockwise and so, hopefully, intercept them. Without a word to
olly, Jean kicked Shandy into a canter. Fred followed suit and Molly settled into his
ide whilst still watching the distance trespasser. Suddenly, the strangers
:appeared! Jean pulled Shandy up and, a few strides later, Molly succeeded in
opping Fred and turned him back towards the Clydesdale mare.
Vhere did they go?" Jean scanned the hedge-line but there was no sign of the
rse and rider. "Come on Molly, let's go and have a look."

They rode side by side, at a walk, scanning the ground for hoof prints.
ddenly, Molly spotted some churned up ground ahead of them.
ook there" she said to Jean, pointing at the ground.
lere, hold Shandy while I have a look." Jean dismounted and handed Shandy's

reins to Molly. Molly watched as Jean went closer to the churned up area, then she went up to the hedge and peered at the ground beneath it. "Good grief!" Jean exclaimed.

"What is it?" Molly stood in her stirrups to try to see better.

"Well, it appears our trespasser is either very brave or a complete idiot!" Jean walked back over to Shandy and took the reins from Molly. "It seems they stopped suddenly just here – probably spotted us coming to head them off – then pushed through the hedge to get away."

"Oh!" Molly was puzzled, "What was stupid about that?"

"There's a ditch and a barbed wire fence in the hedge-line Okay, so the fence is low here, a couple of poles have rotted and fallen over, but it still means having to jump the ditch and the barbed wire whilst under the hedge! Pretty crazy eh!" Shaking her head, Jean lowered the stirrup on Shandy's saddle as far as she could so that she could scramble back onto the mare's back. "The ground's too hard on the other side to see which way they've gone so, I guess we'll just have to keep our eyes open in case they ride round here again. Ah well, so much for our quiet walk out!"

As they rode back towards the farm, Molly pondered on what she had seen. Somehow, she got the impression that the horse wasn't very big. It was also a skewbald – brown and white patches. For some reason, someone riding on Sam and Jean's land on a 'coloured' horse gave Molly a deep sense of foreboding. Yet again, the spectre of a possible conflict over Tyke's legal ownership reared it's ugly head and caused a churning in her stomach.

*   *   *   *   *

10

Saturday morning dawned and it was wet and gloomy outside. The rain was bucketing down and there was a strong wind howling through the trees as Molly, with a miserable looking Fizz at her heels, struggled against the wind on her way to the farm. Despite her waterproof jacket, Molly was soaked through and she had to screw up her eyes to peer through the downpour from under her hood. The foul weather suited her mood. She hadn't been able to stop thinking about the stranger riding in the stubble field the day before and she was certain it had something to do with the traveller who kept accusing Molly of stealing his horse. As Molly and Fizz passed the place where she had found Tyke and his dead mother, she shivered. Was taking in the dumped foal really stealing? Had they not taken him in, he would have surely died, of that, Molly was certain.

Molly was grateful for the warmth and shelter of the barn when she finally arrived at the farm. Taking off her jacket and shaking it out, Molly saw that Jean was already there with the water for washing down the foals. She also had a large, faded towel which she handed to Molly with instructions to rub Fizz down with it. That done, Molly went into Tyke's pen and checked him over. There was hardly any blood at all on his legs today and the wound looked clean and dry. Gently, Molly clean the few spots of blood off Tyke's legs and dabbed at the wound. When she had done, she looked across at Jean.

"We won't be able to turn them out today, will we?" as Molly spoke, a low rumble of thunder joined the noise of the howling wind outside. Fizz gave a whine and wriggled into the pen to get to Molly, pressing her still damp body against Molly's legs.

"Doesn't look like it." Replied Jean. "Although it's supposed to clear up a bit later." Jean came out of Buster's pen. "I need to go and help Sam feed the calves. Why don't you give the gang a good grooming? It will warm you up at least!"

"Okay." Molly nodded. "But I won't be able to reach the top of Pepper and Shandy!" Jean laughed. "There's a plastic step that I use over by the wall. You should be okay if you use that. I'll see you later, for lunch. Okay?"

Molly smiled and went to get her grooming kit as Jean, now wrapped up in a Barbour jacket, went out into the wind and the rain.

By the time she had groomed all five horses, Molly felt as though her arms were going to drop off. She had done the two foals first, then Fred, then Shandy and she was now using a mane comb on Pepper's feathers, having already brushed the rest of the big Clydesdale's body. There were still rumbles of thunder outside, although not as loud or frequent as they had been. It seemed to Molly that the wind was dying down too, although she could still hear the staccato drumming of the rain on the roof of the barn. Fizz was still cowering in Tyke's pen, having tried to bury herself in the straw bedding. As Molly straightened up, the barn door opened a few inches and Jean stuck her dripping head through.

"Lunchtime Molly." she called.

Molly packed her grooming kit away, gave Pepper a pat and left the pen. Calling Fizz, she grabbed her still sodden jacket and headed out into the storm. The dog slinked out, clinging close to Molly's legs and then, as Molly closed the barn door, Fizz ran swiftly towards the house, desperate not to be out in the weather. Molly ran swiftly after her.

Jean was right about the weather. As Molly tucked into the cheese and chutney sandwiches on her plate, the rain began to finally ease off and, occasionally, the ragged clouds allowed the sun to peek briefly through. The thunder was a low, distant, occasional rumble now and the wind was barely audible. Sam looked out of the window with a critical eye.

"Glad I got all my crops in before this lot arrived." He muttered. Jean nodded in agreement. Then Sam noticed Fizz, who was hiding in the corner by the Welsh dresser, trembling. "Some sheepdog that is." He said, jerking his head in Fizz's direction. "First drop of rain and she's hiding away! Not like her mother at all."

"Where is Meg?" Molly asked.

"Out there in the yard, waiting to see if there's any work to be done." Sam replied. "We were moving the ram this morning so she had her work cut out there. He's a bit of a handful, that fella." Sam turned his attention to a large slice of apple pie that Jean had just placed before him. "But he's a good ram. We get some good stock from him."

"The ram's been moved into the field with the main flock." explained Jean to Molly. "Now the rain is stopping, we could walk the foals up to the top field to see them if you like?"

Molly nodded, her mouth full of her own apple pie.

"Right then." Jean bustled around the kitchen, clearing up the debris from lunch. "We'd better get on whilst the weather holds off.

Both foals were on their toes today, probably due to a combination of having been cooped up all morning and the strong gusts of wind under their tails. Jean had anticipated this and had fitted 'stud chains' to their headcollars. The chains went across their noses, just below the noseband of the headcollar, and threaded through the ring under their chins and then were attached to the lead ropes. It meant that, when the foals got too strong, the chains would tighten and enable Jean and Molly to bring the young horses back under control. It only took Tyke a few minutes to realise that there wasn't much point in fighting Molly with the chain in place but Buster seemed determined to argue with Jean. As they splashed through the puddles left by the storm, Molly had to laugh at Tyke. He seemed to think that every puddle held a crocodile and deftly dodged around it, despite Molly's efforts to make him walk through. Buster, however, had no such worries. He was so busy arguing with Jean, he splashed though every puddle with his large feet, soaking Jean, Molly and Tyke with spray.

They were almost at the top field and could hear the flock of sheep bleating when they came to a puddle which stretched all the way across the track, with no space between it and the fence-line on either side. It was at least eight feet across to the far end, where the track showed through again. Jean halted Buster and turned her head to face Molly.

'The ram hated this – Sam, a couple of the men and myself had to carry him over! He's quite heavy, especially with his fleece wet from the rain!"

Molly looked at the puddle apprehensively, then looked at Tyke. He was already snorting at the surface of the water, apparently convinced that the loch ness monster was lurking in there, waiting to grab him. She rubbed his neck and spoke quietly to him to try and calm him down.

"Okay," Jean said, "I'll take Buster through first." With that, Jean clicked her tongue at the young Clydesdale and marched confidently through the puddle. Despite it's size, the puddle was only a couple of inches deep, even in the middle. Buster splashed joyously through. He had been impatiently to keep moving when Jean had halted him. He wasn't impressed either when Jean halted him again, after they had walked out of the water, but then Jean encouraged him to munch the long grass by the fence-line whilst she called out to Molly to encourage her and Tyke to tackle the obstacle.

Molly took a deep breath, gave Tyke a pat and strode confidently forward into the puddle, allowing the leadrope to lengthen so that Tyke didn't feel he was under too much pressure. When she got to the knot in the end of the rope, she felt the resistance of Tyke planting his feet, flatly refusing to follow her. Molly gave a gentle pull on the line and clicked her tongue. "Come on Tyke" she said. "Walk on." Tyke dug his heels in harder. Molly glanced back at him, careful not to look directly in his his eyes. Gary had told her that looking a horse in the eyes was a sure way of stopping it coming towards you as it was the action of a predator. Keeping her eyes down, Molly gave another gentle pull and clicked her tongue. Tyke leant back against the rope, sinking his quarters slightly, his ears back and the whites of his eyes showing.

"Just keep up a steady but gentle pressure, Molly, just let him make up his own mind." Jean advised.

Molly nodded, keeping her eyes averted from Tyke's. She gently pulled on the rope and, as soon as she felt Tyke's resistance, she held it there. Tyke dug his heels in and leaned back even more as he felt the pressure.

"Come Tyke." Molly said quietly, clicking her tongue again. "It won't hurt you. Buster wasn't scared." She kept up the gentle pressure, resisting the temptation to pull harder and try to force Tyke to step forwards.

Suddenly, with no warning at all, Tyke leant back even further then launched himself forwards in an almighty leap, obviously hoping to clear the puddle. He had misjudged it however and landed in the water, about two thirds of the way across. As he landed with an almighty splash, Tyke panicked and leapt again but this time his leap seemed to be forwards and sideways at the same time. He crashed into Molly, knocking her down into the muddy water as his forward leap carried him out of the puddle. Molly's hand tightened instinctively on the rope and she felt the burn as it slid through her hand, stopping when her hand reached the knot at the end. Molly was then dragged a few feet through the water before she couldn't hold on any longer and she let go. As she lay in the puddle, winded and soaked to the skin, she was dimly aware of the sound of Tyke's galloping hooves fading into the distance.

"Molly! Are you okay?" Jean's voice jolted Molly back to her situation. Still laying in the water, Molly mentally examined her body. Apart from her sore hand, there didn't seem to be any pain elsewhere as she gasped and refilled her lungs with air. Slowly, she got to her feet.

"Erm. I'm okay, I think." Molly brushed her wet hair away from her face with a muddy hand. "Where's Tyke gone to?" Molly looked around worriedly.

"He headed up the track." Jean jerked her head in the direction Tyke had gone. She was having trouble with Buster who obviously wanted to follow his friend. "Here, call Sam and get him to come and help" Jean pulled her phone from her pocket and thrust it at Molly.

Sam arrived within ten minutes, in the landrover with one of the farmworkers. It was quickly agreed that Sam would take Buster back to the farmyard whilst Molly and Jean went to find Tyke. Jean tried, at first, to persuade Molly to go back in the landrover so she could get out of her wet clothes but Molly got so upset, Jean gave in and agreed that Molly could accompany her on the search.

"I'll pop this fellow away then drive up the lane to the back field to see if he's there." Sam said, taking a firm hold on Buster's lead rope. Buster was trying to go in the same direction as Tyke and was calling frantically. "Come on, son." Sam gave the rope a small jerk, getting Buster's attention back and then he led the big foal back through the puddle and down towards the farm. As they walked away, Buster kept trying to stop and call for Tyke but Sam managed to keep him moving towards the distant buildings.

Before the farmworker drove off in Sam's wake, Jean made Molly take off her sodden jacket and put it in the landrover. She then gave her own jacket to Molly and made her put it on. "At least have something dry on." Jean said. As they set off up the track to find Tyke, Molly's feet were squelching in her boots and the water was still dripping from her hair and running down her face. She was glad her mother couldn't see the state she was in. As they trudged along, Molly tried to apologise to Jean for letting Tyke go.

"I simply couldn't hold him!" Molly cried, a sob rising in her throat.

"Don't worry about it, child. Not many people would have held him, especially after he had knocked you down like that! Are you sure you're okay?"

"Yeah, I'm fine, apart from this." Molly opened her right hand and showed Jean the rope burn. "It hurts a bit."

"When we get back, I have something to put on that, so don't worry. Now, where's this foal of yours? I tell you, Tyke is a good name for him!"

They trudged along the farm track, eyes scanning the horizon for signs of the young horse. Molly had never been this far up this track before – she had never realised just how much land there was on the farm. Suddenly, it occurred to her that this track led round to the back of the stubble field where they had ridden the day before – which would explain why there was no proper entrance to the field from the bridleway. Molly was startled out of her musings by a sudden exclamation from Jean.

Oh no!" Jean cried.

"What is it?" Molly asked, suddenly feeling scared.

"The gate! It should have been closed!" Jean pointed along the track.

Molly looked where Jean pointed. There was a gate but it was wide open which meant that Tyke, in his wild gallop, would have just carried straight on into the field and, basically, had access to the entire countryside. Her heart leaping into her mouth, Molly rushed forwards, Jean hurrying to keep up beside her.

At the entrance to the field, they halted and scanned the open space. At first they couldn't see any signs of Tyke but then, suddenly, Molly spotted something in the hedge-line on the far side.

"Over there! Look!" As Molly's eyes focussed properly, she felt a flutter of dread in her stomach. There was Tyke but there, also, was the person with the skewbald they had seen riding out here the day before. As Molly turned to point this out to Jean, the older woman cupped her hands around her mouth and called out "Hey there!" and then waved her arm high above her head. Molly held her breath, fully expecting the person to disappear, taking both horses with them but but, to her relief, the person waved back and began to make their way straight across the stubble towards where Molly and Jean were standing.

"Shouldn't they stick to the headland?" Molly asked stupidly.

"Doesn't really matter when it's just stubble like this." Jean chuckled. "You wait until you see the mess the hunt makes of it! Besides, Tyke's already made his mark!"

Molly looked down. It was true. There were hundreds of hoof prints in the field. Tyke had obviously had a good gallop around before being caught by the stranger.

The horse and rider were closer now. With surprise, Molly noticed that the rider was a young girl of about her own age, mounted on a stocky little skewbald that was only slightly smaller than Fred. Tyke seemed happy to plod beside the pony after his adventures. As they approached, Jean stepped forwards.

"Oh, thank you so much for catching him." She said to the girl who, now Molly looked closely, looked almost boyish. The girl had short cropped, dark hair and piercing blue eyes. She was dressed in jeans and a boy's shirt that were a bit too big for her. She was riding the pony bareback, with just an old rope halter on it's head with the rope tied round to both sides. As the pony jogged sideways when Tyke nipped it's neck, the girl sat easily, going with the movement whilst almost absent-mindedly flicking Tyke on the nose with a finger to discourage him trying to nip again.

"It was nothing." The girl said. "He was a bit scared though and I think he's bleeding at the back, near his legs."

Without taking Tyke from the girl, Jean stepped forward and examined the foal.

"Damn." Jean muttered.

"What is it?" Molly asked.

"He's reopened that wound." Jean peered closer at the geld site. "Doesn't seem to be bleeding too much though." Jean straightened up and patted Tyke then thanked the girl again. "However," Jean said "I do need to ask you how come you were riding in this field? It's private property you know."

The girl shrugged. "I didn't think anyone would mind with it being stubble and all. It's the only place I can ride Pat."

"Pat?" Molly asked, wondering about the girl's accent and where she had heard it before.

"This is Pat." The girl straightened the pony's mane. "And I'm Mary."

With a nod, Jean introduced herself, Molly and Tyke. Then, after a minute's thought, agreed that Mary could still ride in the field, as long as she stuck to the headland. It seemed a good way of showing their appreciation for the girl catching Tyke for them. As they heard the landrover approaching along the bridleway, Jean and Molly repeated their thanks. Jean took hold of Tyke's leadrope as they said goodbye to Mary before heading along the edge of the field to meet Sam.

"Right, young lady." Jean said as Sam climbed out of the vehicle. "You and I will drive back to the farm and Sam will bring Tyke."

"Oh but..." Molly began.

"No buts. We need to get you out of those wet things as soon as possible." Jean turned to speak to Sam. "Take it steady, he's reopened the geld."

Sam had a quick look between Tyke's hind legs and nodded. He took hold of the rope then held Tyke to one side of the track whilst Jean started the landrover and turned it around to drive back to the farm.

"Oh!" Molly suddenly exclaimed. "I've just realised something!"

"What's that dear?" Jean said, her attention on controlling the landrover as it bounced over the many potholes on the track.

"Mary! Her voice!" Molly cried. "It's the same accent as that strange man who keeps asking about the mare! Mary's one of the travellers!"

*   *   *   *   *

11

Tyke was looking very sorry for himself when Molly walked into the barn later. She had, at Jean's insistence, had a hot shower and then put on some dry clothes that Jean had dug out for her. The track suit bottoms she was wearing were her own – she had worn them on Wednesday morning over her jodhpurs to keep clean whilst getting ready for the show and had forgotten to take them home. Other than that, Molly had on an old T-shirt of Jean's together with a jumper of Sam's that Jean said had shrunk in the wash. It was still a bit baggy on Molly though. It hung almost to her knees and she'd had to roll the sleeves a few times. At least she was clean, warm and dry though and that was all that mattered. Molly's own clothes had been washed by Jean and were currently in the tumble drier so that they would be ready for Molly to change into before she went home.

Molly looked at Tyke, a worried frown on her face. He was standing in his pen, head drooping, not interested in his hay or the feed that Jean had just put in front of him.

"I've just called the vet" Jean said quietly. "She's going to pop in on her way back to the surgery, just to check him over."

"This is my fault!" Molly cried. The tears that never seemed to be far from the surface sprang into her eyes.

"No it isn't." Jean said quietly. "If it is anyone's fault, then it's mine for deciding to walk the foals up to the top field."

"But I should have held onto him!" Sobbed Molly.

"I doubt even Gary would have held him in that situation. Besides, if you hadn't let go, you would have been dragged and probably been seriously injured!" Jean looked down at the young girl beside her. "I know we say that you should always try to keep hold of a horse but there will be times, my dear, when the best thing is to let them go – for your safety and theirs! So please, don't blame yourself." She handed Molly a wad of kitchen roll from her pocket. "I hear a car." Jean said as Molly blew her nose and wiped her eyes. "Hopefully, that's the vet."

Poor Tyke didn't move as the vet examined him. She cleaned up the wound and gave the foal a couple of injections, explaining to Molly that she was giving the little horse something for pain and also an antibiotic. Her conclusion was that his antics that morning had not only re-opened the wound but also that he may have pulled a small muscle somewhere. She left some powders with Jean for Tyke to have in his feed, explaining (for Molly's sake) that they were more antibiotics and also an anti-inflammatory pain relieving drug. She then asked Jean if she had Tyke's passport.

"Why do you need his passport?" Molly asked. "You know who he is."

"I need to sign him out of the food chain." the vet explained.

"The food chain?" Molly was puzzled now.

"Yes. You see, if a horse has been given 'bute', which is one of the drugs I've given you for him, it can't go into the human food chain when it is euthanised. So we have

to sign the passport so that people know that."
"You're not going to put him down!" Molly yelled.
"No, no! It's not for now. It's for any time in the future. It's the law."

After the vet had gone it took Jean a while to calm Molly down and reassure her that Tyke was not going to have to be put down. Eventually, Jean took Molly indoors and showed her a website that explained all the rules about horse passports and signing a horse out of the human food chain if it had ever had certain medications.
"A horse can still be used for animal food though." Jean explained.
"I didn't think we ate horses." Said Molly.
"Not really, not in the UK we don't but there is a market for horse meat in Europe. There's a lot of problems with it actually, to do with the treatment of horse that are being shipped for meat whilst they are still alive. The better meat dealers have them put down here in the UK and just ship the carcasses.
"Urgh." Molly shuddered. The thought made her feel sick. "I'm never going to eat horse meat, ever." She shuddered again.
"Come on." Jean patted Molly on the shoulder. "It's almost time for you to go home. Let's go and check on young Tyke again then you can come back and get changed before you go."

Tyke was looking a bit brighter when Jean and Molly walked into the barn. He whickered at Molly and rubbed his head against her, almost as if he was apologising for the morning's fiasco. Molly spent some time grooming the young horse, then topped up his water and hay before giving him the feed Jean had prepared for him. With a final hug, she patted the foal and then followed Jean back to the house. As she changed into her now clean and dry clothes, Molly was aware of a stiffness in her leg and her arm, and her hands were still sore from the rope burns. She suddenly realised that it could have been a lot worse!

Despite her efforts to act normally, Jean noticed that Molly was limping slightly when she came out of the downstairs cloakroom.
"Would you like a lift home dear?" Jean asked. Molly shook her head.
"I'll be fine. Fizz needs to run anyway, she hasn't done much exercise today." Molly bent and patted the dog.
"No, she was too busy hiding from that thunderstorm!" Jean laughed. "I'll see you tomorrow then."
"Yep. See you!" With a wave, Molly set off for home, Fizz trotting beside her. At least the rain had stopped and a watery sun was peeking through the clouds.

Molly groaned as she woke up on the Sunday morning. Her hip was sore, her leg and arm felt stiff and her hands were throbbing. Slowly, painfully, she climbed out of bed. Hobbling over to the dressing table, she pulled down the top of her pyjama bottoms and surveyed the large multi-coloured bruise on the skin across her hip bone. As she touched it with her fingers, she winced. Molly could hear her mother moving around in the kitchen downstairs. With difficulty, Molly had succeeded in

iding her bruises from her mother the evening before, thereby avoiding the
earching questions about how they had come about. Not only was her mother still
naware of Tyke's existence but, also, Molly really didn't want Mrs Peters worrying
bout Molly being around the horses. If she knew Molly had been hurt, albeit not
eriously, she would obviously worry. It was bad enough that Mrs Peters worried
bout Gary all the time. Molly knew her mother was on tenterhooks every day in case
;ary had to go to fight or something.

Molly had told Gary what had happened. She had spent an hour 'chatting' to
er brother on a social media site the evening before, after all, he had another vet bill
n the way now! He had been fairly philosophical about Molly's injuries, simply telling
er to try to be careful. Luckily, spending every day around horses himself meant that
e fully understood the risks involved. He'd asked lots of questions about Tyke and
aid he would phone Jean for a chat later. Gary also made Molly understand that,
'hatever she herself thought, what had happened to Tyke was not her fault. She had
one to bed last night feeling a lot calmer about the whole thing. Gary had even
uelled Molly's concerns about the fact that Mary was obviously a member of the
aveller community, pointing out that, if Mary had wanted to steal Tyke, she could
ave simply ridden away from the field with him in tow, rather than seeking out his
wner. All in all, Molly felt much better about life in general this morning, despite the
:tiffness in her limbs.

Molly dressed carefully, wincing as she pulled on her jodhpurs and jumper.
ending down to pull her socks on was uncomfortable too. At last, she was dressed
nd then struggled to brush her hair as she raised her stiff arm up. With a sigh, she
ecided to leave her hair loose today. Calling Fizz, who had been laid on the bed
atching her young mistress, Molly headed downstairs to breakfast.

Entering the kitchen, Molly was surprised – and slightly shocked – to find her
iother sitting at the table, blowing her nose and wiping tears from her eyes as she
obbed quietly to herself. With a lurch of her heart in her chest, Molly rushed forward
nd threw her arms around her Mum.
Mum! What's wrong?" Molly cried. "What's happened? Is Gary okay?"
Irs Peters sniffed and then blew her nose and wiped her eyes again.
Gary's fine, as far as I know." Mrs Peters sniffed again. "It's just that..." she glanced
own at the table where there was an opened envelope with a greetings card sticking
it of it. Taking a deep breath, she looked up at her daughter. "Today would have
een our Pearl wedding anniversary." she said with a rush, before bursting into tears
gain.
Oh Mum! I'm sorry! I didn't know!" Molly hugged her mother tight.
No reason for you to remember." Mrs Peters said, wiping her eyes again and
miling wanly at Molly. "I was coping really well, I thought, but then...." She gestured
 the card on the table. "This arrived. It's from some old friends of your dad's who
'e in Australia. I didn't have their address so I couldn't let them know when your
ad.... when he.... died." Mrs Peters gave a hiccuping type of sob.
Oh Mum." Molly hugged her mother again. "Do you want me to stay home today?
ather than go to the farm? I can phone Jean and tell her."

"No, no, you go on." Mrs Peters shook her head. "I'll be fine, I have to sort out the rest of your school stuff for a start. You go and see that pony of yours and I'll see you this evening." Mrs Peters gave her eyes another wipe then seemed to compose herself. "Tell you what, I'll make a lasagne for dinner – your dad's favourite!"

"Well, if you're sure." Molly said uncertainly.

"I'm sure." Mrs Peters nodded and smiled at her daughter again. "Now, off you go!"

Molly arrived at the farm to find Jean looking Tyke over. The foal seemed to have recovered from his adventure the previous day and Jean confirmed this to Molly as she left the pen. "I think a gentle stroll round the yard will suffice for this chap today." She said with a smile. "I can do that for you if you like. Oh, and you've had a visitor!"

"Really?" Molly looked puzzled. Who would come to visit her here, at the farm?

"Yes. That young girl we met yesterday. She didn't come into the yard, just stopped by the gate and asked after Tyke. She was on foot but said she would be riding out on Pat this afternoon and she said for me to ask you if you wanted to join her? Seems she's spotted you riding Fred a few times."

"Oh, okay." Molly looked at Jean. "What do you think?"

"Well, it's up to you of course. I know she is a traveller and that some folk think they can be a bit dodgy but, at the end of the day, they arn't all bad. In fact, Sam has some of them working on the farm at busy times."

"Really?" Molly was surprised at the news.

"Hmm. Trusted lads who come back year after year to help with the harvest or lambing, stuff like that. Means he doesn't have to pay people in the quieter times."

"So, what shall I do about Mary then?" Molly asked.

"Well, I think it might do you good to ride with someone your own age. You'd have fun I reckon. Just be careful about what you say to her – you know, about security on the farm, stuff like that." Jean said.

"Okay then. I'll give it a go. What time shall I ride then?"

"Well, Mary said she'd be passing here about two o'clock so you need to be ready then I would say. Now, shall we take this young man for a little walk?"

*   *   *   *   *

12

Shortly before two, Molly tacked up Fred. The pony seemed to sense
at Molly was in a different mood today. Molly herself was feeling a mixture of
xcitement at the thought of hacking out with Mary, and apprehension about being
vay from Jean's supervision. This was very different to riding around the top field –
least there, she had still been enclosed by a fence and knew that Jean would be
ple to check on her occasionally. Molly felt that she was entering a new phase in her
ding, even more so than at the show on Wednesday. Her fingers shook slightly as
ne buckled up the noseband and throatlash on Fred's bridle. It wasn't helped by the
ct that Fred kept tossing his head impatiently as Molly fumbled with the straps.

Finally, Molly was ready. Jean help her mount outside the barn as Mary
ppeared at the gate riding Pat. As Jean opened the gate to let Molly ride through,
olly suddenly felt shy. She didn't really make friends easily, preferring her own
ompany. Fizz had always been her best friend and now she had the horses too, it
eemed strange to have a human friend of her own age. Thinking of Fizz, Molly
anced back to see the dog sitting obediently by Jean's side, having been told to
ay with Jean'. Molly knew that her dog would now follow Jean around until such
ne as Molly arrived back at the farm. As Jean closed the gate, she turned to Mary
th a friendly smile.

Don't overdo it today please, Molly is still a novice you know." Mary nodded
lemnly as Jean continued. "Do you know where you'll be going? And how long
bu'll be? Just in case, of course."

ith a glance at Molly, Mary said in her thick accent, "ah, we'll just have a little jog
ound the big field then through the wooded track, if that's okay? Just an hour or so I
nk."

an nodded and smiled again. "That's fine." She looked at Molly. "You enjoy
ourselves and take care now." With that, Jean walked off towards the house, Fizz
otting beside her.

To begin with, the two girls rode along the lane in silence, neither knowing
lite how to open a conversation. Molly looked at her new companion out of the
rner of her eye and noticed that, again, the girl was riding Pat bareback but, rather
an just a halter, today she had a simple bridle on the pony. Just the headstall with a
owband, bit and reins but no noseband. From Jean's lessons in the tack room,
olly knew that the bit was just a simple loose ringed snaffle. And here was she,
ddle, bridle, martingale, Dutch gag. Molly felt quite inadequate all of a sudden. She
ked out of her reverie when Mary suddenly spoke.

hat's a nice colt you've got back there." The girl jerked her head back slightly in the
ection of the farm.

olly thought for a moment before she replied. She was still worried about Tyke's
gins and she really wasn't sure how much she could trust Mary. "He's my brother's
tually. He's away at the moment though so I'm looking after his foal." Molly paused.

"Tyke's just been gelded actually."

"To be sure, I guessed that." Mary laughed. She turned Pat onto the stubble field. "Now you'll be up for a little canter here I think?"

Molly agreed a canter would be fine. With a whoop, Mary kicked Pat in the ribs and shot off along the headland. Not to be outdone, Fred set off in hot pursuit, Molly holding onto his mane with one hand as the pony leapt forwards.

They did a full circuit of the stubble field at a fast canter before pulling up near the gap where they had entered the huge field. Both girls were laughing and windswept, both ponies were sweating and blowing hard. Molly was impressed at the easy way Mary had sat on Pat, controlling him with her body as well as her reins.

"A little walk though the woods to cool these off I think." said Mary. Molly glanced at her, mildly surprised. She had heard stories of how some of the travellers would ride or drive their horses until they were all but dead from exhaustion. Yet Mary was suggesting doing the same as Jean or Gary would, cooling off after fast work. Molly found herself feeling intrigued by this strange girl. Loosening her reins slightly, to allow Fred to stretch for a moment, Molly rode after Mary towards the woods on the top of the hill.

The girls spent about half an hour in the woods, walking at first then trotting through the trees, jumping small logs and generally just enjoying having fun away from adult supervision. Yet all the time, Mary obviously had Pat's – and Fred's – welfare at heart, making sure the ponies had plenty of cooling off time and didn't overtax themselves. Eventually though, Mary asked Molly what the time was. With surprise, Molly looked at her watch and realised it was already five past three! As Mary rightly pointed out that they should head back to the farm now, Molly felt a mild twinge of disappointment. It had been so much fun, she really didn't want the ride to end! As they headed back down the track towards the lane, the girls chatted freely, the ice now broken by the fun they'd had together. By the time they got back to the farm, Molly had discovered that Mary didn't go to school and that her father had several gypsy cobs, including a stallion, that he kept on the common land on the other side of the hill. As they halted by the gate of the farmyard, Jean came across to let Molly and Fred in. Molly dismounted and ran up her stirrups before turning to say goodbye to Mary.

"Thanks for a lovely ride, it was fun!" Molly grinned.

Mary grinned back. "That it was. You'll be at school in the week?"

Molly nodded with a grimace.

"We can ride on Saturday if you like? If you're allowed?" Mary suggested, looking across at Jean. Jean nodded and smiled.

"That would be great!" Molly grinned even wider. "I'll see you then!"

"Same time Saturday then. Bye!" With that, Mary turned Pat around and trotted off up the lane, her legs forwards over the pony's shoulders and her upper body leaning back, almost touching the pony's quarters. Molly watched her for a moment then turned to Jean.

"I wonder why she leans back like that in trot?" Molly said.

"Oh, some folk call that the 'gypsy seat', it's easier to stay on in trot like that when you ride bareback, especially on driving horses which have a strong, bouncy trot."

Molly nodded as she led Fred into the barn. As Molly untacked the pony, Jean looked at him critically.

"Did he sweat up a lot today?" Jean asked.

"A bit yes, after the first canter." Molly admitted.

"Hmm.... Okay" Jean handed Molly the grooming kit. "Give him a good brush down to get all that dried sweat off then. I'll be back in a minute."

Jean reappeared just as Molly was putting her grooming kit away. She was carrying a small plastic case in one hand and an electrical extension lead in the other. She smiled at Molly. "Pop his headcollar on for me dear." Jean said.

Intrigued, Molly did as she was asked. As she put the headcollar on the pony, Jean plugged the extension lead into a plug socket on the wall then unrolled it until the end was by the pen. She then opened the case and removed a set of large clippers. The blades were huge with long teeth. Molly's eyes widened as Jean made a tutting noise. "I'll be having words with Sam when I see him." Jean muttered.

"Er, why?" Molly asked, still looking at the vicious looking blades. Jean deftly removed them and replaced them with a much smaller set.

"I've told him hundreds of times not to leave the blades on these." She noticed the expression on Molly's face. "Those are sheep shearing blades. Nasty looking things aren't they?"

Molly nodded then looked at the blades now on the clippers. "What are those ones for then?"

"These are for horses." Jean explained. "I've just spoken to Marion and she has agreed that Fred can have a small clip, get rid of some of that thick coat he's growing."

Molly was puzzled now. "Surely that's his winter coat? Why are you clipping it off? He'll catch cold!" She rubbed her hands through the thick fur on Fred's shoulder.

"If he were living out and not working we'd leave it because yes, he would need it to keep warm. Thing is, when he works hard and gets sweaty, with a thick coat he won't dry off as quickly and there is more chance of him getting a chill. So we'll give him a clip and then, when he's not working, he can wear rugs to compensate for his missing coat. Okay?"

Molly wasn't sure she fully understood the concept but she nodded anyway.

"Right." Jean said briskly, plugging the clippers into the extension lead. "Let's crack on and give this chap a posh haircut."

An hour later, Molly helped Jean rug up the freshly clipped Fred. Jean had decided to give him a 'blanket clip' which mean his head, neck, chest and under belly were shaved, leaving hair on his body as though a blanket had been laid across him. His thick stable rug covered him from his ears to his tail and, before Molly left, she felt the base of his ears with her hand to check he was snuggly warm but not *too* warm. She then went in to Tyke and check he was warm enough too. She looked at his wound and was happy to see that it looked clean and dry. Putting her arms around the foal's neck, she hugged him and whispered that she would see him on Friday. Then she left the pen and, patting Fred on the way past, she headed out of the barn. Jean and Sam were in the hay barn so Molly called out to them and waved before whistling to Fizz and starting to jog out of the farm yard. The evening had a distinctly

Autumnal feel about it. It was dusk already and there was a chill in the air. The dry leaves in the lane rustled as Molly walked through them. In the twilight, under the hedges, there was a strange eerie feel in the air. Molly broke into a jog again, Fizz close by her side.

As Molly entered the house, she could hear voices in the kitchen. Kicking off her boots in the porch, she opened the door to see, to her surprise, that her brother was sitting at the table chatting to their mother as the woman fussed around, tossing a salad in a bowl.

"Gary!" Molly ran to her brother and threw her arms around his neck. "I thought you wouldn't be home until Christmas!"

Laughing, Gary hugged his sister. "I managed to wangle a 48 hour pass." he grinned. "How's that pony of yours?"

Pulling up a chair so that she could sit next to Gary, Molly sat down and told Gary all about her ride with Mary. She was careful not to mention Tyke. There'd be time for that later, she hoped. As Mrs Peters set the table, she smiled at her two children although there was a definite sadness in her eyes. Making a comment about how proud their father would have been, she turned to retrieve a large lasagne from the oven.

Dinner was eaten with mixed emotions. They spoke of Mr Peters and the way he loved his wife's home made lasagne. They laughed about some of the happy times they'd had and they all shed a few tears as they thought about him and how it was for him to not be with them any more. Eventually, they finished the meal with a treacle sponge with custard. As Mrs Peters began to clear the table, Gary shrewdly suggested that he and Molly do the washing up. With a smile, Mrs Peters made them all cups of tea before heading off to the lounge bearing her cup and the latest copy of a TV listings magazine. Before long, Molly and Gary could hear the signature tune of a well loved game show. With a conspiratorial grin at his sister, Gary started filling the sink with hot water, adding washing up liquid before stacking the dinner plates in the sink. Molly grabbed a clean tea towel as Gary plunged his hands into the water.

"So," Gary said quietly, "how's Tyke?"

*   *   *   *   *

13

Molly set off to catch the school bus the following morning with mixed feelings. She had wanted to spend more time with her brother but she did enjoy school and she knew that her doing well at school was important to her mother. She had also wanted to check on Tyke again, however Gary had promised to pop into the farm during the day so that made it less of a worry. At least Gary would be there when she got home that evening. He didn't need to go back to camp until Tuesday lunchtime.

Molly spent her school day thinking about her week. She didn't really have any school friends so she spent her break times writing in a spare exercise book. It had occurred to her that, when she was grown up, these times would just be a distant memory so she had decided to keep a diary so that she could relive her happy – and her sad – times when she was older. By the time she was on the school bus heading homewards, she'd already filled about a third of the notebook, just with all the stuff about half term! She sat on a seat on the back of the bus, re-reading what she had written during the day. It was a shame she couldn't illustrate the diary with photographs.

Gary wasn't home when Molly walked in through the front door and Mrs Peters wasn't really sure where he had gone, only that he had taken Fizz for a walk a couple of hours ago. Molly thought she knew where her brother was but her pleas to her mother to be allowed to go and meet up with him fell on deaf ears.
I'm sure you have homework to do, love." Mrs Peters looked at Molly. "That was the deal if you remember? If you do your homework promptly, Monday to Thursday, you can go to the farm on Friday evenings, as well as both days at the weekend." Grudgingly Molly conceded her mother's point and headed up to her room. As she glanced out of the window, she saw that it was already dusk. Of course, the clocks had gone back the first weekend of half term! That meant, Molly was sure, that her mother wouldn't let her go to the farm on Friday evenings, not for much longer anyway. Mrs Peters didn't like Molly being out after dark. Hearing the front door slam, Molly changed out of her school uniform quickly and headed downstairs to see her brother and find out if he had been to the farm, as she thought.

Molly didn't get a chance for a proper chat with Gary until after dinner. Even then, it seemed unlikely they would be able to talk about Tyke and Fred as Mrs Peters reminded Molly about her homework and banished her upstairs to her bedroom.
The sooner you get started, the sooner you'll finish." Mrs Peters pointed out, infuriatingly. Fighting down an angry comment, Molly stormed upstairs. She had just taken out her 'homework diary' when there was a knock at the door. Before she could call 'come in', the door opened a crack and Gary's voice asked if she were 'decent' and if it was okay for him too come in. Welcoming any excuse to delay trying to write

a stupid essay for English, Molly got up from her little desk and plonked herself on her bed as Gary and Fizz came into the room.

"So, how was your day?" Gary asked as Fizz, jumping on the bed, rolled onto her back for Molly to scratch her belly.

"Okay, I guess." Molly said, sulkily.

"Hey! What's up with you?" Gary peered at Molly, his voice full of concern.

"I just realised something." Despite her best efforts, Molly felt tears pricking at the back of her eyes. Why was she always so close to tears these days?" She took a deep breath, sniffed loudly and looked at her brother. "Now the clocks have gone back, it will be too dark for me to go to the farm on Fridays after school!" Molly sniffed again.

"Oh. Well, it can't be helped I guess. We can't move the seasons just because you want to go and see Tyke and Fred!" Gary gave a rueful grin.

Despite herself, Molly smiled, albeit sadly.

"I went to see them today." Gary went on.

"Oh! I thought that might be where you had gone! How's Tyke?"

"He's fine." Gary said, nodding. "In fact, he was a bit full of himself today when I took him for a walk! I got him through that puddle though!"

"Really!" Molly was astounded. She wriggled around into a better position. Fizz, realising her belly rub had finished, gave a martyred sigh and curled up at the bottom of the bed. "How on earth did you manage that?"

"Bribery!" Gary laughed. "I took some carrots up with me and, every time he put a foot in the water, I let him have a bite. It took a good half an hour but eventually, he walked through. By the time I'd finished, he was splashing through quite happily! Even seemed to be enjoying it after a while!"

"Ah, cool!" Molly was delighted, although there was a little twinge at the back of her mind that made her wish it had been *her* who had solved the problem, rather than her brother. "So he's okay then?"

"Yep, he's fine. Vet came and checked him again today. She's not charging cos she was really there to look at some of Sam's calves. She just popped in and had a quick look at Tyke on her way out. Oh, and I took Fred out for you."

"You? But you're too big for him!" Molly suddenly laughed aloud at the vision of her tall, handsome brother on the chubby Fred.

"I didn't ride him, silly!" Gary gave Molly a playful push on the shoulder. "Jean wanted to exercise Shandy and Pepper under saddle so I rode Shandy and we decided to take Fred along for a leg stretch." Gary suddenly looked thoughtful. "We saw that friend of yours too."

"Who, Mary?" Molly looked at Gary with interest. "She did say she didn't go to school. I guess she was riding Pat?"

"Actually, no." Gary frowned briefly. "She was with some bloke in a sulky."

"A what?" Molly hadn't heard the term before.

"A sulky. It's a lightweight, two wheeled cart that they use for harness racing. I was a bit angry with them to be honest, they went belting past us at top speed and scared the life of of our horses!"

"Oh!" Molly tried to picture the scene Gary had described. "I guess you were all okay though?"

"Yeah, they went past so fast that the horses just reacted and then realised there as nothing there any more!"

"But surely," Molly said with a frown, "they shouldn't have been galloping along on the road?"

"Oh! They weren't galloping!" Gary gave his head a shake. "They were only trotting but you need to remember, those trotting horses can go at over thirty miles an hour!"

"A trot? Wow!" Despite herself, Molly was fascinated by the thought of trotting at a speed faster than Fred could canter or even, possibly, gallop!

"To be honest," Gary went on, "I don't think it was your friend's fault. In fact, from what I glimpsed of her face, she seemed a bit scared herself. It was the bloke who was whipping the horse up as they went past. Mary was just hanging on tight!"

Molly found this information comforting in a way. She hated to think that her new found friend had almost caused an accident but, if Mary was a reluctant passenger, that threw a different light on things. Gary interrupted her thoughts.

"Well, I'd better let you get on with your homework, otherwise Mum will be on my case. See you in a bit." He patted Molly lightly on the head with a grin and left the room. Molly sighed then headed back to her desk, trying to concentrate on the essay she had to write.

As she got on the school bus the next morning, Molly was quite pleased with her essay. It had been easier than she thought in the end as her teacher had, basically, wanted them to write down a favourite daydream. Molly had written about when, in four years time, she would be riding Tyke, winning at shows all over the country, even at the Horse of the Year Show! Smiling to herself, she waved to Gary at the bus window – he'd walked her to the bus stop to say goodbye since he would gone by the time she got home that afternoon. As the bus took Molly out of sight Gary, she suddenly felt gloomy again. Although her brother had pointed out that, after Christmas, the nights would be getting lighter again, Molly still had to face the prospect of over four months of not being able to go to the farm on a Friday evening except, of course, during the Christmas holidays. Molly's gloom affected her all day she collected yet more homework from her various lessons. Even trying to write her diary during her breaks didn't lift her spirits and she was in a grumpy mood as she walked home from the bus stop at the end of the day.

For once, Molly didn't head straight to the kitchen when she got indoors. Giving Fizz, who had come to greet her, a perfunctory pat, Molly was about to head straight upstairs when Mrs Peters called out to her. With a heavy sigh, Molly dropped her school bag on the hall floor and, dragging her feet, answered her mother's summons. Her mother greeted her with a wide smile.

"Sit down dear." She said cheerfully.

Molly wasn't feeling very cheerful as she sat at the table, looking sulkily at her mother. Mrs Peters frowned at her daughter.

"What's wrong love, is everything okay at school?"

"Yeah, I guess." Said Molly, still feeling grumpy.

"Well." Mrs Peters sat herself down at the table where there was a pile of potatoes and a saucepan of water. "I think I have something to tell you that will cheer you up!" She picked up one of the potatoes and began to deftly remove it's skin with a small, sharp knife. Molly didn't say anything, just looked at her mother, warily. What would

© Chrissie Turner 2017

cheer Molly up and what Mrs Peters *thought* would cheer Molly up, were probably two very different things, she was thinking to herself. Mrs Peters glanced at her daughter before starting to peel another potato. "Anyway. Gary popped up to the farm before he left this morning. He and I had a chat last night about there now being a problem with you playing with that pony on a Friday and he said he had an idea of trying to solve it."

Molly suddenly sat up straighter. This was interesting, she thought. "And did he?" she asked, trying to sound less grumpy. She wasn't sure it had worked as her mother gave her a quick look and a brief frown passed over her face. Mrs Peters sighed heavily.

"Hopefully, you will be in a better mood when I tell you what has happened." Mrs Peters said curtly. Molly held her breath, not daring to hope that something good was about to happen. Mrs Peters began to explain. "When Gary came back, he had got a lift from Jean and she came in for a cup of tea and a chat. She agreed that it would not be a good idea for you to be wandering around in that lane after dark, even if you had Fizz with you." Molly's heart sank. "However," Mrs Peters went on, we all agreed that you would easily be able to get to the farm before dark, it was coming home that's the problem."

"I know but..." Molly started to protest. Mrs Peters held up a hand.

"Hold on girl, I said you'd like what I have to tell you." She cut the potato in her hand into quarters and dropped the pieces into the pan of water. She started peeling another one. "So, it's been decided that, yes, you can go to the farm on Fridays still but Jean will be bringing you home in the landrover."

"Really? Oh! That's brilliant! Thank you Mum!" Molly ran round the table and hugged her mother tight.

"Steady on, you nearly got stabbed then!" Mrs Peters brandished the knife that Molly's arms had just missed as she had flung them around her mother. "It's Gary you need to thank, not me. Oh and Jean as well. Now, go and get on with your homework whilst I finish making dinner. After all, the deal is that your homework is up to date if you want to go to the farm on Friday, remember! Off you go!"

After giving her mother another quick squeeze, Molly ran upstairs, her gloomy mood having dissipated at her mother's words.

*   *   *   *   *

14

On the Friday, Molly ran home from the school bus and quickly changed into her jodhpurs, not wanting to waste a second of the precious daylight. Calling Fizz, she gave her mother a quick peck on the cheek before racing out of the house and ran all the way along the lane, arriving at the farm totally out of breath. To her surprise, Jean was waiting with Fred and Shandy already tacked up. She was holding Molly's hat in her hand, together with a 'hi-viz' waistcoat, similar to the one she was wearing herself.

"There you are dear, hop on quickly. We've still got enough light to have a bit of a hack, especially if we come back through the top field where there won't be any risk of meeting any traffic. It won't matter if we're losing the light then." Jean led Shandy over to the mounting block and climbed onto the Clydesdale's back.

Still trying to catch her breath, Molly quickly checked Fred's girth then led him to the mounting block as Jean moved Shandy out of the way. Finally on board, Molly became more relaxed after all the rushing around and she grinned up at Jean.

"Thanks loads for this." she said. Jean just smiled down at her then rode towards the farm gate. Glancing around, Molly was suddenly struck by a thought. There was no sign of Sam or any of the farm workers and the gate to the lane was firmly closed! Molly knew this for definite, she had just closed it herself! She opened her mouth to point this out to Jean when she suddenly realised that Jean had ridden up to the gate and, using her legs, persuaded Shandy to turn so that she was standing sideways on to it. Jean then leaned down and grabbed the top of the gate latch before asking Shandy, again using her legs, to move sideways, away from the gate, so that the gate opened as Jean held it steady. Jean then nodded to Molly and told her to ride Fred through. When Molly and Fred were in the lane, Jean followed them then turned Shandy back to the gate. She grasped the latch again and asked Shandy to move backwards then to turn again so that the latch sprang into it's catch.

"There." Jean said with a satisfied smile. "Just checking that Shandy still remembered how to do gates. We use that trick a lot when we go out with the hunt."

"That was wicked!" Molly looked at Jean in awe. "Can I learn how to do that?"

"Of course!" Jean laughed. "That can be your winter project, learning how to do laterals."

"Laterals?" Molly looked puzzled.

"Yep." We can have a go over the weekend if you like?"

"I'd love to!" Molly replied, then had a sudden thought. "Oh, I'm supposed to be riding with Mary at two o'clock tomorrow though."

"That's not a problem. We can tack Fred up, say, about half past one and then do a few minutes whilst you're waiting for Mary to arrive. It's not good to do too much at once with the lateral work anyway, or the horse can get bored."

Molly nodded at the sense of this idea and then shortened her reins to follow Jean as Shandy broke into a trot.

Even though they only rode for about 45 minutes, cumulating in a long canter around the top stubble field, it was almost dark as they headed down the track back to the farm. The gate across the track was closed today but Jean deftly manoeuvred Shandy and opened it, closing it again behind them. She looked down at Molly as they walked their mounts along in the dim light of the rising moon as the last of the sun's rays faded away.

"Remember the rule, Molly. If a gate is open, leave it open. If a gate is closed, close it again." Molly nodded then briefly thought about how Fred would react to the big puddle until she saw, to her relief, that the lack of rain during the week meant that the puddle had almost dried up. She suddenly remembered something.

"Gary said he managed to get Tyke through that puddle on Monday." Molly said, looking up at Jean.

"Yes, he did." Jean laughed suddenly. "Took him a while though! Was better on Tuesday morning I gather."

"He took him through again on Tuesday?" Molly asked.

"Yes he did, didn't he tell you?"

""I haven't spoken to him." Molly confessed. Why did she suddenly feel grumpy because her brother hadn't let her know he'd taken Tyke out again? With a jolt she realised that he didn't have to tell her anything he did with the foal. After all, Tyke was officially Gary's, even though it was her, Molly, who had saved the foals life. She felt a sudden surge of resentment towards the brother she adored. After all, he was hardly even here to look after Tyke so what right did he have? Then she gave herself a little mental shake. She was being stupid. If it wasn't for Gary, she wouldn't be able to have Tyke or, for that matter, Fred! If it were not for Gary paying all the bills for both the foal and the pony, there was no way Molly would have been able to pay for their keep nor Tyke's vet bills. As they halted in the stable yard, Molly dismounted with a sigh then realised Jean was speaking to her.

"Tyke's been out in the small paddock with Fred today so I'd just spend some time grooming him this evening. You've got about half an hour before I need to take you home." Jean said with a gentle smile. Molly nodded, not really trusting herself to speak. She had a weird, possessive feeling in her stomach when she thought of the foal and didn't want Jean to pick up on her mood. Following Jean into the barn, she was cheered slightly when Tyke greeted her with his high pitched whinney. What did it matter whose name was on his passport or who paid all the bills? At least Tyke knew who he belonged to and that was what mattered the most. Quickly, Molly untacked Fred and rugged him up then she grabbed her grooming kit and went into Tyke's pen. Tyke whickered as he rubbed his head against her and she hugged him for a moment before selecting her body brush and curry comb and starting to brush the foal's coat.

Back home, Molly was impatient for dinner to finish so that she could go to her room and email Gary. She wasn't too sure of what she was going to say, she didn't want to sound like a possessive, spoilt brat yet she wanted to try and clarify Tyke's status and get it straight in her own head exactly who his owner was. It seemed a bit rude though to simply ask, outright, who Gary considered to be the owner of the foal. She decided to say that her friends at school had been asking her how many horses he had and she had answered 'two' because [and she tried to make it sound light earted] she had got two for most of the time. Still using the lighthearted tone, she ommented that, come Christmas, she would only have one whilst Gary was on eave as he would be there to take charge of Tyke.

Gary's reply made it clear that he had worked out the reason behind her omments. He also made it clear that, as far as he was concerned, Tyke was Molly's nd that he was only helping her out. He even joked that he couldn't wait until she left chool and started work so she could pay for Tyke herself. He then pointed out that, ad their father still been alive, it would have been Dad who paid the bills. Gary was, asically, just acting 'in loco parentis' and taking Dad's place. Although Gary's email lade Molly feel a lot better about Tyke, it also saddened her. Before his untimely eath, Dad had promised Molly that she could learn to ride one day and that maybe, she was keen enough, they may eventually get her a pony. Strange how it had still appened, despite Dad's death. Or was it? Molly was unsure about her feelings with egards the 'spirit world' although her mother maintained that Dad was still there, omewhere, watching over them all. In which case, was it Dad who had made her ecide to go up the lane that morning and led her to where Tyke was laid in the ditch eside his dead mother? Or was that just wishful thinking on Molly's part?

Saturday morning dawned and brought with it the first really heavy frost. 1olly shivered as she left the house with Fizz, well before her mother had come ownstairs. It was not even fully light yet. Molly jogged along the quiet lane, her dog otting beside her, until she came to the spot where she had found Tyke. Wriggling 1rough the frosted grass and the dried, dead stalks of cow parsley, Molly sat for a 'hile, hugging Fizz to her, trying to sense if there really was a spirit watching over er. It was almost deathly silent, just the occasional chirp of a bird as the daylight 1creased. Eventually, Molly felt her limbs becoming chilled and stiff so she crept ack out into the lane, breathing deeply and watching her breath steaming in the osty air. Feeling subdued, she walked slowly in the direction of the farm.

The contrast between home and the farmyard this early in the morning was evere. The yard was alive with activity, not least the noise and the smell of the huge actor as it lifted giant bales of hay onto a flatbed trailer. Then she heard the sound f horses snorting and turned to see Jean and Sam leading Pepper and Shandy out f the barn. Both horses were wearing their full working harness and the wintry sun linted on the shining brass work as the horses moved across the yard. Spotting lolly, Jean called her over.

Morning! You're bright and early." Jean smiled as she spoke.

I woke up early and couldn't get back to sleep." Molly explained.

Okay, well, you can lend a hand then." Jean grinned. "We're taking hay up to the ittle and sheep. This heavy frost will strip the goodness out of what little grass there left now."

How come you're using the horses?"

Keeps their hand in and also cheaper than filling that monster of a tractor with esel." Jean laughed. "Come on, I'll show you how to put them into the cart."

1olly looked again at the trailer and realised that it wasn't the one she had seen the tractor pulling but slightly smaller with different tyres and a long pole with a cross piece on the end. It was obvious now that this was designed to be horse-drawn.

As the sun rose higher in the sky, Molly sat beside Jean on top of one of the giant hay bales, relishing the snorts of the horses and the jungle of their harnesses. As they came into the field where the sheep were, Molly saw that the big ram was wearing some sort of harness. In answer to her query, Jean explained that the harness had a device on the front which would mark the ewes when he mounted them. That way they knew which ewes were likely to be pregnant. As Pepper and Shandy strode across the field, pulling the trailer with ease, Jean and Molly busied themselves with throwing slices of hay off to either side. When the first huge bale had all been thrown off, Sam turned the mares back towards the gate. As she had when they had come into the field, Jean jumped off and ran ahead then opened the gate wide, and shut it behind them then ran forwards, jumping back onto the cart, laughing breathlessly. "You can do the next one." Jean said to Molly. Molly agreed, looking at Jean in amazement. She was certain that Jean was older than Mrs Peters but Molly really couldn't imagine her mother leaping on and off a moving farm cart like that.

The sheep field had been noisy with the ewes bleating loudly as they followed the cart but the cattle were louder. They also jostled around the horses and the vehicle in their eagerness to get to the food source. The two horses, obviously used to this game, kept striding forwards, shouldering the young heifers out of their way. As they left the field, Molly jumped down off the cart, almost stumbling, then did the gate. She then discovered it was harder than it looked to get back on the moving vehicle. As she sat on the last hay bale, she looked at Jean in awe. This woman was a lot fitter than she looked!

The final field had the cows running in it. They still jostled the cart but in a more sedate fashion than the younger animals. Jean and Molly flung the hay far and wide as the horses strode on. Eventually, the last of the hay was finally flung off the cart and as Sam turned the horses towards the gate, Jean and Molly clambered over the boards to sit beside him on the high wooden bench. Looking down at the quarters of the pair of Clydesdales, Molly felt that using horses for this job was so much better than using a smelly old tractor. She began to daydream about, one day, when she was grown up, having a farm like this and only using horses to do the work. She wasn't even aware of Jean doing the gate as she dreamed of using, not Clydesdales but Shire horses. She'd seen a programme on the television about working Shires and felt that they were even more majestic than the Clydesdales were.

As they meandered down the track towards the farm, Sam offered Molly the reins. He carefully showed her how to hold them then sat back as she took control of almost two tons of horse as the two mares trudged forwards. Molly grinned to herself. She knew, deep down, that she wasn't really in control – the horses knew the routine so well that Molly was almost superfluous to requirements, but it still felt good to be sitting up high, listening to the jingling of the harness and watching the two mares moving in unison. Back at the yard, Molly helped Sam and Jean unharness the mares and then they gave all the equines their breakfast before heading into the use to have something to eat themselves. Molly helped Jean prepare the food. hilst Jean stood at the Aga, frying bacon, eggs, sausages, black pudding, shrooms and bread, Molly made sure that the pans of beans and of tomatoes dn't burn by stirring each alternately. The sound of stomping boots and men's ices by the back door heralded the arrival of the farm workers. Molly hadn't alised it but Sam and Jean fed everyone breakfast, every morning. She hadn't ally noticed before since, during the summer months, the working day on the farm arted much earlier so breakfast was earlier too! As the men seated themselves ound the table, Molly helped Jean carry the heavily laden serving dishes across the chen then sat down and helped herself to the delicious food.

When all the men had finished eating and headed back outside to carry on eir working day, Molly helped Jean with the clearing up. When they'd finished that ore, they both headed out to the barn where the horses were housed. Molly quickly rted out her grooming kit and began grooming Tyke. She had discussed with Jean r plans for the morning which was mainly working with Tyke to get him to listen to r more whilst he was being led. She didn't notice Jean leaving the barn and mped in surprised when Jean's voice suddenly announced, "It's ready!".

Vhat's ready?" Molly asked, packing her grooming kit neatly back into it's box.

ou'll see" Jean gave Molly an enigmatic smile. "Pop this on Tyke then bring him t to the small paddock."

olly looked at the halter in her hand. It was quite basic but, where it went across hind his ears, there were four brass 'bumps'. Slightly puzzled, Molly put the halter Tyke, clipped the rope on and then led him out to the paddock.

Both Molly and Tyke stopped in surprise when they walked through the gate of e paddock. Scattered around were various things such as a tarpaulin spread out on e grass, several poles raised on bricks, another pole resting across two oil drums, me cones in a line, two posts with a washing line between them – complete with shing – and several other posts with plastic carrier bags attached which were owing in the wind. Whilst Molly was simply surprised, Tyke had planted himself, ad high, eyes on stalks, and was snorting loudly. Molly went to tighten her grip on e rope. Jean, spotting her, walked across.

on't tighten your hand like that, try to stay relaxed and ignore him if you can. It's e for this chap to learn to trust you implicitly so that, when you say it's okay for him go, the word 'no' doesn't even enter his head." As Jean spoke, Molly forced herself relax and instinctively scratched Tyke's neck to try and help him relax too. Jean nt on to explain. "To begin with, just walk around the paddock, getting as close to the scary stuff as possible, talking to him and not making a fuss about anything. st act as though all this is perfectly normal and see how it goes."

olly nodded, gave Tyke a pat and then walked off with him towards, first of all, the nes.

They spent over an hour in the paddock with Tyke, getting him used to all the ferent noisy, flappy, scary things that Jean had set out. By the end of the session, ke was happily trotting along behind Molly, weaving in and out of the cones, going ross the tarpaulin, trotting over the poles. Molly hugged him tight. As she did so, she suddenly remembered the strange halter Tyke was wearing. She asked Jean about it.

"It's what is known as a 'be-nice' halter." Jean explained. The idea is that those brass lumps are uncomfortable if the horse pulls back or resists. As you saw, they soon learn it's easier to move forwards rather than resist. Very often, when a horse is wary of something, we just need to encourage them to have a closer look and examine things, rather than just giving way to panic. So, now it's Buster's turn."

"Buster?" Molly looked around the paddock. "I thought this was just because of the problems I had with the puddle?"

Jean laughed. "Not really, though the puddle incident meant it was important to do this lesson sooner rather than later. No, this is part of my standard foal education routine. So, as I say, Buster's turn now although he'll need the bigger halter."

By the time they had finished with Buster, it was almost lunchtime. Whilst Jean went into the house to start preparing lunch, Molly gave Fred a quick groom, ready for their ride with Mary that afternoon. Fred was so much easier to brush now that he had been clipped. Molly found the atmosphere in the barn so peaceful, with the soothing sound of the horses munching contentedly on their hay. She rugged Fred up again then packed away her grooming kit before heading across to the house.

Over lunch, Jean spoke to Molly about Fred. "Remember, now that he's clipped, you don't want him standing around in the cold without a rug on, especially if he's hot – for example, after fast work. Okay?" Molly nodded, a serious expression on her face. "In fact, I think I remember....." Jean tailed off then disappeared out of the back door. Molly, slightly puzzled, finished her blackberry pie and custard and then, in order to be helpful, began to clear the table. She was just wiping down the pine surface of the huge 'farmhouse kitchen' table when Jean returned.

"I thought I'd spotted this amongst the stuff Marion brought over." Jean flourished a bright yellow, oddly shaped, fleecy lined horse rug. "Oh!," she said, seeing the cleared table, "Thank you dear... Now, let's go and try this on."

The horse rug fitted on Fred perfectly, going over his quarters and then tucking under the flaps of the saddle and fastening across his withers. A fillet string went under his tail to stop the rug blowing up in the wind.

"What about the front of him?" Queried Molly.

"Oh, don't worry about that." Jean said. "It's the quarters – behind the saddle – that's important. It's where his kidneys are. That's also why, if he stales – has a wee in other words – when you're riding, you should stand in your stirrups to take the weight off his back. You see?"

Molly nodded then sorted out her hat ready to get on the pony.

"Come on then," Jean grinned, "let's do some lateral work first whilst you're waiting for Mary."

'Lateral work' wasn't as easy as it looked. Even though Jean explained that 'lateral was logical', poor Fred wore a very confused – and martyred – expression as Molly tried to get him to go sideways when she applied her leg aids. It wasn't helped when both Molly and Jean got the giggles. Eventually, Molly managed a passable 'turn on the forehand' with Fred only stepping back a few inches, then she managed a few strides of 'leg yield' in walk. She was just giving Fred a pat and a long rein when a shout from the gate heralded Mary's arrival on Pat. Eagerly, Molly rode Fred towards her new friend, Jean opening the gate for her as she went. With a smile and a wave at Jean, Molly and Mary trotted off along the lane. Neither girl noticed Fizz sneaking out through the hedge to follow them.

*   *   *   *   *

15

Molly was curious as Mary took 'leading file' and rode, not up the lane towards the bridleway but actually in the direction that Molly always took when she went home. Mary didn't volunteer any information as to their destination though, instead she began chatting to Molly about her week and asking what Molly had got up to at school. Molly's curiosity was further aroused when Mary suddenly turned off the lane, ducking to avoid a low branch, and headed through the undergrowth and down a narrow path. So well hidden was the track that, in all her treks to and from the farm, Molly had never even noticed it! Ducking often to avoid the branches, musing that there was no way that Shandy or Pepper could get though here, Molly guided Fred closely on Pat's heels. They still hadn't noticed Fizz trotting silently behind them as Mary turned into an even narrower track.

As they made their way along the overgrown path, Molly noticed the smell of wood-smoke and, in the distance, the sound of dogs barking and unidentifiable voices calling. Her curiosity intensified along with the smells and the sounds that filtered through the trees. Where on earth was Mary leading her?

Suddenly, the trees and the undergrowth cleared and, following close behind Pat, Fred burst out into the winter sunshine. Molly caught her breath in surprise. In front of her were about a dozen caravans of various sizes. Some were just like the usual 'holiday' caravans that people had but others were bright and garish with a lot of shiny chrome on them. There were several camp fires in the clearing and, it seemed, dozens of children and dogs playing happily in the winter sun. Mary rode Pat across to a particularly large, shiny caravan and dismounted. Somewhat apprehensively, Molly followed. She could feel the stares from both children and adults as she rode Fred forward. Fred, feeling her tension, moved hesitantly towards where Mary was securing Pat's lead rope to the caravan's tow hitch. As Molly halted Fred next to Pat and tentatively dismounted, Mary grinned at her before yanking open the caravan door and calling out to someone inside.
"Mam, I've brought Molly to meet you!"
In response to the summons, a woman appeared at the door. Her clothes were clean and her hair tidy and she smiled broadly at Molly.
"Ah, there you are m'dear. We've been hearing a lot about you. Now, how about a drink after yer ride?"
Molly mumbled a 'yes please' and then, when the glass of orange squash arrived, mumbled a 'thank you' and then looked around her with widening eyes.

Molly had always been led to believe that travellers [or, as some folk called them, 'pikies'] were dirty, messy and uncouth but she could see no evidence of that around her here. Everyone was friendly and clean and the caravans were immaculate. The children crowded around her, firing questions at her about Fred and patting any part of the pony they could reach. Fred bore it all quietly, looking omewhat bemused. When the children all started clamouring to have a ride on him hough, Mary intervened and chased them away.

"Well," Mary turned to Molly, "yer met me Mam, shall we go off up the big field fer a allop now?"

Molly looked at Mary in amusement. Her friend's accent was so much more ronounced here than usual. She smiled and nodded her agreement, checking 'red's girth before she swung up onto his back. Molly looked on enviously as Mary imply vaulted up onto Pat and then turned the pony and, with a call of 'Ta-ra Mam', otted off through the camp.

To Molly's surprise, Mary didn't go back down the narrow track but crossed to he other side of the caravan site and went down a much wider track, obviously one nat had been used for vehicles judging by the deep ruts. Disconcertingly, the crowd f children ran after them, shouting and laughing, causing Fred to take hold of the bit nd break into a canter. Mary must have heard the change in the rhythm of Fred's oofbeats as she glanced back. Seeing Fred and Molly gaining on her at speed, 1ary laughed aloud and leant forward, urging Pat into a gallop in order to keep her lace in the lead. As Fred surged forwards to keep up, Molly reverted to her tried and usted tactic of grabbing hold of the pony's mane and clinging on for dear life. More 1an once, Molly closed her eyes as Fred galloped along, slipping occasionally on the ght turns. Luckily, the passage of the vehicles and caravans had cleared away the w branches so there was no need for either girl to duck.

Molly was grateful that Fred was clipped as she headed back to the farm later 1at afternoon. The two girls had cantered through the woods, jumping logs as well s having a race around the stubble field and even splashing through a small stream. s usual, Mary rode back to the farm gate with Molly then, declining Jean's offer of a ot drink, Mary and Pat trotted off down the lane in the dusk.

16

The next few weeks seemed to fly by as Autumn turned into Winter and Christmas approached. Molly felt a mounting excitement mixed with the bitter-sweetness of this being the first Christmas without Dad. Gary would be home though and, apart from Christmas, there was also the excitement of the Boxing Day meet to look forward to! Molly had asked Mary about the meet but her friend seemed, if anything, embarrassed when she said she couldn't go. However, Molly wouldn't be dwelling on her friend's absence. Gary was taking Shandy, Jean would be taking Pepper and Sam was going to bring Mrs Peters along to the meet in the landrover! So it looked like it was going to be a fun morning. How Gary and Jean had managed to persuade Mrs Peters to come along, despite her prejudice again hunting, Molly had no idea but at least the trip out would stop her Mum brooding in an empty house all morning. In the meantime, Jean and Molly had their work cut out getting the horses and Fred fit enough for the big event.

On Christmas Eve, Molly and her brother made their way up to the farm early. It was going to be a busy day – not least because Mrs Peters wanted her two children home early in the afternoon to finish all the preparations for Christmas Day itself. Gary and Molly, together with Jean, spent a hectic time riding out the two Clydesdales and Fred, then working with the two foals before applying themselves to some extensive grooming and tidying up of their mounts for the hunt. Brother and sister had walked up to the farm and were surprised when, just after 3 o'clock, Mrs Peters drove tentatively through the farm gate to pick them up. Molly felt a surge of tension. Her mother still didn't know about Tyke but Gary walked across to his mother, smiling, and led her into the barn to introduce her to the whole equine gang.

Mrs Peters was wary of the horses, even Fred and Tyke [the latter was simply introduced as a rescued foal – no mention of his ownership] but the horses regarded her calmly and happily accepted polos from her outstretched, albeit it trembling, hand. Even so, both Gary and Molly heaved a sigh of relief when Jean bore Mrs Peters off to the house for a cup of tea whilst her two children finished up in the barn.

Back home that evening, Molly was aware of a lot of whispering and soft laughter between her mother and Gary which tended to stop every time Molly came near. When she queried it, there were shrugs and exchanged glances but no enlightenment. Eventually, Molly went up to her room in a sulk, Fizz trotting behind her. It was nine o'clock before she ventured back downstairs to find the other family members watching a gameshow on TV and munching mince pies, chocolate log, cream crackers and cheddar cheese. Wondering what was going on, Molly seated herself on the sofa next to Gary and took a mince pie from the plate. Mrs Peters grinned broadly at Molly.
"There you are!" Mrs Peters beamed. "Guess what? I'm not going to be cooking dinner tomorrow!"

th?" Molly looked at her mother in amazement. "Why ever not?" She asked.
Because Jean has invited us all to the farm! So I'll do ours for New Year's Day and
an and Sam will come then!"

Really?!" Molly looked incredulously at Gary, who was grinning. "That's brilliant!"
sn't it just?" Piped up Gary. "So, you'd better get yourself to bed early before Santa
aus turns up!"

olly aimed a playful punch at her brother. He knew she hadn't believed in Santa for
ars! Then she hugged him and her mother, said goodnight to them both and raced
ck up the stairs.

Christmas Morning dawned bright and sunny, albeit freezing cold. The empty
ow case Molly had left at the foot of her bed was now bulging and Fizz was
citedly leaping on and off the bed, a squeaky reindeer in her mouth. Molly gave the
g a quick hug before turning her attention to the pillow case.

By the time Molly could hear her mother calling out that breakfast was ready,
olly had opened all her presents and was surveying the haul. Her favourite by far
is a mobile phone! She had wanted one for ages but her mother hadn't had the
oney for one so, although the label on the package had said 'from Santa' [ha ha,
ought Molly], she rightly guessed that it was Gary who had bought it for her. She
is pleased with the new riding gloves and breeches too but the phone fascinated
r as she plugged it in to charge up. Engrossed in the phone's instruction booklet,
olly dragged on her dressing gown and headed downstairs as her mother called out
ain.

In the kitchen, Gary was already seated at the table, wearing a new jumper,
ilst Mrs Peters busied herself piling a 'full English' breakfast onto three plates.
en the family were all seated, there was a pause, a mutual thought as they all
ked towards where Mr Peters would have been sitting – where, last year, he had
en sitting., smiling at his family, laughing with them and tucking into his meal. Molly
d her brother heard their mother whisper softly 'Happy Christmas, darling' as she
dded at the empty chair. She smiled at her children as they too whispered 'Happy
ristmas, Dad' and then, all with tears glistening in their eyes and with sad smiles at
ch other, they began to eat.

Breakfast eaten and cleared away, the Peters family sorted through various
rcels that Mrs Peters had had the foresight to wrap up ready to give to Sam and
an. Gary added a couple of packages he'd brought with him and Molly had added
r own gifts for the farmer and his wife. Mrs Peters carefully packed the bright gifts
o carrier bags as Molly raced upstairs to get dressed in jeans, a T shirt and a new,
ck, woollen jumper. When Molly came back down, Gary handed her a small
ckage. "Santa left this for Fizz I think" he chuckled. At the sound of her name, Fizz
ed forwards. Molly tossed the package to the dog and she began to tear eagerly
the paper. Eventually, the last scrap of paper fell away to reveal a brand new red
lar, part webbing, part chain, with a new tag stating that Fizz was microchipped
d giving two telephone numbers. One number Molly recognised as the house
ephone but the other was a mystery. Gary smiled. "That's the number for your new

phone." He grinned.

"Oh! My phone! I forgot it!" Molly gasped and she raced back upstairs.

Gary and Molly spent the next hour working out the various features on Molly's new phone until Mrs Peters announced that it was time to walk up to the farm.

"Why are we walking?" Molly asked, curiously.

"Because it's Christmas!" Gary laughed. "I expect Jean will be handing out the alcohol so we're walking so Mum and I can both have a drink. That okay with you?" He said, giving Molly a playful punch. Molly laughed back then called out to Fizz, who was now sporting her new collar, before racing out of the door with Gary chasing her. A call from Mrs Peters made them both stop and turn.

"Hey you two, lend a hand with these bags please!"

Giggling together, Gary and Molly went back to take some of the burden from their mother before they all set off towards the farm.

When they arrived at the farm, Mrs Peters went into the house to help Jean whilst Gary and Molly went into the barn to give the horses their Christmas presents. Molly had bought them all 'horsey Christmas stockings' with treats in, as well as a bag of carrots and another of apples for them to share. Gary had bought a white webbing show halter each for Tyke and Buster, a leather headcollar for Fred and he had got Pepper and Shandy sparkly brow bands. Molly giggled. "The mares will look like proper dressage divas with those on!" she said, grinning at Gary. Gary had also got Tyke a stable rug. The foal had been wearing a small rug that Jean had found in the rug store but had outgrown it. Molly took the rug from her brother and fitted it on Tyke. That done, she gave the foal a last pat before following Gary out of the barn and across to the house.

Christmas dinner was a merry meal. Even Molly felt a bit tipsy, having been allowed a small glass of wine with her meal as well as a small glass of port after it. They had pulled crackers and were wearing a variety of silly hats that had been found in the brightly coloured tubes. The jokes and mottos had them all in fits of giggles too. Fizz and Meg, patiently waiting for the inevitable left overs, were wearing tinsel on their collars. Eventually, everyone had reached the stage where they couldn't face eating another bite. Jean and Mrs Peters began clearing the table as Sam heaved himself from his chair and headed over to the sink.

"Come on then lad" Sam jerked his head at Gary.

"What's up?" Gary looked puzzled.

"It's traditional, Lad." Sam explained. "Women cook on Christmas day, men do the washing up!" Everyone joined in the laughter at the look on Gary's face. Even more so when a tea towel hit Gary in the face. "There you go, I'll wash and you can dry."

With a grimace at Molly, Gary plucked up the tea towel and joined Sam at the sink. Giggling, Molly and Jean headed out to the barn to give the horses their evening feeds and hay. Jean explained to Molly that the Meet wasn't until twelve noon the next day so they didn't need to leave the yard until eleven o'clock. So not too much of an early start.

Christmas day ended with the Peters family wending their way home from the farm, singing Christmas carols and waving the torches they carried to chase away the spookiness of the unlit lane. Suddenly Fizz, who had been running on ahead, stopped and growled low in her throat causing the little family to halt and look around warily. As Gary went to make a whispered comment, Fizz suddenly began wagging her tail and ran forward. A small figure stepped forwards into the torchlight. It was Mary! Molly ran forwards to hug her friend.

"Merry Christmas Mary!" Molly laughed, with relief.

Mary gave Molly a perfunctory hug in return and stuttered softly, "Um, merry Christmas."

Molly frowned and looked closely at Mary. In the light of her torch she could see that the traveller girl had been crying and that there were still tears glistening in the corners of her eyes. There was also a bruise on Mary's cheek and her face was, unusually, streaked with dirt.

"Mary! What's wrong?" Molly asked worriedly.

Mary sniffed and wiped her nose and her eyes on her sleeve. "Nothing." Mary sniffed. "Just wanted to wish you a merry Christmas, that's all." She sniffed again.

"But Mary....."

"I gotta go. See you!" With that, Mary turned and ran off into the darkness.

"Mary!" Molly called, "Come back!" but the girl had disappeared.

"Who on earth was that?" cried Mrs Peters.

"Just a friend." Molly replied, peering into the darkness.

"She looked like one of those dirty traveller brats!" Mrs Peters was appalled "I told you not to have anything to do with them!"

"She's just someone I ride out with." Molly retorted. "Gary's met her."

Mrs Peters turned on her son. "So you know about this?" she demanded angrily.

"Er, yes, I do. There's no harm in Mary. She's just a kid." Gary looked as worried as Molly felt as he looked from his mother to his sister then back again.

"Well. If I had known who Molly was mixing with, I would never have allowed it!" With that, Mrs Peters stormed off down the lane.

The atmosphere in the Peters' house was very subdued when Molly and Gary got home. There was also a tension in the air. All the jollity of Christmas seemed to have been sucked away, despite the bright glitter and the Christmas songs being sung on the television. Molly said a quiet 'goodnight' to Gary and her mother then escaped with Fizz to her bedroom. Flinging herself on the bed, she felt like she should be crying but simply didn't feel like it. She could hear raised voices downstairs. Gary was obviously arguing with their mother and it didn't take Sherlock Holmes to work out that they were arguing about *her*, Molly, herself. Eventually, the shouting subsided into a low rumbling of voices. They may have stopped arguing but there was still a heated discussion going on.

With a sigh, Molly pulled her new phone from her pocket. She had, with Gary's help, put a lot of contacts into it. Mum and Gary's mobiles, the house number, the farm number, Jean's mobile number and even Sam's mobile number. so now she amused herself by giving each their own ring tone and photograph. She'd taken a few photos today, including one that Gary had helped her set up. It had Fred, Tyke and

Fizz on it in a group so she decided to set that one as her screensaver. Suddenly the phone beeped and vibrated in her hand. It was a text from Gary. 'Sleep tight, sis. See you in the morning.' She read it and felt the pricking of tears although she wasn't sure why. After a few false starts, she managed to send her first text in reply. 'Night bro.'

17

Molly and Gary headed towards the farm early the next morning, mainly ecause of the tense atmosphere at home. Fizz trotted ahead of them as usual. Vhen they arrived, Jean was busily doing a 'running plait' in Fred's mane and was reaving tinsel into the hair as she went. Shandy and Pepper already had stunning isplays of tinsel and raffia running along the crest of their necks.

Oh Jean! They look gorgeous!" Molly enthused.

Yeah, they do." agreed Gary. Plaiting isn't something I know much about – most of urs are hogged out!" He laughed and then picked up the grooming kit outside handy's pen, let himself in and set to work grooming the big Clydesdale. Following ary's lead, Molly went into Fred's pen, folded back his rug and started brushing his ready gleaming coat.

At nine o'clock, they went in to breakfast. Sam was filling hipflasks by the sink ut he seemed to be spilling more port than he was getting in the flasks. Eventually nough, he completed the task and joined the others at the table to help polish off the latters of bacon and eggs. Gary was telling Jean about their encounter with Mary e evening before.

It's a bit odd." Jean pointed out. "Surely the child would have come to the farm if she mply wanted to wish Molly 'Merry Christmas'."

Hmm." Gary mused. "It's wound Mum up no end. She was all for banning Molly and going to the meet today!"

Gary!" Molly was horrified. "You didn't tell me that!"

No need." Gary looked at his sister. "I talked her round in the end." He patted olly's shoulder. "Don't worry about it Sis."

Is she still coming with me to follow in the landy?" piped up Sam.

No idea." Gary shrugged. "She didn't mention it."

Ah well." Sam replied. "I'll drive down there when you've set off. If she wants to ome, she can. If she doesn't..." Sam shrugged in his turn.

At eleven o'clock, dressed in full show kit, Molly clambered onto Fred's back. ary was already mounted on Shandy, wearing his army tunic, breeches and boots. an came out, also dressed in full show kit and brought Pepper over to the ounting block. Then Sam appeared, wearing cavalry twill trousers, a tweed jacket nd a matching flat cap. The winter sun shone, albeit weakly, in a cloudless sky. The orses, sensing an occasion, fidgeted and snorted plumes of steamy breath into the r as Sam handed each of the riders a full hip flask. Gary grinned at Molly.

Don't you go drinking that all at once, Sis." he laughed. Molly giggled as she popped e flask into her pocket. Jean called out, asking if they were all ready yo go and Sam ent across and opened the gate wide for them to head out into the lane. The uickest way to the meet was along the bridleway at the end of the lane and then wn through the woods to the next village where the hunt traditionally met on the ommon opposite the pub.

Molly was experiencing that familiar mixed feeling of excitement and fear as they came out of the woods and trotted down the village high street. There were hundreds of people around on foot, many with various dogs on leads. There were also an awful lot of horses and riders around, all smartly turned out, all greeting each other cheerfully. Several people waved at Jean and a handful of young girls on ponies called out to Molly, having recognised Fred. Suddenly, a voice hailed them and, turning, Molly saw Marion walking across on foot with Andrea following behind on a flashy, over-excited fourteen two pony.
"Good morning!" Marion called out. "My word, Fred does look smart!"
Andrea said a quick 'Good Morning' as she rode past on the jogging pony. Marion explained that the pony was only five and it was it's first hunt, hence the excitement. Giving Fred a pat, Marion headed off in her daughter's wake.

A lady was walking around with a tray laden with glasses of port, sherry and orange squash, followed by another with a platter heaped with sausage rolls and fruit cake. Just as Molly picked up a glass of squash, her attention was caught by Sam walking towards them, holding the arm of Mrs Peters. Molly's eyes opened wide as she saw that her mother was wearing a pair of bright pink wellies. Molly turned to her brother who was grinning broadly. "Where on earth did Mum get those?" she asked. Gary shrugged and shook his head, obviously suppressing his giggles. Molly took a long drink from her glass to hide her face as her mother approached the group. Molly was pleased that Fred was the sort that stood calmly amongst all the horses and people milling around them. Shandy and Pepper stood quietly too, meaning their riders could easily manage food and drink without having to worry about about controlling their mounts. Unlike Andrea, mused Molly. It looked as though neither Marion nor her daughter could relax for a second as the pony Andrea was mounted on skitted around, more than once knocking into another horse.

As the hunt secretary approached to collect the money from Jean for their 'cap', Molly noticed the stern expression on the woman's face. She overheard the secretary mutter to Jean about asking the 'bad mannered' pony's rider to remove it from the meet and felt a pang of sympathy for Andrea who, she was sure, was wishing that she were mounted on good old Fred. Subconsciously, Molly patted the pony. Suddenly, Fred pricked up his ears and raised his head as high as he could, turning rapidly to face the main road, almost unseating Molly in the process. As Shandy and Pepper copied Fred, all thoughts of Andrea and her problems fled from Molly's mind as the hunt came trotting down the road towards the pub. The huntsman was blowing short notes on his hunting horn as at least twenty large foxhounds milled around his horse's legs. Molly realised that it was true what people said, the sight and sound of the hunt really did stir the soul.
"I thought hunting had been banned" Mrs Peters said in a loud voice, causing Molly and Gary to cringe as dozens of people turned to see who had spoken. Jean, in a lower tone, explained that, although hunting with the pack was banned, they were permitted to use a 'couple' of hounds to flush a fox which would then be shot by a marksman with a rifle. The hunt itself did a sort of 'mock' hunt with the hounds following a pre-laid trail. With a quiet "Oh, I see." Mrs Peters sidled up to stand beside Molly and Fred, looking embarrassed at the attention she was getting from nearby

ople. In the meantime, Jean came across and explained to Molly and Gary that, fore going off to follow the trail, the hunt were going to go into the fields of a nearby m where there was a cross-country course. People would then be allowed to 'do eir own thing' for about twenty minutes before the hunt moved off properly. "Would u like to do that before we head home?" Jean asked. Both Gary and Molly nodded ppily.

Whilst the hunt staff drank their 'stirrup cup' in the pub car park, the hounds eandered through the crowd, greeting the spectators with friendly enthusiasm. Mrs ters drew Fizz, who was on a lead for obvious reasons, close to her as half a zen hounds approached curiously. Fizz was not good with strange dogs when she s on the lead. In fact she was known to be 'lead aggressive'. However, whether it s their size or their numbers that overwhelmed Fizz, no one knew but Fizz just vered herself to the ground and flopped onto her back, tail wagging slowly as the unds investigated her. When one of the hounds reared up and put it's front paws Mrs Peters' shoulder, Molly and Gary could barely suppress their laughter. At first lly was worried that her mother would react badly to the friendly hound but, after r initial shock, Mrs Peters recovered enough to give the big doghound a friendly t before saying "Get down now, there's a good dog." and gently pushing the hound ay.

1um, don't call them 'dogs' whispered Gary. "They are hounds and should never be led anything else!"

s Peters gave the hound, now back on the ground, a final friendly pat. "Good boy, you go now." With a final sniff at Fizz, the hound turned and trotted over to other group of people, waving his stern, his five pals following closely.

Suddenly, the horn sounded and all the hounds around them pricked up their rs. Whilst the huntsman blew the horn, one of the 'whippers in' called out various und names as he gathered the pack together. Sam approached Mrs Peters with g trotting beside him.

ome on love, we want to go into the crowd by the road to see 'em off." He said.

s Peters patted Fred, told both her children to 'have fun' and followed Sam across the roadside where hundreds of people were lining up on both sides of the road. an looked at Molly and Gary.

eady? We're moving off!"

th a surge of excitement, Molly gathered up her reins. Fred tossed his head, fully are of what was going to happen next. Even Shandy managed a little jig as Gary ne to ride beside Molly. All the horses and riders were going to the very furthest d of the common ready to file out onto the road. There seemed to be hundreds of m! As Molly rode forwards, she realised that Gary had dropped back to ride side Jean and that Andrea had suddenly appeared on her sweat soaked, jogging ny. Molly couldn't help but feel envious of the way Andrea sat quietly, hands light the reins, keeping the pony in check – just – using her seat and back. The girl en managed to flash Molly a bright smile as they rode out onto the tarmac ether.

Molly felt she would burst with pride and excitement as she and Andrea trotted down the road side by side, following dozens of others doing the same with Jean and Gary just behind. The crowd were cheering and waving as they passed and even Andrea's pony had now consented to trot beside steady old Fred, albeit with his head as high as his martingale would allow, his eyes on stalks and his nostrils flaring. Fred was trotting merrily along, flicking his toes out with every step, with his neck curved and his nose tucked in, obviously showing off to the crowd. Finally, they passed the last few straggling groups of people and were riding past the dozens of parked cars which were still lining the route the hunt was taking. As they turned off the lane into the farm, Andrea's pony leapt into the air but Andrea sat quietly and concentrated on keeping him calm. Molly was even more impressed. She so hoped that, one day, she would be able to ride like that.

Molly's musings came to an abrupt halt as she realised that the riders ahead of her were filing through a gate into a huge field and that, as soon as the horse's hooves hit grass, the riders kicked them forwards into a fast canter, fanning out across the expanse before them. Molly shortened her reins very slightly and prepared herself. Andrea's pony leapt forwards onto the turf and galloped off in a flurry of mud. Fred, being more sensible, broke into a fast canter and followed a big grey cob that had appeared, it seemed, from nowhere. Just as Molly felt that the excitement was beginning to settle down, she realised that the cob was heading towards a line of three logs of differing heights. The cob's rider was aiming her mount at the middle sized log which, to Molly, still looked huge! Molly quickly tweaked her left rein and Fred, ever obliging, took the hint and trundled merrily towards the smaller jump. As they soared over, Molly became vaguely aware of another horse jumping beside her. Landing, Fred galloped on after the field and Molly glanced sideways. Gary grinned back as his Clydesdale thundered across the grass.
"Who'd have thought a carthorse like this could jump!" he yelled across. He whooped loudly then leaned forwards to encourage Shandy towards the line of sheep hurdles ahead of him. Laughing, Molly gathered up her reins and set off in pursuit of her brother.

Three sweating animals and three mud spattered happy riders came together as the huntsman blew his horn to call the field to order ready for the proper hunt of the day. As they patted their mounts and headed back towards the gate leading back to the road, Jean, Gary and Molly each told their tales of the jumps they had jumped, the riders they'd seen fall and how many friendly people they had met. With loose reins, they allowed their horses to stretch and relax on the walk back home. Pulling onto the grass verge to allow vehicles to pass them, they waved as Sam and Mrs Peters drove past in the old landrover, Meg and Fizz standing in the back, tails wagging wildly.

18

They were all three tired but elated as, half a mile from the farm, they dismounted, ran up their stirrups and loosened their girths so their horses could properly relax before arriving home. Molly's legs were aching as she walked along beside Fred but she was happy and content, albeit tired. All three were too tired to talk any more, now the adrenaline rush had died away. The only sounds were the clip clopping of the horse's hooves and the occasion snort of a tired but contented horse. The watery winter sun was sinking rapidly down towards the horizon and the temperature was dropping. Molly, her mind still full of the day's excitement, shivered in the chill air. Suddenly, She heard a distant shout and looked up. Running towards them as fast as his old legs could carry him, flanked by Meg and Fizz, was Sam. Even from this distance, it was obvious he was distressed about something. With a worried glanced at Molly and Gary, Jean flung Pepper's reins at Gary then ran forwards to meet her husband.

"It's Tyke!" Sam's breathless gasps reached Molly and Gary, even from this distance. "He's gone!"

Molly heard her own voice scream, although she wasn't aware she had. She went to run forwards, not towards Sam and Jean but to the farm, to check for herself the horrible truth. It couldn't be true! Sam was mistaken! As she went to run, dragging suddenly on Fred's reins, Gary grabbed her shoulder, having put both the mare's reins in one hand.

"Molly! Stop!" he yelled.

"Let me go! I need to find Tyke!" Molly tried to wriggle out of Gary's grasp but his arm was encircling her, pulling her into his body. Suddenly, Molly couldn't struggle any more and she buried her head in Gary's chest, sobbing uncontrollably. Dimly, she was aware of the three adults talking urgently together but she didn't care. She didn't care about anything any more.

Molly had no clue as to how she came to be sitting at the kitchen table in the farmhouse with a blanket around her shoulders and a mug of tea in between her hands. She could hear quiet but urgent conversation but couldn't make out the words. She was aware that her mother was sitting next to her, making soothing noises, much as you would to a frightened horse. She was also aware of Fizz, ever faithful, ever understanding, resting her head on Molly's knee and whining softly. The kitchen seemed to be full of people. Through eyes reddened and blurred with tears, Molly gazed numbly around the room. Apart from her mother, there was Gary standing talking quietly to two policemen. There was also Sam, adding his words to the conversation. Jean, on the other hand, was sitting at the table opposite Molly, looking old and drawn, her eyes also filled with tears.

Finally, the police left and Sam put the kettle on to make fresh tea as Gary seated himself on the other side of Molly. He hugged his sister to him.

"We'll find him Sis, don't worry."

"But what if they won't give him back?" Molly sobbed.

"Who?" Mrs Peters asked, looking confused. "Do you know who took the foal? And why, Molly, are *you* so upset about it. It's not as though it's *your* horse, is it?"

Through fresh sobs, Molly was aware of Gary taking a deep breath and glancing at Jean and Sam. It couldn't be avoided, not now. It was time for Mrs Peters to know the whole story. Silently, Sam placed fresh mugs of tea in front of each of them and placed a plate piled high with mince pies in the centre of the table. Then he took a seat next to Jean. Gary hugged his sister again and said softly, "Molly, I think it's time to tell Mum about Tyke'"

Raising her reddened eyes to look, first at Gary and then at her mother, Molly hesitantly began to tell the tale of how Fizz had found the dead mare in the ditch, of how the foal had still been alive and of how she and Sam had rescued the little colt.

"So, who owns this foal then?" Mrs Peters asked as the story was finished. Gary looked at his mother steadily.

"According to his passport, I own him but, as far as I am concerned, he will always be Molly's."

"But, she *stole* him!" Mrs Peters snapped. "It sounds to me as if, whoever has taken him, they have simply taken back their own property! So that's the end of it!"

"Not really." Sam suddenly spoke. "He was abandoned. Dumped and left to die. I reckon, if ever it came to court, they would deem Gary, or rather Molly, the rightful owner. Thing is though, if it *is* the travellers that have taken him, we'll probably never find him again."

"So why bother looking?" Mrs Peters looked around the table. "He's gone, it's over!"

Molly leapt to her feet, her eyes blazing as she faced her mother.

"Tyke is mine!" She yelled. "I'm going to find him and I'm going to get him back!" Molly turned and ran out the door, Fizz close behind her, fresh tears pouring down her cheeks.

It was almost dark as Molly ran across the farmyard and out of the gate into the lane. She ran, not towards home but up the lane towards the wide track that Mary and she had traversed so recently. She had a stitch in her side, her legs ached and her breath was coming in short gasps but she didn't notice any of those things. She didn't notice how cold it had got either now that the sun had gone in. All she knew was that she had to get to Mary. Mary would know what to do. In fact, Mary probably knew what had happened! As she ran down the wide track through the darkening woods, Molly didn't have the energy to be frightened and, anyway, Fizz was running close by her side. When Fizz was around, Molly felt that nothing could really scare her, ever. The naked winter trees arched eerily above her as she ran.

Molly burst out of the trees into the clearing and stopped so suddenly that Fizz ran on a few strides before spinning round and running back to her young mistress. The clearing was empty. Gone was the collection of sparkling caravans and brightly painted carts and traps. Gone were the lines of bright, clean clothes. Gone was the 'corral' where half a dozen horses and ponies – Pat included – had lived. All that was left were the cold remains of campfires, a few piles of junk and rubbish and an old, rusting estate car which rested on it's axles, all four wheels removed. In the bleak, fast fading light, Molly collapsed, sobbing hysterically, onto the wet ground. They had one. Even Mary and Pat had deserted her. Her friend was gone. Tyke was gone. Hugging Fizz to her, Molly rocked back and forth, giving rein to a tide of emotion.

It was fully dark when Molly realised just how cold she was. She had only been wearing her show shirt and a thin jumper when she had raced away from the arm. The thin jodhpurs she wore were no shield against the frozen ground beneath her. She shivered and hugged Fizz closer, the dog's body heat providing a little comfort. Her night sight showed the dark bulk of the abandoned car on the farthest edge of the clearing. Slowly, easing the aches in her limbs, Molly got to her feet and went across to the rusty wreck. Opening the door she could see, in the gloom, that it was relatively clean inside. Calling Fizz, she climbed into the back seat and there, out of the wind and the worst of the chill, Molly wrapped her arms around her faithful pet and fell into an exhausted sleep.

So deep was Molly's slumber that she didn't hear the ping of the phone in her pocket, nor the insistent ringing, nor even feel it vibrate against her hip. She slept, exhausted by the excitement of the morning and the despair of the afternoon. It was hours later when Fizz, wriggling out of her arms and whining loudly, dragged Molly from her exhausted, wretched slumber. Even then, Molly just lay there, neither awake nor asleep, shutting out the sounds around her. It wasn't until Fizz let out a loud bark, startling Molly into consciousness, that she managed to force herself to sit up in the rusty car. The windows were steamed up and Molly couldn't see what had disturbed the dog. Suddenly, she felt a surge of fear. She had no idea of the time and it was a few minutes before she fully registered where she was. She grabbed Fizz's collar and hushed the dog, putting her arms around the furry body once more and ducking down low in the seat.

The car's driver's door was suddenly yanked open, causing Molly to jump and Fizz to give a yelp of surprise. A head popped into the opening.

"Sis? You there?"

"Gary!" Molly burst into a fresh onslaught of tears. "Oh Gary, they've gone!"

"Come on Sis," Gary pulled open the rear door and held out his hand to Molly to help her out of the car. "Don't worry, we'll find them." He hugged his little sister close until her sobbing faded away. "Come on, let's go home." Gary took off his jacket and wrapped it around Molly's shoulders. As she drew the coat around her, feeling the warmth seeping through her skin, Gary pulled out his mobile phone and sent a quick text. Then, putting his arm around Molly, he led her though the darkness, lighting their way with a small torch. Fizz trotted ahead, knowing the route even without the light, the white tip of her tail and the white ruff on the back of her neck guiding them home.

"Did you know," Molly said between sniffs, "that the white patches on a sheepdog have been bred into them so that farmers can see them in the dark?"

"No, I didn't." Admitted Gary. "But I can see the sense in it. I can see Fizz quite clearly and probably would still be able to see her if I turned the torch off."

"Yes." Molly said softly as, like a guiding star, Fizz led them through the darkness until they could see the glow of the lights of the farm in the distance.

Molly could sense that her mother was on the verge of scolding her as Gary ushered her into the farm kitchen. Instead, after a pointed look from her son, Mrs Peters hugged her daughter awkwardly then hustled her into a chair whilst Jean heated up some tomato soup and placed it, along with a mug of hot, sweet tea, in front of Molly. Despite not feeling very hungry, Molly ate the soup and began to feel it's warmth seeping through her chilled body. No one spoke as Molly ate. Eventually, Molly could bear the silence no longer and looked at Gary, the expression on her face showing her despair.

"How are we going to find him, Gary? How are we going to get him back?"

Her brother sighed and looked at her sadly.

"Well, we've notified the police and we've also put out an appeal on all the social media sites so, with a bit of luck, someone will spot him. After all, he's quite distinctively marked."

Molly nodded and blew her nose.

"Will they be horrible to him do you think?" Molly looked up at her brother, her eyes filling with fresh tears. Gary shrugged.

"I really don't know, sis. But, think on this, he was stolen because he's valuable to them. So, hopefully, they'll treat him right." He bent to give her a hug. "Now though, I think it's best if we head off home and try to get some sleep."

Numbly, Molly nodded. Remembering her manners, she thanked Jean for the soup and the tea then turned towards the door.

"I'll run you all home." Jean said.

Mumbling their thanks, Molly, Gary and their mother followed Jean out into the yard. Molly was surprised to hear, through the winter darkness, the beginnings of the 'dawn chorus'. She realised that, thanks to her, everyone had been awake all night! As Jean drove them home, Molly struggled to stay awake. She didn't want to sleep. Not whilst she was living in such a nightmare.

As Jean halted the landrover, she turned to Molly and, in a very serious tone, pointed out that, in spite of the nightmare of Tyke being stolen, Molly still had a responsibility to Fred. Molly shrugged lethargically. Gary turned to her, speaking in a stern tone. "Look Molly, Jean's right. You still need to see to Fred properly."

"Not today though love." Jean said kindly. "After the hunt, they will all be having a rest day so you can have a day off. But I'll see you tomorrow, okay?"

Silently, Molly nodded then climbed out of the vehicle and walked, zombie-like, towards the door of the house. She felt disjointed, like she didn't belong here – or anywhere come to that. She wondered where Tyke was and a fresh wave of despair washed over her.

19

Afterwards, Molly had no recollection of the remainder of that day. She
d in bed, drifting in and out of sleep, not wanting to eat, get up or do anything. She
s vaguely aware of her mother and Gary coming into her room at intervals with
d and drink but, although she drank several cups of tea and got up to the go to the
throom, she couldn't face the food. After her mother had remonstrated with her for
t eating, Molly began clearing the plate by feeding the food to Fizz who was curled
 on top of the duvet. Fizz seemed to sense her young mistress was upset and lay
se to Molly, offering silent comfort. Every so often, waves of despair would swamp
lly and she would hug Fizz tightly to her, sobbing into the dog's shoulder until the
or animal's fur was sodden with salty tears. The day dragged by.

In the afternoon, Gary persuaded Molly to come downstairs to talk to the
lice. There was no point in hiding Tyke's origins now so the whole story had to be
plained all over again. However, the police seemed to be sympathetic although
y did point out that the correct thing to do would have been to have contacted both
mselves and the RSPCA when Molly had found the foal. However, they seemed
think that there was a clear case of abandonment in the way the foal had be left
side it's dead mother. Whilst the police were still there, an RSPCA officer also
ived, having been alerted by the police. They too felt that abandonment was the
se although, technically, Sam and Jean should have tried to find the owner. The
neral feeling was, however, that if Tyke was found and it became a legal issue, it
s likely to go in Molly's favour.

After the officials had left, Molly wandered back to her room. She didn't see the
nt in talking to the police or anyone else since no one seemed to know where the
vellers had gone. Throwing herself on the bed with fresh tears springing from her
s, she wondered again where Tyke was now. Then she felt a different emotion, a
xture of anger and pain at the betrayal Mary had obviously displayed. It was clear
Molly now that the whole 'friendship' with Mary had been to lull everyone around
e into a false sense of security and to spy out the layout of the farm. Convinced of
ry's guilt Molly punched her pillow angrily several times, imagining that it was
ry's face. Eventually, totally exhausted now, Molly fell into a restless sleep.

It was still dark when Molly awoke. She had a vague, half remembered
ollection of Gary coming into her room and covering her with the duvet before
ing out the light but she had no concept of how long she had slept for. Glancing
er bedside clock, it's LED display bright in the darkness, she could see that it was
w minutes after six in the morning. It was almost time to get up anyway since she
ally headed off to the farm around half past seven. As she thought of the farm, a
sh wave of emotion washed over her and she swallowed hard as a choking sob
e in her throat. Gritting her teeth, Molly slid out from under the duvet and realised

that she was still fully dressed in the clothes she had worn to go hunting! Tiptoeing out onto the landing, she made her way to the bathroom to have a wash then went back to her room and changed into jeans with a T-shirt and a warm jumper. With Fizz padding beside her, she crept downstairs towards the kitchen.

As Molly passed the closed lounge door, she noticed a faint strip of light shining beneath it and could hear an erratic tapping noise. Slowly, she opened the lounge door and peered inside. Her brother was sitting at their mother's computer, totally engrossed in something on the screen and rapidly tapping at the keyboard, obviously writing something. Molly opened her mouth to speak but, before she could, Fizz had trotted forwards and put her head on Gary's knee, making him jump.

"Good grief, Fizz, you nearly gave me a heart attack then!" He looked up and noticed Molly in the doorway. "Morning Sis, glad to see you're up and about. Come and look at this." He nodded towards the computer screen. Molly crossed the room to join him. Looking at the screen, Molly opened her eyes wide in amazement. Gary had set up a page for Tyke on a social media site with dozens of photographs of the young horse, plus a description and details of his disappearance. Already there were hundreds of comments and it was apparent that people were sharing the page over and over again. With his distinctive markings, Tyke would be spotted instantly if he was out in the open somewhere. Then a thought occurred to Molly.

"Erm, won't this put him at risk though?" she asked with a worried frown.

"It may, but let's face it Sis, he's at risk anyway if the travellers have got him and they decide he's not right for the job they have for him."

"What do you mean?" Molly was eve more worried now.

"Well, I would say that he's a gypsy cob Thoroughbred cross which means he was probably bred for 'trotting'. If he can't move fast enough, being a gelding, he won't be much use to them I'd guess."

"So they might kill him?" Molly's voice rose as tears sprang to her eyes again.

"Shh. You'll wake Mum." Gary hissed. "They'd be more likely to dump him I guess."

"Again." Molly whispered. "Poor Tyke. He'll be cold and hungry and no one will care."

"Ah. But think Sis. If he does get dumped, after this," he nodded again at the computer screen, "he'll be found quickly. Don't forget he's microchipped and it's in my name so, when he's scanned, they'll know who he is."

"Someone told me they cut the chips out sometimes." Molly sniffed and wiped her eyes on her sleeve. Gary shrugged.

"Well, maybe. If they realise he has one." he said. "But let's not think about that. Go and pop the kettle on whilst I shut this down and then we can have breakfast and get up to the farm to see if there's any news." As Gary turned back to the computer, Molly turned and resumed her journey to the kitchen. It occurred to her that Gary must have been working on the social media page for a long time, perhaps even all night! She really should be grateful to him for what he'd done.

They arrived at the farm as the weak, watery winter sun was climbing over the horizon. Jean greeted them and confirmed that, as yet, they had heard nothing about Tyke. Molly dreaded going into the barn and seeing the empty pen where Tyke normally stood but she steeled herself. As Jean had said yesterday, there was still Fred to see to. It wasn't his fault. Fred's whinney of greeting cheered Molly a little but it was sad to see Pepper and Shandy looking at Tyke's pen and then calling loudly for the foal. Buster too was upset but whether that was because he was picking up vibes from the two mares or not, no one could tell. Either way, there was a gloomy atmosphere in the barn as they tended the four animals.

Despite her concerns over Tyke, Molly found it helped to have to see to Fred. His quiet understanding of her mood helped as she groomed him and tacked him up for a walk out around the lanes with Gary and Jean on the two mares. "Just a leg stretch" Jean had explained. It was a routine they followed for the next three days, the frost making the ground too hard and slippery for riding on the fields so they simply exercised by walking and trotting around the lanes. Molly felt, most of the time, as though she were on autopilot.

Three days had passed in a numbing monotony with no news about Tyke. New Year's Eve dawned and Molly and Gary went up to the farm early as normal. The day was overcast with heavy, dark clouds and a needle sharp icy wind that numbed their fingers, toes and faces. But at least it was dry.

As they worked the horses, Jean explained that she would be spending the evening in the barn that night. There was a big party locally and they would be setting off fireworks at midnight. Gary volunteered to do the job as he was used to doing what he called 'stag' duty – standing guard – so that Jean and Sam could see the New Year in properly. By the time they rode back into the farm yard, it was arranged that Gary and Molly would sit with the horses and that Jean would call Mrs Peters and invite her to see the New Year in at the farm too! Molly couldn't help wondering if Tyke was going to be protected in a similar way, should there be firework displays anywhere near wherever he was. She realised she didn't care about the New Year. It would be the first time Dad would not be there to 'First Foot', just to humour his wife. And now there was no Tyke either! Seeing in the New Year with Gary in the horse barn was as good an activity as any other, Molly felt.

In the afternoon the weather turned as the clouds gave up their burden in the form of ice laden sleet, driven like needles across the farm yard by a blustery wind. Sitting snug in the tack room with his sister, Gary commented that if the weather kept up the way it was, it would put paid to the fireworks at midnight. Molly simply shrugged, not caring either way as she lethargically rubbed saddle soap into Fred's saddle. She used to love every job involving the horses, even mucking out. Now though, she felt there was no real point. Listening to the sleet hammering on the roof and windows, she pictured Tyke, hungry, cold, and soaking wet. She shivered at the thought and felt fresh tears pricking the back of her eyes. As she put the saddle back on it's rack, Gary 'put up' the bridle he'd been cleaning by passing the throatlash across the front, through the reins at the back and then back across the front and fastening it. Then, after glancing round to make sure everything was neat and tidy, he gave Molly a rueful smile before they plunged out into the weather together and ran through the icy storm towards the house. Even in the short fifty yard sprint to the back door, they were both soaked through. As they came through the door into the warm kitchen with it's well fuelled Aga, Jean leapt from her seat and put the kettle on before grabbing a couple of towels which had been warming on the stove and handing them to Molly and Gary.

As they towelled the freezing water from their hair, the back door opened again and Mrs Peters struggled in with two large bags, Sam following on her heels. He'd been to pick her up and, thankfully, she'd brought clean, dry clothing for her children to change into. As their mother set to helping Jean prepare dinner, Molly and her brother took turns in the hot shower before changing into the fresh clothes. In the spare room, Molly pulled on the dry jeans, T-shirt and jumper, listening to the wild weather outside still buffeting the house. Not quite sure why, she crossed to the window and opened it, looking out across the now dark farm yard. The security light flicked on as it's motion sensor was triggered. Molly saw Jean and Sam, muffled in their waxed jackets, dashing across to the barn, obviously going to feed the horses. As the wind slammed the barn door shut behind them, Molly heard the high pitched whinney of a horse. Her heart skipped a beat and she peered out into the night but, as the light flicked off, there was nothing to see. Swallowing a fresh sob, she realised it had probably been Buster in the barn, greeting his dinner.

20

Dinner was over. Although, due to her age, Molly had only been allowed half a glass of wine [topped up with lemonade] with the meal, she could already feel the strange effects of the alcohol as it coursed through her system. She felt light-headed and somewhat detached from everything around her. She sat in silence as the conversation of the four adults seemed to wash over her. Dimly, she was aware that the others were rising from the table, Jean clearing away the remnants of the meal and Sam leading her mother and Gary out though the hall and into the little used lounge. Feeling uncoordinated, Molly followed. Sam switched on the television as Molly sank into a chair, not caring about the comedy program showing nor the rumbling conversation around her. Even after Jean came into the lounge, Molly still sat there in a semi stupor, finally glancing up only when Jean placed a glass of plain lemonade into her hand. Distantly, she heard Gary chuckle.

"I think my little sister is a tad tipsy" he laughed. "Luckily, she has a few hours to sober up before our 'Stag Duty' otherwise I'd have to put her on a charge!" All the adults laughed at this. Molly just felt odd and disconnected.

The evening wore on, the clock ticking towards midnight. Slowly Molly began to feel better, although she still didn't take part in the conversation, just stared mindlessly at the television, her brain numb. It was about half past ten that Gary, sitting nearest to the window, suddenly cocked his head.

"Perhaps the fireworks won't be such a wash out after all" he said. "Sounds like the rain has stopped and the wind has died down." He got to his feet and went out into the hallway. They heard him open the front door, close it and then he returned to the lounge. "Yep. It's clearing." he announced, sinking back into his chair with a sigh.

An hour later, Gary and Molly made their way across to the barn, dodging the puddles that had formed in the farm yard. Following her brother through the door, Molly again heard the distant, high pitched whinny. It was definitely not one of the horses inside the building.

"Come on sis." Gary urged. "Close the door, it's freezing!"

"Didn't you hear it?" Molly looked at her brother.

"Hear what? Come on!"

"The horse? Calling?"

"What horse?" Gary frowned. "Come on Sis, you're hearing things now. The only horses near here are these ones! I think that wine has gone to your head." With that, he began setting up a portable CD player then flicked through a pile of CDs before selecting one. As the music started, at a low volume to begin with, Molly strained her ears, listening for the horse calling again. She knew she hadn't imagined it. Over the past hour, the feeling aroused by the small amount of alcohol she had drunk had worn off and she wasn't feeling weird any more. She knew there was a horse out there, somewhere. Then again, maybe Gary was right and it was simply her longing for

Tyke that had made her hear the call.

Every few minutes, Gary increased the volume on the CD player, rather than blaring the music out full blast straight away. It was less of a culture shock for the horses that way. Molly busied herself putting extra hay in for them to help distract them from what was going on. The three older horses had an air of 'seen it all before' but Buster was both curious and delighted by the extra attention at a time when, normally, the barn was quiet and dark. His behaviour reminded Molly so painfully of Tyke that the ever present tears flooded her eyes again. She pulled a sorry looking scrap of tissue from her pocket and wiped her eyes. Sniffing, she realise the tissue wasn't much use for blowing her nose so she wiped it on her sleeve instead. She jumped as Gary put his arm around her shoulders. With the music now at full volume she hadn't heard his approach. He hugged her briefly then, so he didn't have to shout, he put his mouth close to her ear.

"Why don't you go outside and watch the display? It's nearly time and Jean said you can easily see the rockets from here. I see enough pyrotechnics when I'm on exercise. I'll stay in here with the horses and I'll call you if I need any help."

Molly nodded and, giving Gary a weak smile, she slipped out through the door.

As Molly slipped out into the dark, dripping farmyard, she shivered slightly as she took a breath of the freezing air. No doubt, before long, all this water would be ice as the temperature dropped during the night. She heard the sound of voices and laughter coming from the direction of the farmhouse. Her mother, together with Jean and Sam, had obviously come out to see the new year in too. As Molly huddled in the shadows in the lee of the barn wall out of the biting wind, she heard the first chime of a distance church bell and, almost simultaneously, a shrill whistle as a brightly coloured stream of sparks shrieked into the sky to burst with a bang into a spectacular spray of coloured light which was reflected thousandfold in the puddles around the yard. As the lights of the firework died away, a second shrieked skywards but Molly didn't follow this one's passage into the sky. She had heard the horse again, distantly, a shrill scream of equine terror. Without thought, Molly turned and ran in the direction the sound had come from, unnoticed by the adults who were watching the dazzling display above them and wishing each other a happy new year.

The horse call had come from the direction of the top field. As Molly pounded along the track, her breath coming in gasps, she wished Fizz was beside her. But Fizz was in the farm house with Meg, tucked up by the Aga with the radio on to cover the noise of the fireworks. As more rockets lit up the sky, whistling and exploding loudly above her, Molly could smell the cordite as it drifted on the wind. The fireworks were both a blessing and a curse. For the few seconds each one lit the night sky, Molly could see the track ahead clearly but it meant that she had no night sight so, as the coloured sparks faded, she had to blunder blindly along, splashing through the mud and the icy puddles. Twice she almost fell into the ditch at the side of the track and several times she blundered into the fence on the other side. Her feet were numb with cold inside her sodden trainers and her legs were soaked up to her knees. Worse still, she hadn't heard the horse again so she wasn't even sure she was headed in the right direction. Yet some inner instinct was pulling her onward.

As Molly reached the top of the track and tried to peer through the darkness
o the open field, her lungs were burning with the effort of drawing what felt like
edles of air into her lungs. The clouds had cleared somewhat but the stars
nkling above her weren't enough for her to see anything. Another firework whizzed
o the heavens, spiralling as it whistled shrilly in the night air. A split second before
exploded in a cascade of brilliant white stars, Molly heard the call again. It was
ich closer now. Jerking her head towards the hedgerow on the far side of the field,
olly thought she saw the tiniest flash of white, a millisecond before the night faded
darkness once more. Yanking the gate open, she ran forward, toward the far
dge then stopped abruptly as her feet sank several inches into the sodden mud of
e field. Sam had ploughed this field a few days ago and now the rain and sleet had
ftened the ground. Yanking her feet out and stumbling forwards, Molly realised that
e was trying to run across the furrows and she was in danger of falling on the
even ground or, worse, getting stuck in the soft, heavy, clinging mud. She stopped,
nking hard. Obviously, if she continued straight across the field, she would have to
lk carefully to avoid sinking into the ruts and the mud would gather on her feet,
wing her down. However, if she went along the headland, it was thickly covered in
iss so, although the route would be more than twice the distance, it would be
sier and safer. As two rockets crossed the sky above her, she turned back to the
d gate then headed along the edge of the field, straining her ears again for any
ind from the horse she was now certain was in the hedgerow on the far side.

Molly slowed to a walk, the stitch in her side painful enough to bring tears to
 eyes, blurring her vision. She was just turning to head along the hedgerow that
d been her goal when she heard the whinney again, so close it made her jump.
other firework lit the sky and Molly looked at the imposing bulk of the hedge,
eking some sign of movement amongst the thick foliage. Softly, she called out in
 darkness.

yke?" She held her breath. Seconds later she heard, not a frantic whinney but a
t whicker, quite close but definitely under the hedge. Curbing the almost
erwhelming urge to rush forwards, thereby spooking the horse she now knew to be
re, she called again and, again, she heard the soft whicker, echoed almost
mediately by a deep noted snort. Were there two horses in the hedge? Talking
tly, babbling nonsense, Molly crept forwards, droplets from the sodden hawthorn
aking her from above. She couldn't even feel her feet anymore.

She almost fell into the ditch. She'd forgotten it was there and her heart
inded as she realised that she had almost fallen into the icy water that now filled it
 overflowing. The fireworks seemed to have ended and, finally, Molly had
veloped some degree of night sight. Trying to work out the best way to cross the
ch, she could see faint flashes of white through the foliage on the other side. Still
ing softly, she eventually found a sturdy branch that stretched across the ditch
d, holding on tightly, managed to get across with only one numbed foot slipping
 the icy water below her. Starlight filtered through the sparser branches on this
e of the ditch and it twinkled in a pair of eyes that were peering at her through the
om. Tyke whickered as he saw his young mistress and didn't even flinch when,
getting all the rules, Molly rushed forwards and flung her arms around the young

horse's neck, sobbing in relief. She jumped when something nudged her in the back. Spinning round, causing Tyke to jump back in alarm, Molly realised that Pat was standing behind her. Both horses wore headcollars and were tied firmly to the hawthorn trees. As she stepped towards Pat, Molly tripped over something on the ground. At first she thought it was a log but, looking down, she saw the white face of Mary, lying there huddled up, eyes closed, unmoving.

Molly dropped to her knees beside Mary's still form. With relief she saw the faint vapour from Mary's half open mouth as the girl breathed shallowly. Mary's face was deathly white and her skin was icy to the touch. Searching through the pockets of her jacket, Molly dug out her new mobile phone and switched it on. The screen lit up but showed absolutely no signal. Molly, her hands shaking, tried Gary's number hoping that there would be some faint response. But there was nothing. Pulling off her own thick padded jacket, she tucked it firmly around Mary's still form then wriggled her way through the clutching thorns of the hedgerow and into the lane. She tried the phone again. Still nothing and, even worse, she noticed the 'battery low' light flashing. She scrambled back to Mary and the horses. Mary's breathing was even fainter now. Realising there was only one thing she could do, Molly made sure Tyke was securely tied and that, if he moved around, he wouldn't step on Mary. Then Molly turned to Pat. Her fingers shook as she pulled the end of the quick release knot, all the while talking to Pat in a soft voice, trying to keep her fear out of her tone. Pat nudged her and snorted as she led him towards the ditch. She had already decided that, although going out into the lane was safer, going back the way she had come would be quicker. Holding Pat's rope, Molly managed to scramble back across the ditch with the help of her sturdy branch. She gently pulled Pat's rope, making a clicking sound. Pat, used to going anywhere he was asked, sized up the ditch in the dim light then popped across, keeping his head down as he had so many times before. Tyke gave a shrill whinney. Molly called softly to him to reassure him then she tied Pat's leadrope onto both sides of his headcollar to make a pair of reins as she had seen Mary do so many times. Out in the open, she could feel the wind biting through her jumper and the first icy needles of sleet stinging her face. Grabbing hold of Pat's thick mane, Molly managed to scramble onto his back. Pat snorted, blowing plumes of steam as Molly clung to him. She turned him along the headland, realising that, if she had sunk into the soft ground of the field, Pat certainly would. Leaning forwards, holding tight, Molly urged Pat into a gallop.

How Molly stayed on as Pat galloped flat out along the headland, she had no clue. As they raced along the last stretch, Molly suddenly remembered the gate. She'd have to get off to open it! She could dimly see the gateway ahead of her and sat up to begin easing Pat back. As the pony dropped back to trot, Molly almost was bounced off! He wasn't as easy as Fred was at this pace. Quickly she pulled on the leadrope to get him back into walk and saw, to her relief, that she must have failed to close the gate properly and it was swinging open in the wind. A twinge of guilt from her oversight was quickly quelled as she kicked Pat into a steady jog towards the opening. As she rode through, a gust of wind caught the gate and slammed it back against Pat's side, causing him to leap forwards. As the gate connected with Molly's leg, she screamed aloud with pain and Pat leapt again in fright. Molly clung desperately to his mane, tears streaming down her face, her whole leg in agony as the pony began to gallop wildly down the track to the farm.

Through the icy tears of pain streaming down her cheeks, Molly could see the farmyard ahead was ablaze with light as Pat galloped towards it. She could see people too, milling around in the farmyard. As Pat raced closer, a figure detached itself from the others and jogged tentatively towards the pony and rider. Even though she couldn't see properly, Molly knew it was her brother. He spread him arms wide and began to call softly to the terrified pony, to calm it so that he could grab the headcollar and stop it's panicked flight.

Molly slid off Pat and into Gary's arms, sobbing with pain and shivering violently as she tried to coherently tell him what had happened. Jean had rushed over to take charge of Pat and quickly grasped the situation.
"Molly love," she said gently, "could you show Gary where Mary is?"
Molly nodded, still numb, her teeth chattering.
"Okay." Jean looked at Gary. "Wait there a minute." Pulling Pat behind her, Jean headed for the barn, Sam close behind.
"Gary!" Mrs Peters bustled up and went to pull Molly away from her brother. "The child needs to get indoors and get warmed up! She'll catch her death out here!"
"Mum, Molly is the only one who knows where Mary is. From what she's said, Mary is unconscious and could die if we don't find her quickly! Give Molly your coat. She'll be fine!"
As Mrs Peters opened her mouth to protest, there was a clatter of hooves across the yard. Jean had come out of the barn, leading Pepper. The big mare was wearing just a riding bridle as Jean jogged across to the small family group huddled in the yard.
"I'm thinking you could get there quickly on the old girl and start first aid or whatever whilst we drive round the lanes. You can flag us down then." Jean handed the mare's reins to Gary before turning to Mrs Peters. "Barbara, could you go into the house and stoke up the Aga? Start preparing hot drinks and stuff? There's some homemade soup in the fridge too. Sam's getting some blankets and the Landy. We'll be back as quick as we can"
Without waiting for a reply from the stunned woman, Jean turned back to Gary and legged him up onto Pepper. Then she turned to Molly.
"Come on love." She said gently. "You need to show Gary where Mary is."
Teeth chattering, Molly allowed Jean to leg her up onto the mare so that she was sitting in front of Gary, his arms around her as he held the reins. As Gary kicked Pepper into a jog, Molly managed to stutter out that the gate at the top was still open and that also they would have to use the headland to get to the far side of the field. Gary hugged his sister closer to show that he understood as he kicked Pepper into a canter. The huge horse responded instantly, sensing the urgency of the situation.

As the huge horse thundered along the track, Molly felt the icy wind cutting into her face whilst the rest of her began to slowly thaw out with the combined body heat of the horse beneath her and her brother seated behind with his arms holding her close. Molly clung to Pepper's mane with one hand as they swung through the open gate and onto the headland. Unable to speak because of the rushing wind in her face, she used her other hand to point Gary in the right direction. Suddenly, Pepper threw her head up, ears pricked as she gave a loud whinney that reverberated across the field. Despite the rush of wind in their ears, Gary and Molly heard Tyke's answering call. As it turned out, Gary actually hadn't needed his sister to show him the whereabouts of the foal and Mary. Calling frantically, Pepper soon located Tyke from his answering calls. Pepper skidded to a halt of her own accord right where Pat's hoofprints came out from the hedge. Gary slid off Pepper's back. Instructing Molly to stay on the big horse and keep her calm, he ducked under the sodden branches of the hedgerow, calling softly to Tyke to avoid scaring the young horse. Molly heard Tyke's answering whicker and Pepper neighed loudly in return.

Surprisingly, Pepper seemed to understand that she needed to stay calm. As she noticed that the mare was sweating slightly, Molly recalled Jean's instructions about not letting hot horses stand around in the cold. Tentatively, she squeezed Pepper's sides with her legs and encouraged the horse to walk up and down along the hedgerow, just for a couple of dozen yards in each direction. Again, the mare seemed to understand and willingly followed Molly's instructions. Molly was warming up nicely from the heat of the horse beneath her.

The sound of the landrover in the lane was a welcome relief for Molly. Drawing Pepper to a halt by where Gary had gone through the hedge, Molly cocked her head to try and hear what was happening. Suddenly, she heard Gary call.
"You okay Sis?"
"Yes, I'm fine. Is Mary okay?"
"She unconscious but alive. Jean and Sam are putting her in the landy now." Gary replied through the branches. "I reckon your jacket saved her. Talk to Pepper. I'm going to try and bring Tyke across the ditch."
Molly began stroking and patting Pepper as she heard Gary encouraging Tyke to jump across the water-filled ditch. She could tell from the sound of Gary's voice that the young horse wasn't keen on the idea. Peering through the branches, trying to catch a glimpse of Tyke, Molly called his name in a soft but carrying voice. Tyke responded with a shrill whinney but, from Gary's continued encouraging noises, was still refusing to cross the ditch. Suddenly, Pepper stepped forwards of her own accord, thrusting her head into the sodden hedgerow. The mare's body shook as she gave a low, rumbling whicker. The sound of branches crashing and a lot of splashing noises follow, together with Gary's voice saying 'steady' and 'whoa'. Suddenly, Tyke shot out of the hedge. Pepper gave a snort and whickered low again as Tyke spotted the Clydesdale and rushed to her side. As Molly reached out to grab Tyke's dangling leadrope, Gary emerged, soaked and muddy. As her shivering brother came over and made a big fuss of Tyke, Molly heard the landrover start up and head off along the lane. She looked down at Gary.
"How are you going to get back up here?" she asked.
"Simple." Gary grinned up at her, muddy water dripping down his face. "Brace your left foot and point your toes up as far as you can."

Molly did as he asked. Gary used her foot briefly as a stirrup and scrambled up onto Pepper's back behind her. As he reached around her once more to take epper's reins, she could feel how soaked he was as the cold water from his jeans eeped into the back of hers. She could hear his teeth chattering as he settled imself on the mare's back. Holding Tyke's leadrope firmly, Molly suddenly felt elated y the fact that the little horse was safe. Then she remembered Mary. As Pepper trode along the headland back towards the farm, Molly found herself dealing with a onfusing mixture of worry about Mary and relief over Tyke's return.

21

Never had Molly felt so relieved as she was when she saw the lights of the farmyard ahead of them. It was only as they were walking along in the darkness that she realised that the sleet was still falling, soaking Gary and her even more. The smell of wet horse surrounded them as they headed down the track. Tyke happily jogged on the end of his rope to keep pace with the long strides of the huge mare beside him. Molly fretted that the gate was still open as they rode through but Gary reassured her that, in view of all that had happened, it really wouldn't matter, not just on this one night. When they rode into the brightly lit farmyard, Sam came out of the barn to meet them. As Gary and Molly slid to the ground, Sam took hold of Tyke's rope and Pepper's reins before informing the siblings that they had better get indoors before Jean and Mrs Peters threw a fit. Stating that he would take charge of the horses, Sam jerked his head towards the house before turning back to the barn, Pepper and Tyke plodding calmly beside him.

The heat in the kitchen felt like a furnace as Molly and Gary entered. Jean and Mrs Peters bustled over, insisting that clothes were changed immediately for the dry ones warming on the rails on the front of the Aga. Even Molly's questions about Mary were ignored until Molly and her brother were both seated at the table, warm and dry, with steaming bowls of thick turkey soup in front of them. As Sam came in through the door, full of reassurance that all the horses were safe and sound, Jean began to explain that Mary was upstairs in the spare room, tucked up in bed.
"May I see her?" Molly asked.
"Not yet love." Jean said gently. "We've called the doctor and it would be best to wait and see what he has to say first I think."
Disappointed, Molly dunked a chunk of bread in her soup. A knock on the kitchen door heralded the arrival of the local doctor and Jean quickly ushered the man upstairs to see Mary.

Twenty minutes later, the doctor was seated at the kitchen table with a steaming cup of coffee in front of him. In a reassuring voice he stated that, in his opinion, Mary was suffering from mild exposure and hypothermia and that she was also underweight.
"The child is exhausted." the doctor went on. "She does have some bruising too and a couple of minor wounds – they could have been caused by a fall, perhaps from her pony or, more likely, they were inflicted by another person. You say she was from the gypsy camp?"
"Yes." Jean confirmed. "We haven't seen her since they moved on. I always got the impression that Mary was troubled in some way, to be honest."
Molly followed the conversation with interest.
"Well, in my opinion," the doctor said, pausing for another sip of coffee, "Mary

esn't need to go to hospital, if you are happy for her to stay here for a few days."
an glanced at Sam and then nodded her assent. "Of course she can stay, for as
ıg as she needs to."
hat's fine." The doctor nodded. "There is one thing though. I will need to contact
cial Services about her. They will probably want to pay you a visit."
)h." Jean's face fell. "So Mary will likely be taken into care?"
ou can't!" Molly blurted out. "It would be like caging a wild animal!"
lush Molly." Jean patted her hand. "I'm sure that they will only do what's for the
st." Jean turned to the doctor with a wan smile. "Thank you for your help doctor."
lo problem." The doctor handed his now empty mug to Jean. "Just see Mary gets
ınty of rest, fluids and good food and I am sure everything will be fine." With that,
stood up and took his leave.

Despite Molly's protests, she wasn't allowed to see Mary that morning.
;tead, Gary and Mrs Peters insisted on the family going home to get some much
ded sleep. As they headed home, Molly was certain sleep was the last thing she
uld be capable of. Surprisingly though, despite all the thoughts whirring around in
r mind, Molly was asleep within minutes of crawling under her duvet, hugging Fizz
se to her.

Molly slowly woke up around midday, enjoy the warmth of her duvet and Fizz's
dy still snuggled against her. It was a few moments before Molly recalled the
ınts of last night. As the full impact hit her, she sat up suddenly, a surge of energy
ırsing through her. Quickly she got out of bed and dressed, Fizz jumping up
:itedly at her young mistress as she sense the urgency in Molly. Racing down the
irs, Molly burst into the kitchen to find Gary and their mother calmly sitting at the
•le having breakfast.
an I go to the farm?" Molly said breathlessly.
fter you have had a good breakfast." Mrs Peters replied, getting up and heading to
• cooker where a pot of porridge was simmering.
n not hungry!" Molly retorted. "I need to see Tyke... and Mary!"
ou get put on a charge in the Army if you don't eat breakfast." Gary mumbled
etly.
n not in the Army!" Molly shouted at him.
ow then young lady!" Mrs Peters turned to Molly, "Calm down! Have something to
: and then we can all go up to the farm together."
lking, Molly seated herself next to Gary and looked down at the bowl of porridge
t her mother had placed before her. As the aromatic steam tickled her nose, she
Idenly realised that she was hungry after all and, picking the spoon beside the
wl, she began to eat hurriedly. Four s;ices of toast and marmalade followed before
lly suddenly realised that her brother was grinning at her.
ot bad for someone who wasn't hungry." Gary chuckled.
h, shut up." Molly gave him a playful shove.
Vhen you two have finished messing around, you can help me clear up and then
'll go and see what's happening at the farm."

For once, Molly didn't protest as she washed up the breakfast things, placing them on the draining board for Gary to dry before Mrs Peters put them away. When the kitchen was back to it's normal tidiness, Mrs Peters went and got her coat and wellington boots. Gary and Molly followed suit. With Fizz trotting at their heels, they set off towards the farm on foot.

Even though it was New Year's Day, the farmyard was it's usual hive of activity. Animals didn't acknowledge holidays. They still needed to be fed, watered, cleaned out, exercised etc. Jean wasn't out in the yard though. As Mrs Peters headed across to the house, Gary and Molly headed instead to the horse barn to check on Tyke. As soon as he saw her, Tyke whickered. Molly went quickly to his pen, let herself in and, throwing her arms around the young horse's neck, she burst into tears. Gary left her to it and busied himself with checking Pat and Pepper over after their nocturnal adventure. When he had finished, he joined Molly in Tyke's pen and checked him over too. Then, whilst Molly gave Tyke a good groom, Gary started to muck out the other horses, leaving his sister alone with her foal.

It was a good two hours later that Gary and Molly headed across to the farmhouse. At Gary's insistence, Molly had groomed all six equines whilst he did their stables and made sure they all had hay and water. Satisfied that they were all happy and content, Gary led the way across the farmyard, declaring that it must be time for lunch.
"A late lunch." Gary stated with a laugh. It's almost three already!"
Molly laughed with him and then stopped. What was going to happen about Mary? Molly wondered.

Lunch was a solemn affair, all in all. However, Jean did impart the information that she had already had a phone call from a social worker who, having spoken to the doctor, was happy for Mary to stay at the farm until the next day at least, when the social worker would visit in person to see what was to be done.
"So can I go and see her now?" Molly asked plaintively.
"The doctor wants her to rest as much as possible." Jean replied in a kindly tone. "However, I'm hoping she may feel well enough to come downstairs later so why don't we all go out and give those horses a leg stretch before it gets too dark? Your Mum has offered to stay to look after Mary." Jean smiled at Molly.
Molly opened her mouth to protest but a warning look from her brother caused her to close it again. With a martyred sigh, she rose from the table and went to put on her jacket and boots.

22

Everyone was in a more light-hearted mood when they all returned to the farmhouse. Pepper, Tyke and Pat had all been walked out in hand, Buster had been put through some groundwork by Jean whilst Gary had lunged Shandy and Molly did the same with Fred. The horses had all now been fed, hayed, watered and tucked up for the night. Sam had put a hefty 'combination' padlock on the barn doors 'just in case'. Now, everyone was gathered around the kitchen table which was laden with a wide variety of meat and vegetables. Best of all, from Molly's point of view, Jean had brought Mary downstairs and the child was seated shyly between Molly and Gary, wrapped up in one of Jean's fluffy dressing gowns.

Molly was bursting to ask Mary a million questions about what had happened the night before but Jean had taken Molly aside whilst they had been doing the horses and asked her to keep her curiosity under wraps until Mary volunteered the information. As it happened, they didn't have to wait very long. Dinner over, they were all sipping hot drinks of tea, coffee or chocolate when Mary spoke quietly.
"I'm sorry." Mary said in a small voice.
Everyone looked at her and she seemed to shrink visibly under their gazes. Jean reached across the table and patted Mary's hand.
"You have nothing to be sorry for." Jean said gently. "I'm sure it wasn't your fault."
"But it was!" Mary blurted out. "It was me who told 'em about him!" With that, Mary burst into tears.
Molly wasn't quite sure what to do or how she was feeling. Part of her felt angry that her friend had obviously been involved in Tyke's disappearance but another, bigger part of her wanted to hear Mary's side of the story and felt that, as Jean had said, it really wasn't Mary's fault. Slowly, Molly put her arm around Mary and gave her a gentle hug. She really didn't know what to say. Eventually, Mary's sobs subsided and she blew her nose noisily on a large piece of kitchen roll that Jean had handed to her. When she had eventually calmed down, she began to speak in a soft voice. She told them the whole sorry tale from the beginning.

It transpired that 'Megan', Tyke's mother, had belonged to Mary's father. He had decided to put her in foal to a good 'blood horse' – a Thoroughbred that belonged to a friend of his – despite Megan being less than fourteen hands high and just two years old. He hoped it would produce a good trotting horse that he could race in harness and earn money from. The stallion was a 'big un', standing at sixteen two. Megan hadn't wintered well whilst in foal and had lost a lot of weight. When Mary's family had moved to the local gypsy camp in the spring, Mary's dad had hoped that the good grass on the common would help Megan pick up some weight before the foal was born. Sadly, it hadn't happened that way. Mary's father had gone away, as he often did, to find some work and earn some much needed money to feed his family. Mary explained at this point that she had five younger siblings and life was hard at times but, when they were low on funds, in the way of the gypsies, the whole camp would help out with food and clothing etc.

It was whilst Mary's father was away that Megan went into labour. She struggled to give birth to such a large foal and it had damaged her so badly that she had died shortly after the colt was born. In a panic, Mary's uncle decided to dump the mare and foal in the ditch and, when Mary's father returned, told him that both the mare and foal had died.

"And so they would have, if Molly hadn't found the little un." Sam muttered at this point. Mary ducked her head, her eyes filling with tears. She sniffed and blew her nose again before carrying her story, haltingly.

"Pa was really mad." Mary sniffed again. "He wanted Barney – that's me uncle – to show him where he'd dumped the mare and foal. When there was no signs of them, he was even madder!"

"But that was ages after." Molly said. "The wild animals would have eaten them by then!"

"Not all of them." Gary cut in. "There would have been something there. Even just bits of the mare's mane."

Mary nodded. "That's what Pa said. Then Uncle Barney admitted that the foal had still been alive when they dumped them so Pa started trying to see what had happened to the colt."

"So how come he knew it was Tyke?" asked Molly, dreading the answer.

"Pa had spotted him in the field when he was walking round looking." Mary blew her nose again. "Some of Tyke's markings are identical to Megan's. It wasn't difficult for him to work out what had happened." Mary looked around at everyone, suddenly looking terrified. "I'm sorry, it was me who told him everyone was going to the hunt. He would never have known there was no one here that day if it hadn't been for me!" and she burst into tears again.

Everyone was silent as Mary sobbed and, eventually, she composed herself again. She took a deep breath then told the story of what had happened on Boxing day. It seemed that Mary's father had moved the whole family to another gypsy camp, fifty miles away, very early in the morning. This one was a permanent site, owned by the gypsies and surrounded by a high fence so 'outsiders' couldn't see in. Then he had taken a truck and a horse trailer and disappeared with Barney. It wasn't until late in the evening when Mary's father had told her to go and see to the horses and she had gone to the only permanent buildings on site – a block of stables – and found Tyke there, looking upset and confused. Mary then described how, three days ago, her father had got drunk with Barney and most of the other men on the site during a big party. When it seemed that almost everyone on site had fallen asleep in a drunken stupor, Mary had taken the opportunity to take Pat and Tyke and make her way back to the farm. The last thing Mary remembered was feeling really dizzy, shortly after she had hidden herself and the horses into the tree-line of the top field. She had ridden almost non-stop, towing the confused Tyke along with her, and was just wondering about the best way to approach the farm when she had slid off Pat's back and almost passed out. In the recesses of her brain, she knew she had to

ecure the horses so she had staggered to her feet, tied them both up securely and
1en given way to her exhaustion and fallen to the floor. It had been getting dark by
1en. The rest of the story, everyone knew.

As Mary sobbed quietly into her tissue, Molly thought about what she had
eard. Her arm still around Mary's shoulders, she gave her friend a little hug.
It really wasn't your fault Mary" Molly said quietly. Even if you hadn't told them about
s going to the hunt, I'm sure they would have worked out a way to take Tyke
nyway.
I think so too." said Gary. "And I also think that, had they not known about the farm
eing deserted that day, they would have come another day, when people were
round, and someone could have got hurt." He reached across and, as Jean had
arlier, patted Mary's hand. "Please don't worry, Mary. After all, you're the heroine
ere because you brought Tyke home!" At his words, everyone around the table
odded their assent. Mary tried to smile in response. Instead, she suddenly went
ale and swayed on her seat, only prevented from falling off by the fact that Molly still
ad her arm around her.
Right." said Jean, briskly. "Back to bed for you young lady." With that, Jean and Mrs
eters gently raised Mary to her feet and helped her out of the room.

Whilst the women were gone, Sam and Gary discussed what they had heard
low voices. They began talking about the risk of the gypsies coming back to look
r Tyke – and Pat and Mary – and Molly was vaguely aware of her brother offering
sleep in the barn that night to keep a look out.
I want to stay too!" Molly blurted out. Both Sam and Gary shook their heads.
No way." said Gary. As Mary opened her mouth to protest, he held up his hand. "In
ct, what we haven't done yet is call the police to tell them that the foal is back. We
an, hopefully, get them to organise a patrol at least."
Aye, that'd be best." Sam agreed.
I'll do it now." Gary pulled out his mobile and a card that the police had given him
ith a direct number to the officer who had been dealing with the case. As he dialled,
ean and Mrs Peters came back into the room. Mary was tucked up in bed and had
llen asleep again.

Gary had explained the situation well. When the police arrived an hour later,
ere were three male officers in uniform along with a young looking WPC who was
essed casually in jeans and a thick jumper. After briefly explaining the situation,
am took two of the men outside to show them the foal and to take them up to the
edge-line where Molly had found Mary. The third interviewed Molly and Gary in the
tchen. Jean and Mrs Peters had taken the WPC to talk to Mary. As the officer sitting
the kitchen asked Gary what had happened, Molly fidgeted in her chair. She just
1ew that the gypsies would come back for Tyke and she wanted to go out and
otect him. It was a second or two before she realised that the police officer had
)oken to her.
Huh.... Pardon?" she asked, breaking from her reverie.
t's okay Molly." The officer smiled. "I just wondered how you knew that Mary and
yke were up in the trees."

"Um. I heard Tyke call. I said to Gary about it but he didn't believe me." Mary threw an accusing look at Gary. Her brother shrugged.

"Sorry. But there are a lot of horses around here and it could have been any of them."

"I know Tyke's call!" Molly glared at Gary again.

"Okay." The officer held up his hand to stop the siblings arguing. "So you heard the foal call. Then what?"

Molly explained how she'd come out of the barn to watch the fireworks and heard the call again. She told about running up the track to the back field and about finding Mary and the horses in the trees. She told how she had ridden Pat back to get Gary. Then Gary took up the story again. As he spoke, Jean came back into the kitchen and started to make tea.

"How's Mary?" Molly asked.

"She's fine." Jean replied. "Sally – that's the policewoman – is really nice and, although Mary was a bit worried at first, she's relaxed now and telling Sally the whole story. Your mum stayed with them just so that Mary doesn't panic again. The poor child is still a bit worried that she'll get arrested I think, even though we've reassured her that she's safe."

Suddenly, the policeman's mobile phone bleeped. He read the text message with raised eyebrows before quickly typing a reply and placing his phone on the table. "Now, there's a result." he said, looking around at the curious faces of Gary, Molly and Jean. "It's a good job we brought two cars as it would seem that my colleagues have just arrested two dodgy looking characters who were hiding amongst the young cattle in the back barn. If you'll excuse me for a moment, I'll go and see what the situation is." As he closed the door behind him, Molly jumped to her feet.

"They've come back for Tyke, I know it!" she shrieked and went to run after the policeman. Gary grabbed her arm.

"Hold on Sis, it's okay! You heard what the policeman said, they've arrested them! They will at least be charged with trespassing, if nothing else! So sit down and wait until that officer comes back!"

Molly plonked herself back in her chair, a sulky look on her face. Jean place a mug of tea in front of her and patted her arm.

"Don't worry love, the police will sort it out, I'm sure."

It was much later when the police finally left. Gary and Sam had gone out to the barn to check the horses and taken both Fizz and Meg with them. Jean had gone to check on Mary. Molly sat in the kitchen, still sulking, whilst her mother busied herself tidying up the farm kitchen. Suddenly, Mrs Peters spoke quietly.

"I still don't understand why you didn't tell me about the foal in the beginning. Then maybe we could have avoided all this upset."

"What do you mean?" Molly asked.

"Well, when you found the foal, it was obvious it must have belonged to someone. I could have helped you find the owner and returned him. I really don't know what Sam was thinking about, helping you to steal him and then hiding him all this time, encouraging you to lie...."

VE DIDN'T STEAL TYKE!" Molly yelled, leaping to her feet.

low then young lady, don't speak to me like that!" Barbara Peters looked at her ughter, her anger plainly showing in her face. Molly glared back at her.

Ve didn't steal him!" Molly repeated. "He was dumped. Left to die with his dead ther. I didn't tell you because I knew you wouldn't understand! If Dad was still ve, he would have understood! You never do! You never care!" With that, Molly ran t of the back door, tears streaming down her face. Blinded by the stinging tears, lly ran across the farmyard, straight into the arms of her brother who was heading ck to the house.

ley!" Gary said as he hugged her close. "What's up?"

bbing, Molly told Gary what her mother had just said. Gary hugged her tight as her s eventually subsided. Unable to hide anything from him, Molly eventually nitted her parting shot to their mother, suddenly feeling a wave of guilt over the tful words. Yet she knew that what she had said was right. Her dad would have ped her save the foal, she was sure of it. Giving Molly a squeeze, Gary suggested t she go and see Tyke, explaining that Sam was still in there with both dogs. "I'll and have a chat with Mum." he said. Wiping her eyes, Molly gave him a watery ile and headed towards the barn. As she entered, Sam glanced up at her from his it on a straw bale and simply nodded at her with a grunt. Fizz trotted over and zzled Molly's hand as Molly gave Pat a stroke as she passed him on her way to ke's pen.

Tyke, obviously still tired out after his adventures over the last few days, was led up in the straw, dozing. He opened his eyes and flicked his ears towards Molly she entered the pen, talking softly to him. He didn't get up but gave a soft whicker Molly sat down beside him and hugged his neck. Fizz curled up in the straw side her young mistress and the foal. A wave of exhaustion washed over Molly I, with a sigh, she laid her head on the foal's shoulder and slipped into a amless sleep.

23

Molly didn't want to go back to school. The last couple of days had been stressful to say the least with yet more discussions with the police, visits to the farm by social workers to talk to – and about – Mary, arguments with Mum about Tyke, long talks with Gary about what might happen in the future. They had even had a man come from World Horse Welfare to discuss the situation with the foal. For the moment, Tyke was still at the farm, the welfare people having decided that, since he was settled and well cared for, it was best to leave him be. Just as good, Mary was officially in temporary foster care with Jean and Sam. It had come as a surprise to Mary to discover that the old farmer and his wife were already registered as foster parents, although they hadn't had any foster children for a while. So, on the surface at least, the situation with Tyke and Mary was okay for a while. It was just the tension at home that was still a problem. Gary had tried his best to explain things to their mother but she still didn't quite get it, Molly felt. Molly was sure things would be even worse after today when Gary had gone back to camp.

Molly was sitting, bored, in her second lesson of the day. Oh, how she hated Maths. She sat, barely listening to the teacher droning on, doodling pictures of Tyke on the front cover of her exercise book, even though she knew she would get into trouble when the teacher saw it. Suddenly, she noticed the school secretary had entered the classroom. Although she couldn't hear what was being said, Molly knew it was concerning her from the sideways glances in her direction from both adults. She shrank down into her seat. What on earth had happened now? Even though she was expecting it, Molly jumped when the teacher called out her name.
"Molly Peters, the head wants to see you. Take your bag and books as you won't be back before the end of the lesson." The teacher's tone was abrupt, obviously disapproving of whatever Molly was supposed to have done wrong to warrant the summoning. Molly flushed as she gathered her things together under the curious stares and mutterings of her classmates. Head bowed, Molly followed the secretary out of the room and through the empty corridors towards the head's office. The heels of the woman's shoes clicked as they marched along. Not a word was spoken and Molly felt the familiar churning in her stomach as a feeling of dread settled in her guts. Whatever had happened, it could not be good. With a start, Molly suddenly felt a surge of fear. What if something had happened to Gary? Or Mum? By the time they reached the head's office, Molly felt sick and dizzy and was sure she was going to black out or something.

The secretary knocked briefly on the head's door before entering in response to a voice calling 'Come in'. As Molly shuffled into the room, she suddenly stopped, eyes opening in surprise. There, sitting to one side of the head's desk was Jean. Beside her, in a nice new school uniform, her head bowed, was Mary! As the head invited Molly to sit in a spare chair, she couldn't help staring at her friend. Then she realised that the head was talking to her so she smiled at Mary then looked at the woman behind the desk.

As the headmistress explained, Molly realised that Mary was going to be coming to school with her! It also appeared that, because they were friends, Molly was going to be helping Mary find her way around and settle into school life. Due to Mary not having spent much time in school over the years, she was behind in a lot of subjects and would be spending most of her lessons in a special unit to help her to try and catch up. Some of the lessons though would be in the same classes as Molly so Molly would be able to help her if needed. Mary was also in Molly's form for registration and similar things. Finally, as the bell rang for the lunch break, Jean stood and, after shaking the head's hand and thanking her, she hugged both Mary and Molly before heading out of the door. The head then suggested that both girls went and had lunch and then, before Molly went to her next lesson, she would show Mary around and then take her to the unit to begin filling in the gaps in her schooling. Chattering excitedly, the two girls headed out into the corridor, which was now teeming with students heading towards the dining room.

Both girls were the object of a lot of curious looks, nudges and whispering as they got their food and found somewhere to sit. At first, it seemed to get to Mary but Molly felt suddenly protective of her friend and brave enough to face the stares and to ignore the gossiping. After a while, taking her lead from Molly, Mary began to relax. Once lunch was over, Molly gave Mary a quick tour of the school before taking her to the unit and introducing her to the 'special needs' teacher.

From Molly's point of view though, the best bit was at the end of the school day. As the girls left the school, there was Jean waiting to take them home! So instead of having to wait for the bus, then have the long walk at the other end, Jean drove them home in less than half the time it usually took Molly to get there. Jean having okayed it with Mrs Peters, she drove the girls straight to the farm so that, although it was too dark to ride, Molly could at least spend some time with Tyke and Fred before Jean took her home.

Molly's relief that no one had tried to take Tyke again was countered by her worrying that it wouldn't be too long before someone did. No matter how much people tried to reassure her, Molly couldn't relax over the situation. Added to that was her worry about Mary and what was going to happen to her friend. Poor Molly really couldn't concentrate on anything. Despite the fact that life had settled into a trouble free routine where Molly spent her school-days helping Mary, then an hour after school at the farm each evening and her weekends riding and having fun with her friend and the ponies, people were beginning to notice changes in Molly. She had lost weight and had dark shadows under her eyes. A visit to the doctor didn't help and Molly, knowing how much the others were worrying about her, worried even more! But, unknown to Molly, things were about to come to a head.

It was the February half-term. Although no one had expected it, Gary came home on leave and he spent a lot of time in the first couple of days closeted with his mother and Jean in the living room up at the farm. The girls were enjoying their freedom from school, making use of the cold frosty mornings to explore the countryside on Pat and Fred. In the afternoons they would play with Tyke and Buster, Jean having handed the task of educating the young Clydesdale over to Mary. Like many with 'Gypsy blood', Mary had a natural affinity with horses.

Half way through their week long break, Molly and Mary returned from their morning ride to find several strange vehicles in the farmyard, one of which was a police car! They girls exchanged worried glances as they dismounted and hurried to put their ponies away. Before they could run over to the house, however, Sam appeared and sternly told the girls they were to stay in the barn, carry on with their chores and work the foals. He'd brought out some food and hot chocolate drinks for them, making it clear that they were to even have their lunch in the barn! Both girls were curious – and now even more worried about what might be going on in the house – but Sam was adamant that they stayed put. Eventually, despite their curiosity, the girls agreed to stay where they were, hoping that Sam would leave the barn and that they would be able to sneak over to the house to find out what was going on. But it wasn't to be. Sam stayed in the barn, grooming Pepper and Shandy, hissing though his teeth as he brushed, just like the old ostlers used to, to keep the dust out of their mouths. So the girls took the foals out into the front paddock to work with them. From there they could at least see the comings and goings in the farmyard.

Sam had a surprise for them when they took the foals back into the barn. Both the big Clydesdales were tacked up with saddles and bridles on and Sam informed the two friends that he wanted them to ride the mares out! It was obviously a distraction technique – and it worked! Right from the start, the girls were giggling as Sam fiddled with their stirrups, wrapping the leathers around to shorten them as there weren't enough holes to accommodate the length of the girl's shorter legs. He then sent them out with instructions of where to ride, for how long and to just walk and trot.

Still giggling at how tiny they both looked on the huge horses, the girls set out with every intention of following Sam's instructions to the letter. However, as they rode along the bridleway, they spotted smoke floating up amongst the trees around the area where the old Gypsy camp used to be. With a glance at each other, the girls reached an unspoken agreement and turned the two mares off the track and onto the narrow footpath that meandered through the wood.

Riding the two huge horses though the path that they had traversed before on the ponies was much harder than the girls had thought it would be. The low branches which, even when riding the ponies, the girls would have to duck under, were now too low for the Clydesdales to pass underneath so the girls had to frequently try to find a way around them. Here, at least, the bulk of the huge horses was a help as the mares forced their way though the undergrowth. Slowly, it dawned on the two girls that they would have been better going round the longer way, the way the vehicles had always used, rather than along the narrow track through the woods. The two orses plodded forwards, forging a fresh path through the undergrowth. Finally, the irls could see glimpses of the clearing ahead of them through the trees. As the learing opened up before them, they drew the horses to a halt and peered through ie twigs and branches. To their surprise, there was a lone caravan parked on the far ide of the open space with a camp burning near it. It was not one of the bright, iodern caravans that Molly remembered seeing on her last visit. This was a true, old ishioned, bow-topped Romany van. Yet there was no sign of a horse for pulling it. That's me granny's old caravan!" Mary exclaimed in a shocked whisper. "What's she oing here?"

lolly shrugged and shook her head. "No idea." She turned to look at Mary's pale ice. "Do you think we should go and ask?"

lary didn't reply. She sat motionless on Shandy's back, staring intently at the scene efore them. Suddenly, the door of the caravan opened and an elderly woman opeared, climbing stiffly down the steps. Although the girls were sure that they were ill hidden by the trees, it seemed to them that the old woman knew they were there. s she tended the fire she kept glancing in the direction of where the girls and the orses were hiding. Suddenly, she threw another log onto the fire and straightened o abruptly, defying her age and stiff joints. She turned to face the trees squarely, en called out softly, "Mary? Would that be you?" The two girls looked at each other, ary going even paler. In another silent exchange, the two friends nodded to each her and nudged Shandy and Pepper forwards and out into the open.

There was a tearful reunion between Mary and her grandmother, during which oth girls were hugged tightly by the old woman. Obviously realising that the girls ould be missed if they stayed too long, Mary's Grandmother asked them both to turn later, if they could, without the horses. Promising to do their best, if not today en certainly in the morning, the friends scrambled back up onto the mares using a rge log and headed out of the clearing. They rode off along the wider vehicle ccess because it was easier for the mares and, to begin with, neither of them spoke. Jddenly Mary muttered "Don't be saying a word about me Granny now, will yer?" olly glanced across at her friend. "Of course I won't!" Molly frowned then asked low are we going to get away to go back to see her?"

don't know yet. But you don't have to come, if you'd rather not." Mary studied olly's face as she spoke.

Of course I'll come!" Molly said, emphatically. "Your Gran said for both of us to go ack, didn't she?"

Ay, she did." Mary nodded. "I wonder why? I wonder why she came back, on her vn and why she needs to speak to us both?"

; the girls rode along the lane in the gathering dusk, Molly puzzled over Mary's ords. Why did an old Gypsy woman want to speak to them both? Why did she want speak to them so badly that she had come and set up camp on her own at the serted camp-site?

24

Back at the farm, there were still several cars in the farmyard but the police car had now gone. As the girls rode up to the barn, Sam came out of the house to help them put the mares away. He didn't mention what was happening at the house and brushed away the girl's questions. Instead, he rattled off a list of chores, most of which were the normal evening routine for the horses, then he gave them strict instructions to stay with the horses until someone came to tell them otherwise. As Sam headed back into the house, the girls looked at each other.
"I wonder what's going on?" Molly whispered, even though there was no one around to hear them except the horses. Mary just shrugged as she struggled to throw Shandy's heavy rug up and over the horse's back. Realising her friend was not in the mood to talk, Molly busied herself with rugging up Pepper, which was just as much of a struggle, before moving on to change the rugs on Fred and Tyke. As she worked, Molly kept glancing at her silent friend. Mary had a worried frown on her face and actually looked close to tears.

They had just finished making up the horse's feeds when, over a chorus of low whickering, they heard voices outside along with the sound of car doors slamming and engines being started. Quickly throwing the feed buckets into the pens, the girls rushed to the barn door and, opening it slightly, peered through the crack. It was almost dark and, despite the bright security lights in the farmyard, neither Molly nor Mary could recognise any of the people leaving. When they spotted Jean heading across towards the barn, the girls drew back and went to sit innocently on a bale of straw near Pat's pen.
"All finished girls?" Jean said brightly as she came though the door. Molly could sense that the cheerful tone was somewhat forced and that Jean was concerned about something. However, Sam's reaction earlier had made it clear that asking questions would get them nowhere so Molly smiled back and nodded. Mary followed Molly's lead. Hopefully, someone would tell them what was going on soon enough.
"Okay then," Jean went on, "it's dinnertime!" with that, she led the way back to the house. The fact that Jean hadn't done her customary 'last check' on the horses clearly meant that she had other, more important, things on her mind. Molly was really curious now – and worried too. A glance at Mary confirmed that her friend was feeling the same.

On the surface, dinner was a normal meal, with normal conversation. Gary asked the girls about their day and, despite the fact that they were bursting with questions over what had been happening in the house, both Molly and Mary talked about their rides and what they had done with the foals, making sure that they didn't mention the old Romany caravan in the woods. Finally, Mrs Peters announced it was

ᵉe for her family to head home. As Gary and Molly stood up from the table, Mary
ᵈddenly blurted out, "Who were all those people here today? And why were the
ᵖlice here?"

ᵉ adults all looked at each other. Finally Gary spoke.

's nothing for you two girls to worry about, honest. Just tying up a few loose ends
ᵇout lots of stuff." He smiled at them. "You two concentrate on enjoying the rest of
ᵘr half-term. Okay?" With that, he headed out to the porch to get his jacket.

ᵘt..." Molly began

ᵘsh child." Jean said quietly. "It's adult stuff and no concern of yours." She patted
ᵒlly's shoulder. "Now run along and get your coat."

ᵒlly glared at Jean. She had come to adore the older woman and trusted her but
ᵉ hated it when Jean took on this patronising tone.

ᵒlly!" Mrs Peters snapped, "Get your coat on please. It's time to go!"

ᵗh a martyred sigh and a quick glance at Mary, Molly did as she was told.

Molly woke with a start. Fizz, laid at the foot of the bed, was growling quietly.
ᵉ sound was so low that Molly could barely hear it. Surely that wasn't what had
ᵏen her? As the soft rumbling stopped, Molly thought back to the evening before.
 the way home she had tried quizzing both her mother and Gary until finally her
ᵗher had lost her temper and ordered Molly to bed early. Frustrated and angry,
ᵒlly had flung herself on her bed, sobbing. Eventually she had undressed, climbed
ᵈer the duvet and fallen asleep. Now she lay in the pitch dark, trying to figure what
ᵈ caused her to awaken.

The rattle of gravel against her window made her jump and Fizz resumed her
ᵍwling. Scrambling from the bed, Molly felt her way across the room. Pulling aside
 curtains, she peered out. There, on the pavement, was Mary! Molly glanced at
 bedside clock. It was only four am! Mary was waving frantically at the window,
ᵛiously wanting Molly to join her outside. Molly gave Mary a quick 'thumbs up' sign
ᵈ wriggled across her bed to turn on her reading lamp. She then grabbed her
ᵗhes up from the floor and dressed as quickly as she could. Fizz wagged her tail
ᶜitedly. Like any collie, she was always ready for a jaunt, no matter how early in
 morning it was.

Once she was dressed, Molly opened her bedroom door slowly, her hand on
ᶻ's collar to keep her quiet. She crept through the silent house, holding her breath
 as long as she could and then trying to breathe silently so as not to wake Gary or
ᵉr mother. Once downstairs, she decided to go out of the kitchen door since the
ᵗt door creaked – only slightly – but enough to sound really loud in the silence of
 early hours and, with his Army training, Gary would be subconsciously alert to
ᵧ unusual sounds. Clicking her fingers, a signal to Fizz to stay close, Molly
ᵒcked the kitchen door and opened it just enough for her and the dog to slip
ᵒugh into the cold night air. Quickly, being as quiet as possible, Molly slipped out
ᵒugh the back gate then jogged round to where Mary was hiding in the shadow of
 privet hedge, away from the glow of the street-lights.

ᵒme on," Mary whispered, "we gotta go and see me Granny."

ᵒn't she be asleep?" Molly whispered back.

"Shh... It'll be fine." Mary assured her as she jogged away along the road. Molly hurried to keep up, Fizz trotting at her heels.

As they approached the track that led through the woods, Molly suddenly realised how dark it was. As she thought about mentioning this to Mary, the girl pulled a small torch out of her jacket pocket and switched it on. As the torch beam lit the way through the trees, Molly began to relax, despite the surreal situation she was in. It was spooky in the woods but, with Mary leading the way and Fizz close by her side, Molly felt brave enough to cope. It seemed no time at all before the girls could see a faint glow ahead of them through the branches. The old Romany woman had obviously managed to keep her fire burning. As they entered the clearing, Molly saw that, not only was there a fire burning brightly on the ground but there was also the soft glow of an oil lantern in the window of the caravan. The old lady must have been watching out for them because the caravan door opened before they were half-way across the open space, the oil lamp behind the stooping figure throwing out long shadows to meet the darkness beyond the camp fire.

Molly was astounded when, at the old lady's invitation, the two girls and Fizz climbed up the steps into the tiny Romany caravan. It was almost like the Tardis in Dr Who! There was no way, looking from the outside, anyone would expect the interior to appear so spacious. It was also scrupulously clean and tidy. The scent of incense filled the air. After hugging both girls, 'Granny' indicated that they should sit on a small, brightly upholstered seat, just about big enough for the girls to sit next to each other. She then lifted a boiling kettle from a primus stove and poured the hot water into three cups sitting ready on a tiny work surface. It suddenly occurred to Molly that the old lady had been expecting their arrival, even at this unearthly hour.

After handing the girls the cups of fragrant tea, Granny seated herself opposite them in the small space. She took several sips from her own cup before setting it down on a small table. She then leant forwards and reached towards Molly, holding out her hand. With a quick glance at Mary, Molly placed her own hand in the old lady's. Granny, using both hands now, turned Molly's hand over so that it was palm upwards and then gripped it firmly for a moment before lowering her eyes and studying it in silence. Molly felt a momentary embarrassment over her bitten fingernails but then suddenly became aware of a feeling of warmth and happiness flowing over her. She realised that Granny was muttering, barely audibly, as she gently ran her index finger along the lines of Molly's palm. Molly sensed that it was best to remain silent. Suddenly, the old lady patted Molly's hand then released it, leaning back in her chair and retrieving her cup. As she sipped her drink, her twinkling blue eyes piercingly gazed into Molly's own. After a minute or two, Molly took a sip of her own drink. It tasted fruity and Molly could feel the warmth flowing through her once more. Then Granny spoke softly.

"It'll be right." she said. "For ye both. Just follow your hearts and let your souls fly. It will be right, for us all." She then looked directly at Molly. "Send your brother to me, before the scales of justice strive to find the right balance." Raising herself out of her chair, she reached out her arms to Mary. Mary stood and her grandmother hugged her close, murmuring into her ear. As her grandmother stepped back, Mary looked at her in surprise but the old lady just nodded. She then shuffled to the door and opening it said, "Off yet both go now. Remember what I said."

As the girls headed back through the wood, Molly was aching to ask Mary what the old lady meant and, also, what she had whispered in Mary's ear but something in the look on Mary's face made Molly bite her tongue and stay silent. It was just coming up to six in the morning as they reached Molly's home. Finally, Mary spoke in a low whisper.

"Go and wake Gary and give him Granny's message. Tell him to go as soon as he can. I'll see you at the farm later." With that, before Molly had a chance to reply, Mary jogged away, disappearing from sight as soon as she was outside the glow of the street-lights. As Molly watched her friend go, she became aware of Fizz nudging her hand. After giving the dog a perfunctory pat, Molly quickly went round to the back of the house and let herself into the kitchen as quietly as possible. She crept quietly up the stairs and then, after a slight pause, opened the door to her brother's bedroom.

Once Gary was fully awake, he got Molly to repeat her story three times before finally announcing that he really ought to check it out. He shooed Molly from his room with instructions for her to go and make some breakfast whilst he got dressed. When her brother arrived in the kitchen, Molly couldn't resist asking if she could go with him to the old gypsy camp.

"I don't think so, Sis. Besides, I know Jean wants you at the farm early today – she'll explain when you get there." He sat at the table and began attacking the plate of toast and marmalade Molly had placed in front of him. As Gary drained the last of his mug of tea, Molly tried, yet again, to persuade him to let her go with him. The answer was a stern 'No!'

"No what?" Their mother asked as she entered the kitchen, wrapped in a warm fluffy dressing gown.

"I have an appointment first thing and little sis here is trying to stick her nose in." Gary replied. He gave his mother a quick peck on the cheek then ruffled his sister's hair, having obviously realised that his tone of voice had been somewhat abrupt and that his sister felt hurt by his attitude. "Don't worry Molly, you'll understand later." With that, he headed out of the door. Mrs Peters turned to her daughter.

"Shouldn't you be heading up to the farm by now my dear?"

Molly looked at her mother in surprise. She'd fully expected the 'third degree' about Gary and what he might be up to. Instead, her mother was acting as though nothing had happened. Before she could reply, however, her mother got up from the table and headed out of the room saying,

"Actually, give me five minutes to get dressed and I'll come with you. I need to speak to Jean anyway."

Molly was so intrigued by her mother's behaviour, she didn't even contemplate sneaking out before Mrs Peters returned. Once her mother was ready, they set off to the farm, Fizz trotting, as ever, faithfully by their side.

25

Something weird was going on - Molly could see that as soon as she and her mother arrived at the farm. For a start, Pepper was standing in the yard wearing her harness whilst Shandy was saddled and bridled and being ridden by Sam. Molly's surprise was echoed by her mother so obviously even Mrs Peters wasn't aware of this part of whatever was going on. Holding the gate open for the horses to pass through, Molly tried to linger to see where Sam was taking them but her mother gently drew her away. They headed over to the farmhouse, Molly's mind whirring now.

In the kitchen, Mary was tucking into her breakfast. As the smell of porridge and toast tickled Molly's nostrils, she realised that, although she had made Gary some breakfast, she hadn't had any herself! Jean, coming in from the hallway, saw the hungry look on Molly's face.
"Help yourself girl." Jean smiled as she spoke. Molly stared at Jean in surprise! Used to seeing the woman in various, often well worn, jeans or jodhpurs, she had never even dreamed that Jean would ever wear a smart skirt, blouse and jacket. Low heeled 'court shoes' were on her feet instead of the usual wellies or riding boots. And she was wearing make-up! Not a lot, admittedly, but enough to make her look very business like. "And you can stop gawking." Jean went on. She then cast a meaningful look at Mrs Peters and headed back out of the room, into the hallway. Molly watched as her mother followed in Jean's wake. She turned to Mary.
"What on earth is going on?"
"Dunno" Mary shrugged. "did yer brother get Gran's message?"
"Er, yeah, he did. He went straight up there."
"That's good." Mary took a bite out of her toast and chewed slowly. "Me Granny will help sort things out."
"What things?" Molly asked.
"No idea really. No one tells me anything." Mary replied.
"Nor me." Molly agreed. "Maybe we could..."
"No, we couldn't." Mary shook her head. "Jean had a long chat with me this morning. She didn't really say much but, what she did say made it clear that we can't do anything that might cause problems. So I agreed that me and you would just look after the horses as normal."
Now Molly was puzzled. It wasn't like Mary to avoid finding out what was going on. She suddenly remembered the horses in the farmyard.
"Oh, by the way, do you know where Sam's gone?"
"Sam?" Mary looked at Molly sharply. "what do you mean?"
Molly explained about Pepper and Shandy in the farmyard, Pepper in harness and Shandy being ridden by Sam. Mary's eyes clouded for a second then she simply shrugged and resumed eating. Even Molly's comment about not having seen Sam on

horse before didn't get a reaction. With a sigh, Molly rose from the table and
grabbed a clean bowl before heading over to the Aga and ladling out a bowlful of
porridge.

Mary and Molly had turned out 'the boys' – Fred, Pat, Tyke and Buster – and
had started mucking out when Sam returned on Shandy but without Pepper. Before
she could stop herself, Molly rushed up to him, a hundred questions on her lips.
Infuriatingly, Sam just patted her on the shoulder, smiled at her then handed her
Shandy's reins with instructions to untack the mare and turn her out. He called Mary
over to lend Molly a hand then turned and hobbled out of the barn, looking somewhat
stiffer after his unaccustomed ride. Molly looked at Mary, even more puzzled now as
her friend quietly got on with the task, not making any comments about all the weird
doings on. Suddenly, Fizz gave a small bark and trotted out of the open barn door.
With a quick glance at Mary, which her friend didn't return, Molly followed her dog out
into the farmyard. She was just in time to see Gary jogging towards the house, Fizz
wriggling around his legs in greeting, almost tripping him up!
"Gary!" Molly called, "What's going on?"
Gary stopped and gave Fizz a brief pat then waved at Molly. "Tell you later!" He
called back. "Can't explain now!" With that, he headed indoors. Molly was about to
run across the yard to follow him when she felt a hand on her arm. She turned to look
at Mary.
"Don't." The gypsy girl stared deep into Molly's eyes. "They know what they're doing
so leave them. We need to to trust them to sort stuff out."
"What stuff? Is it to do with Tyke?" Molly asked, returning Mary's stare. "Or you?"
Mary shrugged. "I trust them." Mary said, her voice barely above a whisper. "So you
should too." Without saying any more, Mary turned and went back into the barn.

Molly followed her friend and watched as the girl got Shandy to lower her head
so that Mary could put the headcollar on. Mary then led Shandy out to the field and
turned her out before coming back to the barn. She looked at Molly who had sat
down on a straw bale with a sigh.
"I thought we were friends, Mary" Molly said sadly.
"And so we are." Mary picked up the muck fork and headed over to Pat's pen to start
cleaning his stable.
"So why won't you tell me what's going on?"
"Because I don't know!" Mary's eyes flashed as she glared at Molly. "Why can't you
just leave things be! They'll tell us when they're ready!" She began furiously throwing
the clean straw up and chucking the soiled bedding into the wheelbarrow.
Tears stuck the back of Molly's eyes. She felt sure that Mary knew what was going
on and it hurt that her friend obviously didn't trust her enough to explain. She felt
angry too but working out why wasn't quite so simple. Was it just because the adults
were refusing to tell her what was happening? She really wasn't sure. Wiping her
sleeve across her eyes, Molly grabbed her own set of mucking out tools and headed
for Tyke's pen.

The sound of a car pulling into the yard drew Molly back to the barn door.
Mary threw Molly a glare but then couldn't resist following her. The girls peered
through the gap between the doors. There was a mini-cab in the yard, it's engine

running as the driver waited patiently for his passengers. The door of the farmhouse opened and Gary, Jean and Sam appeared, all dressed in smart clothes. Molly's eyes opened wide as she looked at her brother. He certainly hadn't been dressed like that earlier! Then she remembered the bag her mother had been carrying when they walked up to the farm that morning. She must have been bringing a change of clothes for Gary! Molly then realised that her mother wasn't joining the group but was instead standing by the kitchen door waving the others off and still dressed as she had been when they'd come to the farm. Almost as if she sensed Molly's eyes on her, Mrs Peters looked across at the barn. As the taxi pulled away, Mrs Peters headed towards where the girls were watching the adults and puzzling over their antics. Both girls quickly ran across the barn and resumed their chores.

"Right girls,"
Despite the fact that they had known she was heading across to the barn, Mrs Peters' voice made both girls jump. "Before you ask, no, I am NOT going to tell you anything more than what you already know..."
"But Mum...." Molly couldn't resist interrupting.
"Molly!" Mrs Peters reprimanded her daughter. "I said that I am not going to tell you – and I mean it! What I WILL tell you is that I am here to keep an eye on you both so please, no sneaking off or anything. Just get on with your jobs and, hopefully, all will be revealed in due course. Okay? Lunch will be at noon – and I expect you both to be there!" With that, she turned and left the barn.

Molly looked at Mary as the barn door slammed shut. "What do you think is going on?" she asked.
"I said before, I don't know." Mary replied. For some reason, Mary's voice sounded small and there was a tremor as she spoke. Molly suddenly felt guilty. Whatever was going on obviously DID involve Mary yet it never occurred to Molly to think about how her friend must be feeling. Molly watched as Mary sank down onto a bale of straw with a sigh, tears coursing down her cheeks. Molly rushed over and hugged her friend. Fizz, ever alert to the emotions of 'her' humans, wriggled over and pushed her head under Mary's hand. As Mary stroked the dog, the tears subsided. She sniffed. Molly rummaged in a pocket and eventually produced a wad of tissues that were relatively clean. She handed them to Mary. After a while, Mary gave Molly a wan smile. "We'd better get on with stuff I guess." she said. Molly hugged her briefly and nodded her assent. Both girls went back to work, both trying not to think about all the strange things that were going on.

26

The girls were eating lunch with Mrs Peters when they heard a ㄷommotion outside. Before they could go to see what was happening, Mrs Peters ㄷd them both with a stern look that clearly told them to stay put. She then went out ㅗ the yard herself to check what was going on. She was back within seconds.

ﾑary, you're needed outside." As Mary went to go out, Molly also rose from her ㅌat. "Molly, finish your lunch please." Mrs Peters instructed her daughter. The girls ㄷhanged a puzzled glance before Mary went out. Molly started to gobble the ﾑains of her meal. "Slow down child," Mrs Peters reprimanded her, "you'll make ㅓrself ill." Before Molly could reply, Mary reappeared, her face flushed with ㄷitement. She looked at Mrs Peters.

 need Molly's help." said Mary, grinning. As Mrs Peters reluctantly nodded her ㄴent, Molly leapt from her seat and headed for the door.

Mary led Molly round the back of the huge barns to a small paddock that Molly ㅓ only glimpsed a couple of times since she'd been coming to the farm. Jean had ㄷe explained that the twenty metre square area had been set aside for Jean to ㅋe a small vegetable garden but she'd never really got around to sorting it out. ﾑehow, she'd never had enough time. Now, however, it had clearly been allocated ㅏ a different purpose for there, by the hedge, was Granny's Romany caravan, ㅗper standing patiently between the shafts. A couple of farmworkers were chatting ㅓthe old lady, obviously discussing whether or not the van was positioned to ㅏnny's liking.

ﾑhat's going on?" Molly asked.

ㅌ Granny's moved in!" Mary giggled. "We need to sort Pepper out." After greeting ㅓold lady, the two girls set to work, unhitching Pepper from the caravan. As Molly ㅓher away, Granny commented that the mare was a 'good un' and Molly turned ㅓsmiled back at Granny, again feeling that those piercing eyes were looking into ㆍsoul. As Mary, having given her grandmother a quick hug, came to help her take ㅡmare away, Molly again had that feeling that yes, everything was going to be ㅑy and a surge of happiness flooded through her once more, just had it had when ㅑhad visited Granny in the early hours of this morning.

Unharnessing Pepper was harder than it looked as the girls tried to figure out ㄷh buckles to undo and which to leave fastened up. The mare stood patiently as ㅜtwo girls, giggling now, worked their way through the maze of straps that made ㅡPepper's working harness. At least Molly remembered seeing Sam loosen the ﾑnes and turn the collar round to get it on and off without catching the horse's eyes. ㅏlly, Pepper stood before them wearing just a headcollar. Grabbing a brush each, ㅡgirls brushed the sweatmarks from the mare then Molly picked out her huge feet ㅓst Mary put on her turnout rug. Together they then walked the mare to the field and turned her out. That done, they went back to the barn and, between them, carried the heavy harness through to the tack room. After a brief study of Shandy's harness, they managed to hang Pepper's up neatly. Molly knew that Sam used different stuff to clean the harnesses so she just rinsed the bit off and made a mental note to remind Sam, when he came back from wherever he'd gone, that the harness hadn't been cleaned.

Still hoping for answers, the two girls decided to go and visit Granny to see if she could enlighten them about what was going on today. They were thwarted however. As they approached the caravan, they could see that Mrs Peters was already with the old lady, chatting quite animatedly. Molly realised that she hadn't really seen her mother relaxed and chatting like this for months. Suddenly not wanting to intrude, Molly put her hand on Mary's arm.
"Can we come back later?"
Mary looked at Molly in surprise. "I thought you wanted answers?" she said.
"Yeah. I do but... Well, Mum looks happy, you know? I haven't seen her like that for ages. Not since... Well.... Not since Dad died really."
Mary studied the scene before her for a minute then smiled at Molly. "Yeah, I see what you mean. Ok, we'll come back later. We can go and finish up in the barn, hay and water and stuff. Then go for a ride after we catch in?"
Molly grinned at Mary gratefully. With a final glance across at her mother, she turned and, with her friend beside her, headed back to the barn.

Trying to keep themselves occupied for the afternoon wasn't difficult. By the time they had got the barn pens ready for the horses, with hay, bedding water etc., it was easily time to start thinking about catching in. They caught in Fred and Pat first and gave them both a quick groom before taking them for a ride. Then, after catching in the two mares and the yearlings, as Tyke and Buster were now categorised, they had just enough light left to spend half an hour working with the youngsters in the paddock before starting the evening routine of grooming and changing rugs ready to settle the horses for the night. The occasional check on Granny's caravan revealed that Mrs Peters was still in situ, chatting away merrily to the old Romany woman - a situation the girls didn't want to intrude on. Finally, apart from the evening feeds, there was nothing left to do in the barn. There was still no sign of Jean, Gary and Sam returning and the girls didn't know whether that was a good or bad thing. As they were trying to decide what to do next, Mrs Peters appeared at the door of the barn, her face looking, Molly thought, younger and somehow glowing.
"I'm just going to start making dinner." Mrs Peters announced cheerfully. She then looked at Mary. "You know, your Granny is a very special lady." With that, she walked off towards the house, her step light. The two girls looked at each other and, with a nod from Mary, silently made a joint decision. Calling Fizz, they headed out to visit Granny's caravan.

Strangely reminiscent of the scene Molly had encountered in the early hours, there was a fire burning brightly in front of the caravan and the glow from the lamp was shining through the window in the dusk. Granny came to the door as the girls approached, yet again as if she was expecting them. Mary spoke first.

"What are you doing here Gran? Are you my surprise?"
Molly glanced at her friend. Mary had been told she was getting a surprise? Why hadn't she said anything earlier?
Granny smiled at her granddaughter. "Maybe. Maybe not." she said cryptically. "Now, would you like some tea?"

There was no talking as they sat sipping their fragrant hot drinks. That was okay though, Molly felt. There was a peaceful air surrounding them all as they sat around the fire. Molly gazed into the flames, daydreaming. Several times, she imagined she could see images of her father in the dancing tongues of fire and she again felt that glow of happiness wash over her. She was becoming more and more convinced that there was something magical about the old lady. Maybe she was a witch? Molly smiled to herself at the thought. As she pondered the idea, Granny spoke softly.
"No, I'm not."
Molly looked up in surprise. It was as if the old lady had read her mind! Mary was chuckling to herself as if she was in on the secret. Before Molly could react however, she heard her mother calling.
"Off ye go." Granny said softly. "I'll still be here tomorrow."
Mary hugged her Gran before the girls raced each other to the farmhouse.

Before they sat down to eat, Mary was given a foil covered plate to take out to her Gran. She was back within minutes, wriggling into the seat next to Molly and starting to eat hungrily. After Mrs Peters and the girls had eaten, there was still no sign of the others. Molly wondered about that but, weirdly, didn't feel worried. Maybe, she mused, it was because her mother obviously wasn't worried – nor was Mary – If they weren't worried, why should she, Molly, worry? The phone ringing in the hallway made Molly jump. Mrs Peters got up from the table and went to answer it, infuriatingly closing the kitchen door behind her so that the girls couldn't eavesdrop. It wasn't long, however, before she returned.
"Okay girls, they're on their way back." Mrs Peters smiled before adding, "Jean said you two know how to do the feeds and stuff so asked if you could go and finish up the horses for her." Both girls nodded.
"Where have they been?" Molly asked, bursting with curiosity.
"You will find out in due course." her mother replied. "Now I don't want you bombarding them with questions as soon as they come home, let them eat first. In fact, it would probably be better if you two girls stayed outside for a while, if you would? We adults will have a lot to discuss." Mrs Peters saw the look on Molly's face. She smiled at her daughter. "Don't worry love, it's going to be okay."
"It's okay, we can visit me Granny." Mary piped up.
"No you can't." The girls jumped as the back door opened and Granny came in. "Cos I'll be in here having a natter and a listen." The old lady had brought her plate back and smiled gently at the girls. "Now you'll do as yer were asked and go and see to those horses. You'll be told when yer can come back indoors." With that she sat down in the old easy chair in the corner of the kitchen, the one the dogs often slept in. The girls looked at each other. There was nothing they could say to that, really. They rose from the table and, at a nod from Granny and a bright smile from Mrs

Peters, headed back out to the barn to do as they had been told.

As the girls ran across the farmyard, Mary suddenly stopped and looked at Molly, an incredulous look on her face.

"Me Granny!"

"What?" Molly was confused. "What about your Gran?"

"She went into the house!"

"So? What's wrong with that?"

"I don't know that anything is wrong." Mary glanced back at the farmhouse with a small frown. "But something really weird is going on. My Gran has never, ever been inside any building – she's known for it! She doesn't even go into shops or anything! Yet she's just walked into that house!"

Molly followed Mary's gaze towards the house and shivered. Was it just the cold that made her tremble? Or was it something else? Whatever it was, the shiver didn't appear to have been triggered by fear. It was more of a shiver of anticipation Molly felt. But anticipation of what, she had no idea. She plucked at Mary's sleeve.

"Come on, lets get to the barn. It's freezing out here!"

Mary tore her gaze from the house. "Yeah, you're right. But I still want to know what's got into me Granny!"

The horses had finished their feeds and were contentedly munching their hay. The girls were sitting on a hay bale, trying not to speculate about what was going on in the house and failing miserably. They had heard a taxi pull up and, peering through the crack in the door, saw Sam, Jean and Gary go into the house. That had been over an hour ago. The girls had groomed all the horses and tidied up the barn but now there was nothing really left to do. They both ached to know what was going on in the house but knew that they had to try and be patient.

27

Gary entered the barn. Both girls leapt to their feet but, before either of
em could speak, Gary looked at Molly.
Come on then Sis, time to go home." he said with a grin.
What? But what's been happening?" Molly asked.
'll tell you later." he said, still grinning. He turned to Mary.
Jean said for you to go indoors now too. She's got a lot to tell you."
ary looked from Gary to Molly and then shrugged nonchalantly, belying the fact that
e was worried about what was going on. With an offhand wave at Molly, Mary said
ee you tomorrow then" before heading out into the dark farmyard on her way to the
rmhouse.

Gary jiggled a set of keys in his hand. "Come on then Sis. Jean and Sam are
nding us the Landy for tonight and we'll bring it back in the morning. Mum's already
it and it's freezing!" With that, he turned and left the barn. Bursting with curiosity
d questions, Molly turned and went to give each of the horses a 'goodnight' hug
d a couple of polos out of her pocket. As she turned out the lights in the barn, she
ood for a few seconds listening to the sound of the horses moving around and, the
und she loved, munching their hay. With a sigh, she closed the barn doors firmly
en headed across to the Landrover as Gary started the engine.

The Peters family were all sitting in the lounge back in their home. Gary was
plaining to Molly that he had, with Sam and Jean, been to court that day. It had
ostly been to do with Tyke and his disputed ownership.
o what happened?" Molly asked in a small voice, terrified that she was going to
ar the worst news ever and have to return Tyke to Mary's dad.
Vell, it seemed to go okay but we won't know for definite until tomorrow morning."
3ut...."
Now Molly, don't get upset. As I said, we'll know tomorrow, hopefully first thing." He
niled at his sister and patted her arm. "Now, get an early night and we'll see what
morrow brings that much quicker."
olly sighed and rose from her chair. She hugged her mother and brother before
dding them goodnight and heading up the stairs.

Molly didn't sleep much. She lay awake, then dozed for a short while,
ɔke up, read a book, tried again to sleep... and the cycle repeated itself. Finally,
ortly after six in the morning, she heard movement from her brother's room. She
ok that as a signal that she could now get up herself. She felt so tired, so worried,
 drained, it was as much as she could do to drag her jodhpurs on. Fizz seemed to
nse her mood and lay quietly on the bed, watching her young mistress. Molly
ard her mother getting up too, much to her surprise. Mum was never up this early
ually and now that made two days in a row! Molly finished dressing and headed

down the stairs.

At the farm, Mrs Peters headed straight into the house whilst Gary and Molly headed to the barn to begin sorting the horses out. They could hear Sam and the farmworkers over with the cattle but there was no sign of Jean or Mary. A quick glance across to the Romany caravan showed that Granny was awake too as the lamp was glowing in the pre-dawn darkness. The birds were starting their dawn chorus as the brother and sister slipped through the barn doors to be greeted by a variety of whickers and whinnies as the horses demanded their breakfasts.

They were just changing the rugs on the horses – stable rugs being replaced by turn-out rugs - ready to put the horses in the field when they heard a car pull up outside. At a glance from Gary, Molly resisted the urge to go and peer through the barn doors. As they led the mares out to the field, however, Molly recognised the social worker's car, parked next to the old Landrover. She wasn't sure whether to be worried about that or not but Gary didn't seem concerned at all so she tried to follow suit and relax. It wasn't easy though. What if they had come to take Mary away? As they headed back to the barn to get the foals, Molly saw that Granny was making her way across to the house too. What on earth was going on? A glance at her brother's face told her nothing. Molly felt the familiar churning in her stomach that always started when she felt things were about to go wrong. Then she gave herself a mental shake. Being in this mood would be no good for Tyke, or any of the horses.

All the horses were out in the field and the social worker was still closeted in the house as Gary and Molly began mucking out. The physical activity seemed to help Molly's stomach churning settle down – or maybe it was just that the job was so familiar to her now that it was a comfort, rather than a chore? She glanced across at Gary who was busy sorting out Pepper's stall. They had agreed that he would do the three Clydesdales whilst Molly did the two ponies and Tyke. Even though Gary had more work to do though, he was still miles faster than Molly.

They had just finished doing the beds and, whilst Molly did the water, Gary was filling the haynets. Suddenly, they heard another vehicle outside. Again, Molly fought the urge to go and peer through the doors of the barn, then she heard Jean calling Gary's name. Gary looked at his sister.
"Stay here, I'll be back in a minute." he said before he headed out across the yard to the house. With Gary not there to stop her, Molly went to the door and looked out. She didn't recognise the vehicle that had just arrived but she could see that the social worker was still here. Suddenly, the door of the farmhouse burst open and Mary came racing across to the barn. Molly stepped away from the door just as Mary burst in, almost knocking Molly flying!
"Molly! Guess what?"
"What?" Molly asked abruptly, after all, she was the only one who had no clue about what was going on.
Mary looked at her with a small frown then suddenly gave her friend a hug.
"Don't be like that, Molly, it's brilliant!"
"What is?" Molly was still feeling hurt.
"I'm staying!" Mary burst out, a massive grin on her face.

.h? What do you mean?"

m gonna live here! Forever!" Mary began to skip around the barn, then saw the zzled look on Molly's face. She skipped over to her friend. "Jean and Sam have plied to foster me long term and are going to adopt me! So, I'm staying! And so's e Granny! And Pat!" Mary began to skip around the barn again.

)h Mary! That's brilliant!!!" Molly ran across and hugged her friend. Then a thought curred to her. "What about your parents?"

Vell, me mam wants me to have the chance of proper schooling and me dad... ell, me dad don't want to know, not really... besides, he ain't got a say in the matter more..."

)m the expression on Mary's face, Molly guessed that Mary really didn't want to < about her father. She sought for a way to change the subject.

o, how come your Gran's staying here?" she asked.

iry shrugged. "I guess she wants to stay in one place for a bit … and she said she nts to keep an eye on me!" Mary gave a small chuckle. "But the best bit is that I'm ying! That's why that social worker woman came, to sort out the papers and stuff!" e girls hugged again, laughing. Sitting on a straw bale together, they made all ts of plans for the summer with the ponies. Then Molly suddenly thought about <e and it felt as though someone had stuck a pin in her balloon of happiness. Mary ked at her and, astute as always, guessed what the problem was. She gave Molly ympathetic hug. There really didn't seem to be anything to say.

Shortly afterwards, Sam appeared and told Molly that she needed to go round the horse paddock. With a worried glance at Mary, Molly raced out of the barn, ry hot on her heels. As she approached the field gate, Molly could see Gary was nding in there, next to Tyke, scratching the yearlings withers as he chatted to a tall n who Molly suddenly recognised with a horrible feeling of dread.

h No!" Molly stopped suddenly and turned to Mary in horror, "it's the horse welfare n! He's come for Tyke!" Molly felt frozen to the spot as she watched her brother king to the welfare man. They hadn't noticed her yet. Tears poured down Molly's e as she realised that Gary must have betrayed her and organised for the welfare n to take the young horse. Unable to face her brother, Molly spun round and ran, iout thought, away from the paddock. Vaguely, she was aware of Mary calling er her, then Gary's voice called her name too. Ignoring their shouts, blinded by her rs, Molly ran as fast as she could across the farmyard. She wasn't even aware of z barking and suddenly appearing beside her. Molly yanked the gate open and ed out into the lane, running until she felt her lungs would burst.

Gasping for breath, the tears still running down her cheeks, Molly eventually wed to a walk. As she wiped her eyes and nose on her sleeve, she suddenly oped and looked around her. She knew where she was. As she looked at the vthorn hedge, she didn't see the bare twigs but was transported back to the eltering months of summer, to the late flowering hedge and the cow parsley iwering their snow-like petals on her, Fizz and a tiny foal lying in the ditch beside dead mother. Sniffing and sobbing still, Molly fell to her knees onto the damp th and crawled forward under the branches, Fizz whining and wriggling by her e. At last she reached the tree trunk and sat with her back against it. As Fizz crept into her lap, Molly hugged her close and silently began to cry again as she relived the last few months in her mind.

Fizz suddenly wriggled out of Molly's arms. Before Molly could call her back, the dog had run out into the lane, barking. Molly froze in her hiding place. Suddenly, she heard what Fizz must have heard – Gary, calling Molly's name. She shrank back against the tree, knowing full well that her efforts to hide from her brother would be futile. Sure enough, after a few minutes, Fizz came running back, showing Gary exactly where his sister was hiding.
"Molly?" Gary called softly. "Are you in there, Sis?"
"Go away!" Molly sobbed.
"Nope. I won't. Mary told me what happened when you came out to the paddock. You've got it all wrong."
"No I haven't!" Molly sobbed again. "I saw you with that welfare man. I know he's come to take Tyke away!"
"As I said, Sis, you've got it wrong." Gary said quietly. "Think about it. Did you see a trailer or horsebox? How the heck was he going to take Tyke? In the boot of his car?"
Wiping her eyes again, Molly thought back to the vehicles that she had seen in the yard earlier. Gary was right. Not one vehicle which could have been used to transport a horse. Maybe she HAD got it wrong!"
"He could have called someone to bring a lorry or trailer. They could be on their way." she said, unwilling to think of any other explanation for the man's visit.
"Sure, he could have." Gary admitted. "But he didn't. All he did was bring some paperwork for us."
"Paperwork?" Molly was puzzled now. "What do you mean, 'paperwork'?"
Gary paused for a moment, then spoke quietly. "He was bringing the paperwork which, basically, clarifies that Tyke is ours. All legal and correct. He's ours, for life."
Molly sat for a moment, trying to take in Gary's words. Then she crawled back through the branches until she was back in the lane. She stood up, slowly and gazed at her brother's face. As she saw his broad grin, she realised that he spoke the truth, but she needed to be sure.
"So he's ours? Truly?"
Gary hugged Molly to him. "Yep, he all ours. Shall we go and tell the little Tyke the good news? That he's here to stay?"
Molly laughed and hugged Gary joyfully. Fizz suddenly leapt up at them both, wanting to be included in their fun. Molly reached down and patted the dog then she grinned at her brother. Gary grinned back.
"Come on then sis, let's get back to our gypsy cob."
"Race you!" Molly yelled as she suddenly turned and began running back up the lane towards the farm, towards her friends, towards the horses … Towards Tyke.

*   *   *   *   *   *   *

Printed in Great Britain
by Amazon